Circle of

Sun

BY KIM LUKE

BOOK I OF A SERIES

CIRCLE OF SUN

Copyright 2012 by Kim Luke

For information:
kimjluke59@gmail.com or kimlukeauthor.com

Published April 2012 by Kim Luke
Republished April 2015 by Kim Luke
ISBN-13:
978-1475148329

ISBN-10:
1475148321

Circle of Sun is dedicated to my husband, Bob. Many of the most intriguing parts of my story came from his imagination. When I told him I was writing a book, he said, "Great!" Bob is my consummate life coach.

Other Books by Kim Luke:

Black Inferno

Prologue

No one will visit his final resting place. In death, as in life, his name had long been associated with broken promises, broken rules and broken lives. He embraced nothing, and was embraced by nothing. His only lasting impression was darkness, keeping even the most forgiving souls from speaking a kind word about him, even in death. A brisk October wind forces a tighter clenching of the scarf covering her throat. The only sound heard is the crunch and swish of fallen leaves as she walks to the pauper's section of the cemetery. She pauses, and kneels with devotion to the memory of Colton LaMont. Melanie clears debris and places a few flowers upon the site. Sorrowful tears fall for her undeclared love, and the parched and thirsty soil drinks.

Chapter One

Brilliant sunlight floods the rock face we climb. The quartz veins in the limestone shimmer near my gloved hand. The two of us scale the forty-five foot challenge with ease. We take pictures of one another.

Alec teases me about my pink camera, and my sloppy climbing technique. We gather our gear and walk across to the next plateau passing crevices and brush. He leads, and I follow. His sandy hair dances with every September gust. Alec's shoulders are broad and he is tall compared to my petite frame. His body is fit and the bronze of his skin reveal seasons of living to the fullest. Alec is beautiful. The adage might be true opposites attract. He is dark, and I am fair. Alec thrives on adventures while I find adventure in books and history. I am not glamorous like the women I would pair with his kind, but his love for me is pure. I don't have to be anything more than what I am, making me love him even more, if it were possible.

The azure sky is a breathtaking backdrop for puffy white clouds to sail by. This day is magical only because I am alone with him.

Alec jogs back in the direction of our last climb when I realize my camera is missing, and I continue on the trek to set up for our next climb. I grow uneasy, does he need my help? He's been gone too long, and I try to stay calm as I make my way back to the top of the ledge.

"Alec...Alec!" I say, but no answer comes.

Eyeing the ledge, my fear mounts and can no longer be ignored. Panic grips me and without hesitation I make my way to the drop off. I slowly peek over. His voice behind me says my name.

"Quinn!"

Turning, I am blinded by the searing rays of the afternoon sun. I see only a tall shadow before large hands violently shove my shoulders with such force I am thrust over the rock wall. My scream fills the canyon. I am free falling down, down. My lungs ache for a breath in this deep darkness. I am suffocating. I experience excruciating pain and ultimate despair. All hope escapes my consciousness.

Sound and sight are extinct now. My world is black.

* * * * *

Warmth surrounds my feet and travels slowly up my body. My afflictions are gone. My eyelids are open, to a foreign place. I rise and begin to walk, but my feet don't touch the sand! I float along a quiet shoreline. The sterling sea is calm. Without sun or moon this place is neither day nor night, but dusk like. Through the mist, a figure approaches.

Her body glides towards me. She is draped in shimmering silver, her face expressionless. Her gaze is not at me, but beyond me.

Curious, I turn ...only infinite shoreline. My quivering hands cover my racing heart.

She seems to sense my fear as she studies me. Large round lapis eyes peer into mine, into my soul. Her blank expression is replaced with tender mercy. Her friendly eyes promise no harm. I am no longer afraid. I can't see, but I feel her smile. She is blissful, her immense joy radiates around her like sparkling crystals.

My face is now wet from the mist; yet her ivory skin is smooth and dry. Before I can form words, she does.

"No one can prepare for a time as this. The sun itself fades in brilliance a bit with each passing day. Eyes look but do not see. Purity drains from the hearts of good men. Find the Circle of Sun. A tender seed must push through bitter soil to survive," she says and points behind me, "let the prints lead you."

The footprints behind me are mine.

She interrupts my thoughts.

"Follow their path to your sun."

I bask in her radiant warmth as her graceful hand touches my face.

Her gaze never leaves me as she glides away.

I watch as she melts into the distance. I want to follow, but she is gone. Few and unclear were her words. All I can do is to begin. I turn and take the first step.

My heavy eyelids open to blurred edges of brilliant color, strange bouquets cover the ceiling. I blink to focus and the scene becomes clear. Taped to the ceiling are vivid crayon filled pictures--children's artwork thoughtfully placed for those awaking here.

Suddenly a face casts a smile down at me.

"Dr. Crenshaw is here to check in on you," says a nurse.

"Quinn, how are you feeling? Your surgical procedure went very well, and with your recent progress, we can begin to discuss getting you out of here after all of these months. I am sure you are ready," the doctor says.

I am completely baffled by this conversation and I struggle to communicate. My confusion is obvious to him and he pats my hand. Me? In the hospital for months? I am disconnected to reality, free falling again.

"You are still groggy, I will be back in the afternoon to check in on you," he says kindly.

My drowsy state can only mean I am still dreaming. The memory of the misty grey ocean beacons and I remember the mystical place. Desperate to return to the silver shoreline, I fall into sleep hoping to see her again.

During the next week reality rolls in like an unwelcomed storm. Added to confusion is loss. Alec is gone! Pain permeates every fiber of my being, and the waves of grief crest and ebb. Hikers found us at the bottom of the rock face, Alec dead and me clinging to life. In death, Alec saved my life, his body breaking my fall. I am horrified at the picture this paints in my mind. Alec is gone, and even though I survived the accident I will need months of recovery. Investigators did not seriously consider what I told them about being pushed. My pink camera was never found, perhaps it never existed. Trauma can produce false memories, they explained. The only logical theory of what happened on the cliff has been difficult to accept. Alec fell and my shock at seeing him dead caused me to fall too. Although I could not identify who the shadowy figure was, I know it was Alec's voice making me to turn. How is it possible? If he pushed me, how could his body break my fall? I can't put the pieces together. As my body heals, answers elude me. I recall the panic as I approached the edge. I heard Alec's voice behind me saying my name. I was blinded by the sun. I remember hands forcefully pushing me. It's not possible, Alec would never hurt me. I reluctantly accept their version of the accident as reality. Logically it makes sense, so I struggle to recapture my confidence and stabilize my mental state.

Chapter Two

Months spent in rehabilitation protect me from the initial rumors. With Alec having been in the world of professional sports, news of our accident created suspicion, gossip and finger pointing. Foul play was not suspected; authorities called the incident nothing more than a tragic accident. Alec fell over the ledge; my fall resulted from the jolt of shock seeing his body lying motionless on the rock floor. Alec's death became the subject of publicity at the publishing house.

My boss attended a symphony benefit, where damaging comments insinuated the tragedy was capitalized for their gain, pretty much sealing my fate. I was let go under the guise of downsizing. Perhaps the competition seized this as an effective way to get an upper hand.

Besides Alec, my career was my identity. With no family, my professional life became the center of my world. I took pride in my work, and had some purpose. But throughout the last several months, my priorities are changed. My life will never be the same. My body is healed, but I am not. I find myself thanking God, after witnessing his astounding mercy. I possess a new level of awareness as a result of my brush with death, a spiritual awakening.

Releasing my old life, I seek courage to embrace what lies ahead. I often think of the silver shoreline, the mystical woman and her mysterious message. Those words and images visit my consciousness time and time again, burned into my memory. Uncertain as I am about this new chapter, one thing I am certain of, a purpose, a reason for my existence. I don't even know what it is. But in my heart, I know without any doubt, I am on a journey to discover it. Although the path is unclear, I have a peace never before experienced. A knowing rises beyond the pain of my loss, supplying sweet stability. The stirring of my spirit is connected to my accident and the haunting and beautiful dream.

The loss of my position changed my course and my passion for collecting books has become my new career. I'm now the owner of a bookstore I renamed Fireside Books. Following my departure from publishing, I was notified of a bookstore for sale. It was curious since the message arrived through publishing house's mail system, and without identification of a sender. Perhaps a few compassionate souls roam within the walls of that place. I inquired about the bookstore and was even more amazed at the hassle free process, making me the newest owner of a main street business.

Nestled among the tree covered river bluffs along the Missouri, lies the sleepy village of White Oak, my new home. Its strong German heritage still preserved in the culture and the architecture of the community. Less than hour from Kansas City, this little village is worlds away. The town square is flanked by Midwestern entrepreneurship. The aroma of roasting coffee beans from Mocha Joe's to one side of Fireside Books, and savory onion pie and strudel from the German bakery on the other. Men in camouflage frequent the archery shop across the street, while a sweet tooth can be satisfied with confections from a little place around the corner. Secondary streets include the City Hall, the White Oak Police Station and a refurbished old theater. The surrounding wineries draw visitors, and the quaint little businesses cash in.

I have the opportunity to meet other business owners and make some new acquaintances. The Chamber of Commerce ribbon cutting ceremony for Fireside Books became front page news, and helped spread the word about my new venture. Through the Chamber of Commerce I met Carolynn Langford of Langford Winery. Strikingly beautiful, Carolynn extended the first welcome. She suggested we team up at some point with a wine tasting at Fireside Books! Another new acquaintance, Rand Jolliet president of a software company, outfitted me with business systems and helped me tackle the technical side of things. He is a smart man and quite sincere. Rand is seriously considering a run at becoming the next Mayor of White Oak and I offered my support to him.

My friendship with Tera goes back many years. She comes in from the city often to help me in any way she can. A crisis reveals who your friends are and I gratefully acknowledge she is true blue. She pulled me through some of the rough times last year. I don't know where I would be without her. Tera is the closest thing to family. My parents both battled serious addictions eventually costing their young lives. I don't even remember them. I left foster care as soon as I was old enough to assume my own life. Tera drives in from the city a few times a week. We stay in close contact through texting and phoning. Hearing from her regularly does give me a sense of security. I am leaning on her less as time goes forward. We enjoy similar passions for antiques, books and wine. Countless girlfriend hours spent roaming the Midwest countryside seeking treasures. We love Langford Winery and their wine room, Bordeaux's, our new favorite place to relax and catch up.

Mr. Edison is my new landlord, tentative about leasing this space this winter, before replacing a window and some other minor concerns. With my grand opening date in mind, I convinced him to allow me to move in. I suggested he delay the repairs until the weather is warmer. Mr. Edison agreed.

It was at my Grand Opening I met Professor Enderlee from the charming coffee shop next door, Mocha Joe's. I love how the fragrant fresh brew waifs into Fireside books and told him so when he sauntered over to greet me from next door. An elderly distinguished gentleman stands at the threshold, pausing to take in the sights. He must be the neighbor Mr. Edison told me about. The proprietor of Mocha Joes' is a wiz with business. I learned that Professor Enderlee formerly a Professor of Business at the university, was disenchanted with higher education in general. His departure came swiftly when he realized the wisdom and experience of a more mature educator was becoming less and less appreciated within the administration at the university. And Mr. Edison also told me concerned alumni committee influenced the administration. When I inquired about the alumni committee, he let me know quite a few alumni live in White Oak. I might want to avoid them.

Professor Enderlee is a distinguished looking man who ducks his head as he crosses the threshold of Fireside Books.

His smile lights up the place.

As I approach him, he holds out his strong hand quivers ever so gently as I grasp it. There is genuine warmth from this gentle giant. No need for introductions, Mr. Edison shared his name with me, and mine with him.

After shaking hands enthusiastically, his wide handsome smile turns more serious as he tips his tweed Gatsby cap and nods.

"I am pleased to make your acquaintance, Ms. Clarke. I wish stellar success for Fireside Books," he says in his baritone voice.

"Please call me Quinn, Sir."

"Quinn it is, and you may call me Professor Enderlee," he says. It's evident from his booming laughter, he finds his response comical. He winks and smiles taking stock of the bookstore. "It is very nice, Quinn. I am an instant fan of Fireside Books and of you!"

His comment seems genuine enough, but I'm surprised by the speed he arrives at his conclusion.

Professor Enderlee says, "A tender place in my heart for the entrepreneur's spirit. You remind me of sweet Rose, my student assistant who I miss terribly since she moved on after graduation."

A tenderness resonates from this humble man, and I too immediately form a favorable opinion of him.

He begins to explore amid the medieval literature, and quickly becomes engrossed. As I begin to turn my attention away, my eye is instantly pulled back to his profile. This refined gentleman, who carries a slight scent of sweet tobacco, produces a large round pink bubble from his lips! And then ....pop! The bubble bursts and he begins to chew. He is quite embarrassed when he realizes I am watching.

"Please excuse my poor manners, Quinn. You have already discovered one of my vices!" His twinkling eyes are charming, and I instantly love this man.

"Any gentleman, who enjoys medieval literature and bubble gum, is welcome to enjoy both at Fireside Books," I tell him.

He continues looking around and I become distracted by a text message.

Tera: How is it going at FB?

Me: Great...Pleased!

Tera: Celebrate after closing?

I turn my attention back to the busy shop. In the afternoon I meet a couple who recently retired from public school education, Hailey and Tripp Atchison. Tripp was a teacher of history, and stout in stature. Hailey, a business teacher is taller than her husband. She is a rather large woman with silver hair and vivid red lips. They immediately introduce themselves and visit at length about their unmet expectations of retirement. I am interrupted a number of times by Hailey who is a bit abrasive. They purchase several periodicals and order even more. Most of the books are spiritual themes, in some form or fashion.

"You've selected some compelling subjects," I say as I process their order.

Hailey fidgets but makes no response. She keeps her red lips pursed as if she has a secret to tell.

"We are exploring spirituality among different cultures, quite interesting," Tripp says rushing his words. The Atchison's' are the best customers of the day thus far.

Before my five o'clock closing, another middle aged man wearing an outdated trench coat enters.

"Hello Ms. Clarke. I am Elliott Kenadie from The White Oak Advocate. May I ask you a few questions for a story I am writing on new businesses in town?"

"Sure," I reply.

Elliott Kenadie's speech is hurried and high pitched delivered through small thin lips. Reading glasses hang dangerously close to the end of his long narrow nose. His small dark eyes peer over their rims at me.

"Have you ever owned a business prior to Fireside Books?" he asks while forcing a smile.

"This is my first venture," I reply.

Mr. Kenadie takes his pencil and quickly licks the lead before making some notes. He asks me about my interest in literature, my inventory and my hours of operation. He scratches his head with his long fingers.

"Are you aware of the staggering amount of businesses close their doors after less than one year here in White Oak?" he says.

"No," I answer, wondering how his line of questioning could be helpful.

"Miss Clarke, may I take your photograph?"

Once again, he is moving from topic to topic, appearing rushed and a bit bored with the whole interview. Before I can respond, he snaps a picture of me, unprepared. He bids me good day and quickly turns and leaves. What an odd character and somewhat rude too! I shudder to think what he will write and I am already anticipating the photo as disastrous. I remind myself the exposure is helpful and will not tap into my advertising budget whatsoever. A cold burst of winter chill rushes in before the door closes behind Elliott Kenadie.

The fire is barely a smolder now. I secure the fireplace doors and prepare for closing. A jingle, jingle of the bells attached to the door, alerts me to yet one more customer.

Carolynn Langford holds a phone to her ear. Her presence commands respect. Her classic features, stylish wardrobe, long red hair and refined elegance paint an impressive picture. I've already learned a few things about her. She has her finger in numerous community circles. She is married with two school aged children. She may be busy, but always seems clam and in control. After finishing her conversation, I am the first to speak.

"Carolynn, welcome to Fireside Books, would you care for some refreshments?"

"No, thank you, Quinn, I wanted to stop over and look around on my way home from the PTA fundraiser and before our soccer team meeting. Good turnout today?" she asks while her eyes dart around the bookstore.

"I am pleased, even with the bitter cold," I say.

"How in the world did you fit them into this miniature shop?" she casually inquires with the slightest of smirks.

"Well, they were not all here at once," I remind her, wondering what her point was, and feeling a trace of inferiority.

Removing any sarcasm from her tone she replies, "Oh, of course. Fireside Books is a charming little place...cozy, with the fireplace and all." She explores a bit while I continue to close shop. She seems anything but a soccer mom. With her back to me, her graceful ivory hand slowly sweeps across titles on the shelf. Carolynn's long flowing copper tresses fall casually down her back. I couldn't help but wonder about the kind of impression she makes at these parent meetings in her tall leather boots and her exquisitely tailored red trench coat.

"Meeting the people of White Oak and a few neighbors was my pleasure! I met Professor Enderlee from Mocha Joe's," I say.

"You mean Mr. Enderlee?" she asks as she scans the shelf by the window.

"Oh, I thought his title was Professor. He is a wonderful man," I reply.

"Yes, I know him. He once was a Professor at the University. I wonder if his poor memory affects his ability to brew morning coffee?" she says laughing at the expense of the Professor.

In the Professor's defense I say, "Out of all the people through the door today, he was the most encouraging, a real gem."

"Good…will you be eventually adding a coffee bar here?" she asks.

"No, not with Mocha Joe's next door. Some patrons bring their cup from Mocha Joe's along to sip and shop. I like the idea of supporting one another in our common interests."

Carolynn smiles and says, "Sounds like you are going to be good for White Oak, and a smashing success!" Carolynn reaches in her bag and retrieves her phone. "Will the fourteenth work for the wine tasting event we spoke about?"

"Let me check," I reply. I am delighted she remembers offering the opportunity. "Yes, the fourteenth is ok."

"Thank you for your support, Carolynn."

"We will schedule time from 6-8 p.m." she says. "I will bring the wine and glasses and some savory snacks." She records the date in her phone.

"Carolynn, your generosity is appreciated, but let me take care of the snacks."

While still making notes she responds, "Yes that would be fine. What kind of promotion do you have in mind?"

"Well, I can distribute the usual flyers around town, post the event to the city's Facebook page, and announce the event at the next Chamber meeting."

She finally finishes making her notes and replies, "Sounds good. I will promote at the winery and give a mention on our radio spot."

"Thanks, Carolynn," I respond.

"See you at the Chamber breakfast meeting in the morning," she says.

Carolynn did not strike me as a very patient or nurturing person, although I have only seen her in a professional setting. She is cordial to me, but not a terribly warm personality.

"Yes, I will see you then," I offer, but the door shuts before I complete my response.

Today had been a good day and after closing up shop, I begin to face the future with hope.

Tera and I planned to meet later at Bordeaux's. The quaint spot quickly becoming a favorite gathering place for us. I look forward to slowing down the pace, while enjoying good wine with my best friend.

After locking up, I peer in Mocha Joe's window while I pass by. Professor Enderlee is at the counter, and I wave to him. A look of panic is on in his face. I quickly enter, rushing to him as he begins to slump down.

"Professor Enderlee, what is wrong? Let me get you to a chair."

He leans on me as I lead him to a bench against the wall. He plops down rather hard, knocking his Gatsby hat off center. His eyes are empty looking and dazed.

"What is it? How can I help you? Are you sick?" I ask as my concern grows.

He is unresponsive and panic begins to rise in my throat. He is in trouble. His face is drained of color. I am feeling fear again, a frequent visitor. I need to stay calm, I need a clear head.

He raises his arm showing the medical bracelet. Insect allergy is the warning.

In dismay, I search his face.

His hand reaches for his neck, and I see large red welts across his throat. He holds a syringe in his right hand and I realize he needs the drug injected.

I have never injected anyone, and the thought is unnerving.

He points to his thigh and I take the syringe out of his hand.

I forcefully thrust the needle into his leg and dispense the antidote.

I immediately call 911 on my cell then turn my attention back to Professor Enderlee.

He is breathing easier and I do my best to calm him. He is visibly shaken and watches wide eyed as the paramedics arrive. He is adamant about avoiding a ride to the emergency room.

The medics check his vitals and give him a second dose of epinephrine. They instruct him to visit his doctor first thing in the morning.

I send a text to Tera, and request a rain check on our plans for celebrating at Bordeaux's, too much of a day for this girl.

I brew some tea for Professor Enderlee while waiting for the paramedics to leave. We sit together quietly, and he thanks me first with his kind eyes, and finally with spoken words.

"Thank you Quinn, thank God you happened to walk by."

"Professor, you must have learned by now the danger of being stung. Why couldn't you inject yourself?" I ask.

"I am not certain," he responds thoughtfully, "I was stung by a bee last summer, while moving into the coffee shop. Pony, a young man who works with me, quickly called 911. I now wear the medical bracelet and keep the epinephrine with me at all times. I nearly forgot about the allergy, and am certainly surprised to be stung in the winter months!"

"Are you sure a bee stung you?" I ask.

"Yes, the bees; they came out of the water faucet! They came right at me and stung me immediately. After attempting to swat at them, I was lightheaded. I reached in the drawer for the epinephrine. Then, I became confused," he explains.

"We will need to talk to Mr. Edison first thing tomorrow morning so he can check the faucet; you need to be safe in your own business!"

He says, "Thank you, Quinn. I will be just fine now; I am going to drive home to rest,"

"No way, Professor, I will be driving you home and bring you back in the morning. I would sleep much better if with you safely at home."

I feel tenderness for this charming man. He seems to be relieved by my offer to take him home.

His home, a sprawling bungalow, is not far from the coffee shop.

I carry his satchel and walk next to him as he ascends the steps to the front door of this grand old home. He apologizes for his housekeeping, as he leads me to a study. His home is in need of some attention. He removes his coat and sits down on the sofa.

"Professor, do you need anything before I leave?" I ask.

"Thank you so much, Quinn. No need to pick me up in the morning. Pony will stop over and give me some assistance. Would you mind bringing me a glass of water?"

His color returned, and his eyes are bright and focused.

I find the kitchen but search for a clean glass. This room like the others is cluttered and unkempt. The wide hallway leading back to the study is lined with photographs. I notice a portrait of a young woman. She is striking. Another time I will ask the Professor about her. Sounds of heavy breathing greet me as I enter the room. I cover the sleeping Professor with a blanket, and quietly let myself out.

Chapter Three

White Oak's main street is lined with beautifully restored old buildings. The Chamber of Commerce breakfast meeting is held at one of them, the McCracken House. I soaked up the history of the building during my first meeting with the chamber. A thriving fur trading industry at the turn of the century called this place home. The McCracken House is not only functional, but a glimpse to a bygone era.

As the room fills, I add some cream to my morning brew at the coffee bar.

Elliott Kenadie joins me at the coffee bar, before I find a seat.

"How are you this fine day, Ms. Clarke?" Kenadie inquires.

His sunny disposition is a remarkable improvement over our last encounter.

"Good, and after this coffee, even better!" I say.

"And I enjoy my tea! I like to quote my old professor who used to say, 'Ah, tea, it is the cup of life!'" he says as he nods and takes his seat.

I sip the coffee as I page through the prepared folder for each member, a calendar of events, member lists, and agenda. I am hoping the meeting will be better than the coffee.

Adam Langford, Carolynn's husband abruptly sits down next to me.

I greet him and in return I receive a somewhat cool and detached one word response.

"Morning," he says.

Carolynn is nowhere to be seen as bank president Delmont Smith, calls the meeting to order. A suit and tie spruce up a rather ordinary man with thinning hair. His demeanor is quite serious, and his face devoid of much expression. Madge Botherme is introduced and given the floor.

Rand Jolliet scribbles on his notebook, then elbows me to show what he has written. "Madge is best in small doses, hang on to your seat!" he has written. I've been warned that Madge is distinctive.

Barely seeing over the podium, Madge Botherme addresses the

chamber wearing extremely outdated fashion. The white blouse with crisp collar means business under a colorful print jacket. That teased hairstyle is plenty stiff, as she smiles through a generous amount of pink lipstick.

"Good morning business leaders of White Oak. I asked our President Mr. Smith, if I could update everyone on our Operation Reach Out program, and he kindly allowed me a few minutes. Although this is a city project, many of our Chamber members are involved," Madge Botherme says.

Mrs. Botherme stops to pose. She continues after Elliott Kenadie snaps a few pictures.

"This project's goal is to involve citizens in all branches of our city. People support that which they help to create. Citizen Involvement will bolster the good of the entire community."

The meeting is disrupted by a loud creaking of the front door. All attention turns to see who is tardy.

Carolynn Langford comes through the door looking composed, even regal. Where other less confident people might appear disheveled and offer a flurry of apologies for their late arrival, Carolynn walks confidently to the back of the room, and nods towards the podium.

"Madge," she says before taking her seat.

Madge Botherme does her best to pick up where she left off.

"If more become involved, we can tackle the issues. This far reaching project will be divided into groups touching every facet of our little city. As of today Reach Out to our Students will be organized and spearheaded by Cindy Arness. Please give a wave when I mention your-."

Adam Langford stands and moves to the back near Carolynn, disrupting the meeting again.

Madge continues, "Dominic Bump will work with our merchants, Reach Out to our Health Community headed by Constance Aster, Reach Out to our Religious Community headed by Blanche Treadwater and finally the last one, Reach Out to our senior's, headed by Edith Craven. I want to unveil our newly designed logo for this unique and historical campaign to improve the lives of every citizen in White Oak."

Madge Botherme steps away from the podium to a showcase a

covered easel.

"Cue the music please!" she orders, as the secretary scurries to the back of the room and starts the music. A boisterous rendition of "America the Beautiful" blares from the rear of the room as the councilwoman makes a dramatic tug on the cloth-covered easel to reveal the logo. Unfortunately, the tugging of the fabric concealing the logo pulls the whole thing down with a crash.

"Oh no!" Madge cries as Dominic Bump jumps up to assist her.

A few poorly concealed chuckles come from the group. Finally the logo is revealed and Madge applauds enthusiastically, encouraging the rest of us to do the same.

In an awkward moment, members glance around, weak hand clapping follows.

Madge signals for the music volume to be increased. Upon the easel is a most unusual looking logo. An aggressive bullfrog poised for a big leap! Lack luster applause fades quickly, and the music is cut.

My quick glance around the room catches more than one set of rolling eyes.

"Why a frog?" Grace Coyville asks.

"They are tasty!" Domonic Bump blurts out. His comment brings more laughs.

A clearly annoyed Mrs. Botherme puts one hand on her hip, while using her other hand to make a few points.

"The North American bullfrog is the official state amphibian of Missouri! Thanks to a local 4th grade class from Chinn Elementary, a brilliant suggestion! May I remind you frog hunting season opens in June, and this species of frog can be found in every county within Missouri?" Mrs. Botherme says, staunchly defending her logo.

Delmont Smith speaks up, "But do we really want a bullfrog on this project?"

Carolynn Langford stands and says, "I don't see the need for a logo at all."

Rand Jolliet addresses the group, "May I remind you a majority is needed from a vote to create this kind of program, and I don't think a vote was taken. There is a more important issue to spend precious time on. I brought up the need or a comprehensive communication system.

This city is growing and the time to prepare for expansion is now. If a catastrophe were ever to occur, this is the best way to insure safety."

"This point has been covered Mr. Jolliet," Madge Botherme says.

Delmont Smith stands and addresses the group, "Rand, I agree with you on this issue. I know a standard communications platform is critical, not only on a daily basis, but especially when command and control is paramount during emergencies, but we will table this issue for the next upcoming city council meeting."

"I am ready for that," Rand says and sits down.

Delmont Smith nods for Mrs. Botherme to continue.

"Ladies and Gentleman, The logo committee chose me to create a face for Operation Reach Out. Unfortunately no one else wanted to take time from their schedules to participate. The logo has been chosen and printed on all of our ordered literature, pamphlets and banners, thank you," she says.

Madge distributes lapel badges of the frog logo, with the words Reach Out printed below the green amphibian. It is obvious few are enthusiastic about the logo, but the meeting moves forward.

Delmont Smith takes the podium back.

"Last year we had a triumph with our Moonlight with Merchants event. The support from the community has been impressive. Our goal is to increase the number of businesses taking part, and patrons. Who will take the reins of this project?" Delmont asks. He looks over the room for takers, of which there is none.

Carolynn Langford says, "I would like to make a motion to nominate our newest chamber member, Quinn Clarke, to organize this event. She will do a fine job."

All eyes are on me as I squirm in my seat.

"I thank you for the nomination Carolynn, but I am new to White Oak and to the chamber. I would like to experience the event before spearheading it. Perhaps next time," I say.

"I was the organizer last year, and it was very simple. I will gladly share my notes, and assist you," Carolynn says.

"Well...then, how can I refuse? Sure I will... take the reins," I say to the group reluctantly before taking my seat, relying on Carolynn's experience and her confidence in my ability.

Delmont Smith says, "Wonderful, thank you Ms. Clarke!"

After a few more items of business, we are adjourned.

While gathering my belongings, I see Carolynn and Adam Langford talking with Madge Botherme. Carolynn is patting her shoulder. No doubt Madge is looking for sympathy and support. My eyes catch Carolynn's, and she motions for me to wait a moment.

Elliott Kenadie is snapping pictures of the logo, but he is the only one showing real interest in it at all.

The room is thinning out and Carolynn is nowhere in sight. While freshening up in the ladies room, I hear muffled voices coming from the floor above me. A voice sounds a lot like Carolynn and a man's voice, perhaps Adam? The conversation becomes louder along with some thumping and scuffling sounds. Is Carolynn in trouble? Immediately upon leaving the rest room, I am met by Carolynn.

"Oh, Quinn, thank you for waiting," she says with a sincere smile.

"Is everything alright?"

"Yes, why do you ask?" she replies.

"From the ladies room, I heard voices and some scuffling," I tell her.

Carolynn's phone begins to ring, and she checks it.

"Adam and I were upstairs helping the secretary move her desk to the sunny side of the room, this place is quite drafty. Adam mostly voiced his opinion loudly. I wanted to thank you for taking the organizational role of the Merchant's night. My hands are full this year with the children's schedules. I will share my notes with you when I am at Fireside Books for our wine tasting event. You will do a fine job," Carolynn says. "See you soon, Quinn."

Rand catches me out front of the McCracken House as I'm leaving.

"Quinn, the chamber is blind to the real issues. I can't figure it out why we are wasting our time with this Reach Out project. It is nothing more than a distraction from the real issues. The next council meeting could run overtime. I'm getting frustrated," Rand says.

"The Reach Out project does seem weakly supported. You are right about the length the next meeting may take. Have a good one, Rand," I say.

My thoughts turn to Fireside books and my day ahead, but I couldn't help but wonder if problems existed between Carolynn and Adam Langford. The wind releases a frog pamphlet tucked under my wiper as I leave.

Chapter Four

Before opening Fireside Books for the day, I stop in to check on the Professor. As soon as I enter Mocha Joe's, he comes from behind the counter and greets me with a big hug and his words of gratitude.

"Thank you so much for helping me last evening, Quinn. I really feel a bit silly. If you had not glanced in the window-" he says.

"You are looking well," I said.

"I am superb!" he says with a big grin. "Quinn, wait!"

He disappears into a back room with the giddiness of a child.

The bistro décor is inviting with seats at tall tables and worn leather chairs and sofa huddled around a cozy fire. Each quaint booth along both outer walls is flanked with a shake covered awning. The cottage inspired awnings provide intimate privacy to those seated within. A beautiful, natural dark wood floor, and the pressed copper tin tiles covering the ceiling lend antiquity to the well-designed interior. Towards the back of the shop lies a walnut bar with brass foot rest. Tall stools offer seating illuminated by art deco pendant lights.

A young man puts pastries into a glass bakery case already richly stocked with biscotti, breads, strudels and bars.

The professor emerges from a back room with a red bag.

"This is my most requested coffee blend, for you Quinn."

"Why thank you professor, but your gratitude is more than thanks."

"I want you to enjoy this small token, please," he says insisting. "Pony, would you kindly serve Quinn some to take along?"

"Sure, I would be happy to," the young man says as prepares a cup to go

"This is Pony Coldstone. He helps me a few days a week here at the coffee shop. He is a former student of mine. Pony this is Quinn, owner of Fireside Books," the professor says.

Pony says, "I'm glad to meet you Quinn; the professor loves your bookstore."

I can't help noticing how young Pony is. He can't be more than sixteen or seventeen.

Pony says, "If you are guessing I'm too young to be a college student, you're right!"

Professor Enderlee says, "Yes, Pony's academic gift allowed him to enter college after graduating from high school at age thirteen."

"My goodness, young man! I am pleased to meet you," I say as I hold out my hand to shake his.

He grasps my hand, humbly lowering his eyes. He serves me the coffee and I thank them both again before making my way out the door.

The winter drags on. Leafless oak branches form a frame around the view from my shop. Traffic changes the once peaceful fallen snow into sloppy mayhem. Shoppers take no time for window shopping as they move their bundled bodies quickly to and fro. Winter's breath forces them to clutch their coats tighter. Lowered heads brace against the bitter wind. I am glad to be on the inside looking out, as I hold the hot coffee from the Professor and warm myself by a soothing fire. A stray cat, I named Thomasena, is now the resident feline. I appreciate the company. Since coming here everything is slower. I'm content surrounded by books like trusted familiar friends. Consistency was not part of my childhood, but one constant was the library. I spent hours amid shelves, finding the atmosphere peaceful and intriguing. Through reading I traveled the world, meeting interesting characters and cultures. Today my only distraction is the vibration of my phone, texts from Tera.

I will be in White Oak tonight, Bordeaux's?

Me: It's a date-6ish.

Tera is a free spirit, with boundless energy. I am not sure where I would be without her this last year. A real friend is one who walks in when the rest of the world walks out. Others simply were too busy to continue our relationship during my rehabilitation. Tera is spending more and more time in White Oak. For the last six months we've grown to love Bordeaux's, a restaurant and wine bar within Langford Winery.

Business was brisk before lunch at Fireside Books, but the sound of jingling bells signaling patrons remains silent since. Growing my inventory to feature everything from current best sellers to rare books is one of my goals. On Tuesday I will be viewing a set I would be interested in purchasing. The collection being offered at Royce Estate would be exciting to own, if the condition is good, and the price is right.

Thomesena rests peacefully next to me. This bookstore was scheduled to shut its doors after thirty years in White Oak, when I purchased it. The old stone fireplace needed updating to pass city code, and adjustments were made, otherwise the shop is the same. Several patrons are relieved it was saved. A constant in life gives a sense of security. Consistency is fleeting. I am relishing this existence after the turbulence this past year, knowing nothing ever stays the same.

Leaving the corporate world was good decision for me. Owning Fireside Books is giving me the time I need to heal. The last thing I recall before dozing off is Thomasena's purring. Sleep comes easily, but doesn't stay long. My dreams of losing Alec haunt me. Today is no different, still seeking answers to the questions about the accident. I don't remember seeing him lying at the bottom. I am certain Alec called my name, but the searing sun blinded me from confirming who. How could Alec's voice be behind me when his lifeless body was already waiting to break my fall on stone floor far below. I struggle for clarity. The jingling door wakes me and alerts me to a customer.

"May I help you?" I say rising to my feet. I've never seen this woman before, and I would surely remember her vibrant red hair.

"Yes," says a woman in a breathless British dialect, "I am looking for anything by Reginald Angelo."

"I am familiar; he will be back this way," I say leading her to the back of the store and leaving her to browse. Her red leather boots are almost as vivid as her hair. The oversized orange handbag dwarfs her already small frame.

My phone signals a text from Tera, I plan to respond to once my customer leaves.

Within minutes, she presents herself at my counter.

"Found the book I wanted," she announces.

Bold ruby red hair surrounds her alabaster skin with striking contrast. Mint colored eyeglasses studded with rhinestones crowd her petite features. She offers a slight smile framed by generous amount of rosy lipstick, and produces payment from the orange leather bag. Exact amounts of cash and coin are taken from a snappy silver pocketbook, and she pauses and studies my eyes while passing it to me. She lingers for a brief moment after being handed her receipt and but says nothing before swiftly collecting her purchase and bag and leaving.

The customer bustles out and a jingle, jingle follows her as the door closes behind her.

I tend to the fire, spreading the smoldering bits and securing the fireplace doors.

Thomesena nudges me to fill her dish.

Like a flash men run past the shop window and pedestrians from the other side of the street are running too.

My curiosity pulls me to investigate. There is some commotion at the end of the block. I quickly gather the receipts and clear my sales counter, when I discover a small note lying where the ruby haired woman purse was. Words written in purple ink simply say,

"You were pushed."

Chapter Five

Traffic is backing up in front of the shop. Voices are raised along with my growing confusion. The shrill of sirens in the distance raises my concern as I make my way to a group formed at the end of the block.

A policewoman is asking curious bystanders to move back.

"Make way for the ambulance" the female officer bellows.

The crowd moves back, and I catch a glimpse of the street. An orange leather bag lies in the snow and slush, its contents scattered all over the snow covered pavement. My heart begins to beat faster when I realize the victim was my customer only minutes ago!

The onlookers block my vision. A reserved silence now, as the rescue squad makes their way to the center of the situation. The throng of people is asked to move again. Everyone is eager to oblige. When the mob shifts I catch a glimpse of the red leather boots. The sight freezes me and the backs of curious heads prevent me from seeing more.

"Did you witness the accident?" I asked a young man next to me.

"Yes," he replies excitedly, "a car peeled around the corner and her as she crossed the street. Horrible, horrible....the old car just kept going...never even stopped!"

The woman is dead, evident when the rescue team covers her face completely.

The cluster of onlookers begins to thin out, but I am still standing in the same spot. Dazed and confused I make my way to the policewoman is clearing the crowd.

"Who was she?" I ask the officer.

"That information is not available yet, are you a witness to the accident?"

"No, but she left my shop minutes before!" I tell her.

The police woman gives me her card.

"Come down to the station and give a statement," she says.

I agree willingly, since I am intending to find out more from Officer Bishop than she would learn from me.

At the police department Officer Bishop begins to fill out a report.

I give her Fireside Books as my address.

She delivers the paper to an office which gives me a few moments to respond to Tera's text...

Bordeaux's at 7, loads to tell you.

Shortly thereafter, a man on his phone wearing a suit and tie approaches.

"You're Mrs. Clarke?" he asks.

"It's Miss Clarke."

"I'm Detective Keefe Remington. I want to ask you a few questions in my office," he says.

His long blonde bangs fall forward and he combs them back with one sweep of his hand. One might expect a short clean looking hairstyle for a detective in a suit, but Remington's image doesn't follow the rules. He leads me into his office mostly taken up by a desk. Before he speaks, his phone rings again.

"Remington here...yup what do you mean?" he says to the caller.

As he listens intently, I take the opportunity to fish in my bag for my cell. After a few attempts I empty the contents, find the phone and put everything back.

Detective Remington says, "Are you certain? Ok." Detective Remington pauses with a confused expression before turning his attention to me.

"Did you know the victim?" he asks.

"No I've never seen her, she purchased a book minutes before the accident," I say, "I would remember her. She was... distinctive."

"Distinctive?" he asks.

"She wore red leather boots and carried an orange bag, her hair was a bold shade of red, and her eyeglass frames were green. You don't see that every day," I say.

Detective Remington makes no comment.

"Is her identity confirmed yet?" I ask.

"The call I received from officers at the scene report no identification found of any kind," says Remington.

"She clearly took cash out of a metallic like pocketbook from her bag," I tell him.

Our conversation is interrupted again by a knock on the door.

Policewoman Bishop enters and hands a folder to Detective Remington.

"Sir, someone is here about the vehicle in the incident," she says.

Detective Remington says, "Thanks, Dawn."

He takes the folder without even glancing at her.

Oddly she lingers. The awkwardness does not affect her. After a few moments the Detective glances up.

"Thanks Dawn... that is all for now," he politely comments.

Dawn Bishop stares intently, eyes fixed on him.

"Sir, shall I take a statement?" she asks.

"I will take care of it shortly, thanks."

She leaves the room and closes the door behind her.

Remington shuts his eyes and pauses with lids closed for a few extra seconds and I am quite sure I sensed frustration and a little embarrassment. When he opens his eyes, he picks up right where we left off.

"The silver wallet was empty, no driver's license, credit cards . . . nothing.

"Could contents of her wallet be stolen during the commotion?" I ask, disgusted at the thought.

"Unsettling as it is, opportunist with such little regard for decency can live in White Oak too. Unfortunately my experiences have taught me that," he replies.

"The woman's accent was British, she was middle aged. She asked about the works of a particular author. She only spent a few minutes shopping, before she brought a book to the counter," I tell the detective. This would be the time to bring up the note, but I must consider this decision carefully, and the public scrutiny I would invite. Did the delivery of the message put the mystery woman in danger? For now the incident remains an accident, so I will not mention the note.

"So, you were not a witness?" asks the detective.

"No, a young man in the crowd saw an older car speeding around the corner and hit her," I say.

"Yes, those are the facts we gathered in our report from the accident scene," he says looking at notes. His phone rings again, he glances and asks the caller to hold.

"Thanks for your assistance Miss Clarke."

He rises from behind the desk with an out stretched hand and a pleasant smile.

I stand and accept his firm handshake.

With Alec's notoriety, our accident became front page news. Driving to Bordeaux's thoughts twirl like a carousel wondering if the mystery woman's note was speculation from someone with too much time on their hands. Tera would hopefully give me some much needed perspective.

I check my visor mirror quickly as I arrive at Bordeaux's windblown. I work my fingers through my hair for a quick lift, and apply lipstick, all the primping I have patience left for today. Tera is a natural Latin beauty with dark eyes and olive skin. Her image will be amazing as usual and she won't say anything about my appearance, under the good friend clause.

Bordeaux's itself is lodge like in design surrounded by large oak trees. The heritage of Langford winery goes back to 1851 when the family emigrated from Germany to join other Germans in Missouri. Langford's is my favorite winery among the several in the area of White Oak, with Bordeaux's being the main reason.

Carolynn Langford is quickly over to my side with questions.

"Is it true, the victim of the crime, left your shop only moments before?" she asked.

"A crime...who told you she came out of my store?" I ask her.

"Councilwoman Madge Botherme, the ear of White Oak was in. Who was she?" she asks.

"No, she was a new customer to Fireside Books," I say, uneasy with her probing.

Carolynn says, "Tera is already here, she asked for a dirty martini again and enjoys making us remind her that this is a winery."

Carolynn leads me to a table in the cavern area.

A portion of Bordeaux's is built into the bluff. Some of the wine storage barrels sit here. Hearty oak booths, low lighting, limestone walls and bountiful faux grape vines create a relaxing ambiance.

Tera steps out of the booth and greets me with an embrace. Her long flowing brunette hair swept up in a casual ponytail, but her exotic dark eyes and full lips are glamorous.

I am genuinely happy to see my friend.

With glass in hand, she nods to the waiter to bring my standard, Chardonnay.

Carolynn brings the wine herself.

"Tera took the liberty of ordering dinner for you. We are preparing the Ziti in Marinara, and a signature Bordeaux salad with house dressing on the side," asks Carolynn.

"Delicious, thank you Carolynn!" I reply.

"I hope you didn't wait too long for me, Main Street was the scene of an accident," I say.

Tera says, "Carolynn filled me in; it is horrible!"

"The poor woman left my shop with a purchase and within 3 minutes she was dead! The car didn't stop, a hit and run. I gave a statement at the police station."

"My, goodness," Tera gasps as she reaches a delicate hand for her glass of Pinot.

"I met Detective Keefe Remington and told him what I knew, basically nothing. The woman paid with cash, but her British accent and her colorful garb, left an impression on me...her hair was ruby colored!"

"What?" Tera asks.

"Unusual, for sure! She wore mint green eyeglass frames, red boots, and carried an orange leather bag."

Tera says, "What could she have been thinking while dressing this morning?"

"Well," I said, "not that she was going to die!"

Tera's face becomes somber.

Carolynn serves our meals, a feast for the eyes. The steaming Ziti, tossed gently in Bordeaux's own marinara and topped with freshly grated parmesan cheese and fresh basil. A toasted baguette with goat cheese rests alongside a salad with frilly lettuce, artichokes and olives and dressed with Bordeaux's own savory recipe of olive oil, basil, oregano and lemon.

"I found something on the counter after the woman left the store, a message." Once again I fish through my bag. I dump everything out on the oak table; "It's not here!"

"Quinn, don't forget what the doctor told you about your memory, you may need more time. Maybe you left the note at the shop," she says.

"No, Tera, I clearly remember putting placing the note inside my bag, so I could show you."

Tera impatiently says, "Tell me the message, Quinn!"

"Written in purple ink it read... you were pushed!"

Panic rises as I verbalize the words, my body tenses up. The old familiar dread starts in my chest and quickly works its way to all parts of my body. In a split second, my recollection of the accident is played out in my mind. No matter what the doctors said about the unlikely scenario I supplied, I can't let it go. Why would anyone want Alec or me dead? What possible motive could exist? My fear and doubt resurface. I feel unnerved by the fact I could still be in danger.

"Good Lord, Quinn!" Tera says.

"What did the detective say about the note?"

"Lord no, Tera," I say "The last thing I need is to be involved in another...accident!"

"But if you withhold this information, you could be risking . . ."

"Perhaps, but I will give it time," I reply as I sip my wine.

Tera's expression reveals her compassion but she is silent for the moment.

I raise an index finger to my lips. With my voice lowered I continue.

"If you will remember, controversy and public scrutiny ended my career. I don't want or need more attention drawn to myself. My feet are firmly planted in White Oak. I want the past to remain in the past. I am making my way back. I believe the mystery woman was a

"I am sure you are right," Tera says. "You are tired. Let's finish our meal and get you to bed. A good night's rest will make a difference."

"Yes, exactly what I need. I almost forgot to tell you, I received an email with an offer about an antique book collection for sale."

"Who's the seller?" she asks.

"It's R. Royce."

"Quinn, are you joking? The Royce family is extremely affluent. Their estate is massive; nothing quite like it exists. The Royce's goodness! Can I come along?" she wails.

"No way, I can't have you asking for a dirty Martini!" I say laughing. "My appointment is at 2pm, the day after tomorrow. They live at the top of Royce's ridge. Pretty great, huh?" I ask.

"Good for you, Quinn. Sounds like an interesting opportunity. Any single men in this Royce family?" Tera asks, with raised brows.

"I'm not even sure who R. Royce is, and knowing your curiosity, I will be silencing my phone. Oh, and by the way, I reluctantly accepted the nomination to organize the merchant's night in White Oak today at the Chamber meeting."

"How did that happen?" she asks sarcastically.

"I'm not sure, Carolynn is going to help me with the organization of the event."

"Why don't you let me help you out too?" Tera asks, a typical response for her.

"Thanks, friend," I say sliding out of the booth.

"No problem. You take care, Quinn, get some rest."

"You're not leaving?" I ask. She looks over my shoulder at a gentleman sitting at the bar and instantly I understand.

"Ok, be good," I say with a wink.

Walking through Bordeaux's, someone touches my arm in passing.

"Hello, Quinn!" Rand says from a table he shares with Cindy Arness.

"Hi Rand, Cindy, are you enjoying a good meal?"

Cindy says, "The food is very good. We are putting together our campaign plan!"

"Campaign plan?" I ask with a smile.

"Rand will be running for mayor in the next election and I'm his campaign manager!" explains Cindy.

"Great news," I say.

Rand says, "I can't do any worse than the current mayor."

"I will do what I can do to help," I say and leave Bordeaux's, thinking it looks more like a date.

The day has been a long one. I turn into my driveway and find dozens of white birds covering my front lawn.

Chapter Six

Winter holds its grip, preventing any thoughts of spring. Weeks pass and still no answers to the questions about the mystery woman's accident. The long anticipated wine tasting at Fireside Books is tomorrow, and I fall asleep hopeful.

Alec moves and I enjoy watching him as he methodically builds a fire, arranging the kindling. His most attractive quality is his confidence He ignites the wood and eager flames grow bright. We sit back mesmerized by them as they dance.The brilliance of the blaze glares, and I blink my eyes awake to daybreak's light.

The morning's first rays of sun beam into my eyes, but this is one dream I don't want to end. Almost immediately the dull pain of loss returns. I will put one foot in front of the other remembering time is my friend; grief's grip loosens with it. Gratefully the promise of the day pulls my spirits up. Morning is beautiful as beams of sun barge through half closed wood blinds casting brilliance on my bedroom of apple green and willow hues. I roll out of bed and sink my feet into the lush softness of luxury. My plush flokati rug was one of the first things I purchased for the house, another lies in the bathroom, a gift from Tera. We burned the midnight oil many nights making this small, picturesque Victorian mine.

By the time I shower and dress, the room is flooded by the radiant luster of a new day. My reflection in the mirror seems as different as my new life. Outside of the corporate world, I wear less makeup and a more relaxed wardrobe and allow my chestnut hair to grow longer. I'm looking forward to the wine tasting event at Fireside Books, and connecting with Carolynn Langford.

The day passes at the bookstore with only a handful of shoppers. Carolynn's voice reaches the back room.

"Hello?" she calls out.

"I will be right there," I say "Hi Carolynn, let me help you get your things in."

"Don't be silly, Adam is getting the rest out of the car for me. Where shall we set up the wine?" she asks as her eyes travel around the shop.

"Wine and glasses on this counter, and the snacks by the window," I say.

"Good," Carolynn comments.

Carrying a tote and basket, Adam Langford comes through the door, and brings a burst of cold brisk winter air with him.

"Thank you, Adam," Carolynn says as he begins to unpack.

Adam nods to us both and leaves.

"Is he displeased about something?" I ask, his demeanor hard to ignore.

Carolynn stands at the counter with her back to me. She flips some of her long red hair over her shoulder and responds without turning.

"No, not at all," she says without concern.

"He seemed upset," I say.

"He was in a… mood when he woke up," she remarks casually.

I stoke the fire as our first patrons arrive. With soft symphony sounds in the background, and our wine and snacks all ready, our event is underway.

Carolynn brings a selection of wines with her for sampling, confident as she communicates with the guests, and answers their questions with ease.

Three other customers arrive as the others begin to shop around the bookstore.

Cindy Arness comes through the door next with a wave hello and with a kind smile she says, "I wanted to drop by to support your event."

"What a kind gesture, thank you Cindy," I comment.

Cindy does some wine tasting, and spends a good amount of time talking to Carolynn, while I help some customers with purchases. The evening flows and I have time to savor the smooth buttery oak of Langford's Chardonnay.

Tera arrives and helps Carolynn with the women's book club

members who come all at once and occupy much of the last hour. Carolynn and Tera visit and laugh when shoppers are not at wine bar. They obviously like working together. I am pleased with the turnout.

Tera stays around to help with the clean- up. Afterward we sit on the sofa in front of the fire with our glasses of wine.

Carolynn takes a folder from her bag with the notes on the merchant's event.

"This should make your organization pretty simple. The entertainment we used last year is listed but I will need to get you their contact information later," she says. "Call me anytime with questions."

"I appreciate the support from you both, thank you," I say.

"I promoted the winery, and sold some wine, so I am pleased!" a relaxed Carolynn says.

Tera chimes in, "I would do anything for my friend! Are you up for a road trip soon? We haven't been antiquing in months."

"Yes, I miss the adventures," I respond.

Carolynn's interest is piqued and she asks, "Have you been to Mason & Murdock in St. Charles? Their gallery is divine, and the antique mall is in the same vicinity. My brother took me last year; I purchased my bracelets there." She holds up her hand. Glistening from her slender wrist are two solid gold bangles, each with a rectangle of smoky quartz.

"Those are beautiful!" I say.

Carolynn explains the quartz stones are special. When worn, they act as a filter to trap negative forces.

"Quinn and I talked about going to Mason & Murdock," Tera adds.

"We should plan a girl's weekend; getting away sounds good to me," Carolynn says as she pours herself another glass of wine.

Tera heads home to the city after saying her goodbyes.

Carolynn and I are left to discuss the evening and she mentions Cindy Arness.

"Cindy Arness tried to dominate every conversation, making communication difficult to with the customers!" Carolynn says.

Cindy always seemed quiet and reserved so this comment surprises me. Carolynn's two glasses of wine are showing their effects.

"She gets away with so much," Carolynn says in a naughty whisper.

"What do you mean?" I ask, completely confused. Carolynn didn't seem the type to gossip.

"Let's just say her former employer asked her to leave quietly."

I say, "I remember she was teaching at a private school."

With her shoes off, and her legs drawn up under her, Carolynn casually adds, "Apparently her skills at raising funds paled in comparison to her skill at skimming from them."

Carolynn's phone rings, and she excuses herself to take a call.

Stunned by the information I wait for her.

Carolynn is gone for at least ten minutes before she emerges from the back room looking visibly upset. Her eye makeup is mostly dabbed off with the tissues she is using to dry her tears.

"Carolynn, are you alright?" I ask immediately.

She sits down, and takes her wine glass in hand.

"Adam is on his way to pick me up, so he can help me with loading. He is...unhappy with me," she says as the tears begin to flow again.

This is a different side of Carolynn.

She says, "He doesn't understand me, he is impatient with me." She let more tears fall and I put my hand on her shoulder to comfort her. She continues, "A few years ago, I sustained a painful injury and had trouble getting off of the pain medication prescribed. Not a good time for us. I finally was able to wean myself away from the drug, but....I had a little relapse. This became the last straw for Adam. He wants out of our marriage. I am trying to convince him to give us some time. I still love him and our family." This last statement brings her emotions to the surface, and I give her more tissues, and as much encouragement as I can.

"Can I help?" I ask her.

She looks at me with tear-stained ivory skin and wet eyes.

"No, I will be fine. I am sorry to share my burden with you Quinn."

"That is what friends do," I say, handing her another tissue.

"Be a friend, thank you."

"I surely will," I say.

Adam comes into the shop, lifts her totes and says goodnight and nods to me as he walks out.

Carolynn follows.

Chapter Seven

The next day as I pour coffee the doorbell rings. No one is there, but on my stoup, standing in the morning light is a small box with a note.

"Thanks for being a friend. C."

I am surprised to find one of the gold bangle bracelets with the smoky quartz stone! I immediately put the bracelet on and gaze at its beauty when I receive a text from Carolynn.

"Enjoy the bracelet. Please accept in the spirit of friendship," the message says.

I text back telling her I'm already wearing it."

White Oak is starting to feel like home. A fine day this shall be. Today is the day I will meet the mysterious R. Royce. After I decide on a black pants suit, my curiosity about the Royce family dominates my thoughts. How extensive is their collection? Who lives in the grand estate? A quick glance to my buzzing phone causes me to pause. Weather advisory is posted. A storm is predicted to move into our area by late afternoon. They are calling for several inches of snow, along with severe temperatures and blowing winds. I gaze outside, the sunny start to my day is giving way to overcast skies. Winter is not my favorite season. I will be able to finish my appointment at Royce Estate and return back to Fireside Books before any weather obstacles begin.

The other two messages are from Tera.

"I met someone new.... fill you in later... C. Langford is coming, looking over my antique collection."

Our conversation about antiques happened just last evening. I'm surprised they've already planned something. She will be impressed with Tera's treasures.

I arrive at the shop and gather items needed for my appointment. I take some time to hunt for my pink camera, before I remember it was lost in the accident and I will need to use my phone for picture taking. The sound of the door chimes signals a customer.

A man enters and after removing his brown scarf, I am surprised by Detective Keefe Remington.

"Good Morning Detective, what brings you to Fireside Books, news about the mystery woman?" I ask.

With a serious tone he replies, "No, unfortunately, and haven't found the car involved. Miss Clarke, are you certain you are telling me everything about the woman?" His brown eyes penetrate my confidence.

His inquiry catches me unprepared for a response. I am afraid my body language tells him what he needs to know as I shift my weight from side to side avoiding his gaze completely.

"Is there anything you would like to tell me?" he asks me a second time.

Not telling him what I know may only reflect badly on me, and as I make eye contact with those eyes, I confess.

"Well, yes, Detective Remington, one small bit of information I didn't mention-"

"You mean this?" he said as he laid the small note written in purple ink on the counter. "Left in my office, after you dumped your bag.

My head lowered as I reread the message. I slowly raise my head.

"I am as puzzled as you are, I don't understand any of this," I explain. Exposed and uncomfortable, I don't want to dredge up the past, or face questions challenging my credibility, my mental state or motives. The panic gripping me when Alec did not return after going back for the camera resurfaces. He said my name. I can vividly feel the utter shock and horror as I fell, realizing the man I love is murdering me.

"Miss Clarke," the detective brings me back to the present. "I am fully aware of your accident last year and the media circus surrounding it. They place a higher priority on selling papers, than fact checking. Where exactly did this note come from?" he asks.

"I believe the ruby haired woman. She left it on the counter immediately after she paid for her book."

Detective Remington says, "'You were pushed' What do you make of this woman, her message?"

I push my hair back and grasp the back of my neck with my hand.

"Maybe she was obsessed with the accident, and was compelled to share her opinion," I offer.

Remington studies my face.

"Or, she was attempting to warn you. She knew something about the case. What kind of investigation was performed on your behalf Miss Clarke?"

"My injuries became the priority; many broken bones, and concussion...a miracle I survived. The authorities discredited my memories of what happened because of the head injury. Discussions remained between my doctors and me. Alec couldn't have pushed me since his body broke my fall and saved my life. No evidence existed of another person on the cliff. Foul play was not suspected in Alec's death. He went back for the camera and fell. I went back looking for him, and the shock of seeing him at the bottom of the rock face caused me to slip," I said.

"Is this what you believe happened, Miss Clarke?"

His tone is sincere, and I detect softness in his inquiry. Perhaps he is the first person who questions the existing theory. His windswept blonde hair surrounds his strong and handsome face. I relax my guard a bit but I don't like showing my vulnerability.

"I don't know what to think, but a warning...." I break from my answer, a cold chill and the familiar fear, confusion, and turmoil washes my façade away. "No answers . . . only questions and . . . fear," I say, losing some control. I cannot stop the rising emotion and my eyes fill with tears. I am embarrassed and turn from Remington. I dab at my eyes catching the tears before they roll down my cheeks. "Sorry, Detective."

Remington confronts me with compassion in his eyes and offers me a tissue from the sales counter.

"Is there anyone who would want you dead, Miss Clarke?" he asks with piqued interest.

"No, I am not wealthy, I have no family. Prior to moving to White Oak, I worked at a publishing company. Alec had many friends and connections from his life in professional sports and his connection with the Kansas City Chiefs organization. He enjoyed the social aspect of his career; he did invest in more than one business venture with bigger players. I can think of no one who would want either of us dead," I stated.

Remington glances around the shop.

"Can you show me what the lady bought?" he asks.

I take him to the back of the store and bring him to the shelf.

"She wanted a particular author. She purchased a book from this collection," I explain.

Detective Remington runs his finger over several of the titles until he comes to the opening left from the missing book. His eyes narrow as he studies the space. He uses his pen to fish out something between the books. Dangling from the end of his pen is a round medallion or amulet on a chain. He inspects the item on the counter. One side is a robed figure and on the opposite side, a series of letters in the shape of a cross.

I am stunned.

"Have you seen this before Ms. Clarke? he asks while continuing to examine the object.

I raise my eyes to meet his and show him nearly the exact medallion around my neck. Although the back of mine is smooth quartz the other side depicts the same robed figure.

"They are nearly identical," I gasp, "I have had this medallion since I was a child."

Remington rubs his forehead and says, "The bigger question is why leave the medallion here for you to find?" He raises the chain around my neck a bit higher for closer inspection. "This is the second message she left before losing her life! Her note and this medallion are significant to you Quinn, I'm sorry, I mean, Miss Clarke." His lack of formality comes as a surprise to both of us.

I reply, "I am not used to being referred to as Miss Clarke anyway. I prefer you call me Quinn, Detective."

"Certainly." His face softens as he smiles--the first genuine smile I've seen from him.

"I'll do some research and see what I can figure out," he says.

I missed three calls and the time has come for me leave for Royce Estate.

"Thank you for coming over, I'm on my way to view some books at Royce Estate in a bit. Again, my appreciation, Detective."

"Call me Keefe, please," he says as he puts the amulet in a plastic sleeve.

I'm surprised but I nod in agreement.

He says, "The Royce Estate . . . not too many area folks have actually seen it; the family keeps to themselves. May I ask you one more question--your camera was never found?"

His comment stuns me; this fact was not publicized.

"That's right," I say.

"Poor weather is moving in late this afternoon, calling for a monster storm- you don't want to be caught in it," he remarks as he leaves.

"Thanks again . . . Keefe."

I am not certain, but I sense a slight note of concern or interest in his tone. I quickly dismiss the notion.

I use the drive to the Royce estate to return a few calls. I raise the phone to my ear just as a ring comes in, startling me.

The voice on the other end of the line is a woman.

"Quinn, hello this is Cindy Arness, may I speak with you for a moment about the Reach Out Campaign?" she asks.

I forgot all about what Carolynn told me about Cindy and her checkered past.

"Sure, what can I do for you Cindy?" I answer.

"The Reach Out campaign is hosting a Community Fair at the high school, with leaders from all five of the areas we are working with--civil duty, health care, business owners, educators and senior citizens. We would love your support," she says.

"What is the date, and what is involved, Cindy?"

"Next Tuesday at 6 p.m. at the high school, and we want you to represent your business with a booth and answer questions from the students."

"Oh sure."

"Thanks, Quinn. By the way, what do you think of the FROG?" she asks with a slight laugh.

"Honestly, it's a little weird, I think."

"My word, I can't believe how terrifying the logo is. But I am not a fan of frogs," she confides.

"I agree. I don't understand why a logo is necessary."

"I volunteered to be the project manager, but they selected Madge. I am busy anyway," she confesses.

"Madge seems . . . gung ho."

"She has good intentions, but she's not the best representation for our city. Where did she find the print suit?" Cindy comments while chuckling a bit.

"She needs some image consulting for sure. But she does appear to be a hard worker and dedicated," I say in her defense.

"She's ambitious too, but confused on the issues. Where her support comes from is a mystery. She dislikes the mayor and the chief of police, that Remington fellow."

My ears perk up a bit when she refers to Keefe Remington.

"Why?" I ask.

"She doesn't think either one are doing their jobs. She isn't happy with anybody else being in charge," Cindy says. "She is threatened by my desire to run for city council this next election, and worried I might get a foothold in the council. I could do some good for this city, balance the budget."

Suddenly I realize I need facts about the gossip Carolynn shared with me about Cindy. I couldn't back her if what Carolynn told me is true.

"Well, I appreciate you calling me, and I am happy to support the event, Cindy. Thank you so much for thinking of me," I say as I hang up the phone. I am nearly halfway to Royce Estate.

Chapter Eight

I enjoy traveling by car, time to think without the distractions. My thoughts turn to Keefe Remington. His comment about the camera caught me off guard. Someone besides Alec and I must have been on the bluffs; in this theory someone could have taken the camera. Little merit is given to what I remember. The police did not recover a camera. I doubt they ever believed one existed. Detective Remington's knowledge about certain details of the accident is confusing. Detectives talk about their cases to other detectives?

The sky grows darker. The blustery winds from the north tell us what is to come. The few published pictures of the estate have fueled the gossip mill in White Oak for years. The Royce Estate is a replica of an existing English estate, built so Mrs. Royce would feel at home. Rumors tell of her unhappiness about moving to the United States. Two hundred and thirty acres of isolation explains why little is known about the Estate or the Royce family.

I keep both hands on the wheel, to steady the car in the strong northern wind. I reduce my speed at County Road Forty-Three, and take my planned left hand turn. The estate entrance should be three more miles from here on the right side. I pull over for an image check and continue on to my appointment.

I slow the car in anticipation of the estate. Strangely, I am offered no option to go right or left; the road simply ends. A fence sits directly in front of my car. Beyond that lies nothing but wind-whipped fields as far as the eye can see. This is puzzling. Perhaps I should have taken road forty- two, or even forty-four. I am glad that I gave myself a little extra time. After I turn to head back, I answer my ringing phone.

"Hello?"

"This is Mr. Edison, is this Quinn?"

"Yes," I reply.

"I will be over on Friday to measure your window for the replacement."

"Oh, sure Mr. Edison, can you hold on a moment? I want to check my schedule." I pull the car over to the edge of the road again. "Yes, the date would be fine. I will expect you then, thanks." I unclick my seatbelt to reach for an unopened bottle of water rolling around on the passenger side floor since I left White Oak. I crack it open and take a long drink.

Continuing on through light snow flurries now, I anticipate the main road soon. It seems to be taking me longer to go back than it did to come. Once again I'm forced to stop. A fence lies directly ahead of my car and nothing but field as far as the eye can see. I look right and quickly left...no options. How is this possible? I raise my hand and lightly rest my fingertips on my forehead. I know that this dead end should not be here, I was JUST here. I KNOW I turned my car around. The flurries are becoming stronger and my internal compass is skewed. I begin my self-talk...remain calm, turn the car around... and don't panic. I doubt my sense of direction. I swallow hard, unnerved. I take a drink of water and struggle to keep my emotion in check. I turn the car around and head the other way, and once again the road seems to go on and on. The blowing snow flurries make visibility difficult. I make the decision to head back to White Oak. Although that decision instantly gives me a small measure relief, it is fleeting. Deeper within me lie unsettling thoughts… am I unstable somehow, are my senses unreliable?

Out of nowhere a dark oject reveals itself ahead on the right side of the road. The shape becomes identifiable as I slowly move toward it. A massive iron gate with two piers tell me what I suspect. This must be the entrance to Royce Estate. But, on the east side of Forty-Three?

Without hesitation I turn in. These towering piers are each topped with round stone finials. The wrought iron gate stands open. Through the blowing flurries, massive trees line each side of the drive. Towering tree lines bend toward the center. Black branches grasp, forming an eerie ceiling above me. Snow is accumulating on the ground now as the lane curves and the front of the car begins an incline. My heart rate rises in anticipation of viewing the notorious Royce Estate.

My palms are clammy and the fingers on my right hand tingle. As the branches begin to thin, I reach the summit and descend.

Through the blowing snow, I can make out the outlines of a castle.

The sensation of electrically charged air has the hair on the back on my neck standing. A strange feeling of hopelessness comes over me. The closer I get to the structure, however my curious symptoms evaporate.

With limited visibility I can still see the estate is two massive stories complete with towers. The lane leads me to a port with three arches, blowing snow swirling violently through them. I stop the car and gather my supplies.

Suddenly I am startled by a face in my window, just inches from mine. My door is opened.

"Miss Clarke, may I help you?" a man asks humbly. He takes my bag and gently escorts me. "Please follow me."

There is no small talk as we hustle across the port to find shelter from the growing storm. As the colossal oak doors are pulled shut, I turn to the man.

"Thank you sir," I manage to say. I am disheveled and harried, as I begin to take stock of this gentleman before me. His wears black trousers and vest, and a crisp white shirt.

"Good day Miss Clarke, we are expecting you. My name is Beef; may I offer you a place to freshen up while I serve some hot tea? Mrs. Royce will see you in a few minutes," he says.

"Yes that would be helpful," I respond.

Beef leads me down the hall and gestures to a door on the left.

I scurry in, grateful for a chance to provide a better first impression. The room is spacious with dual circular gilded mirrors above each of two basins. Displayed are various toiletries, linen hand towels and fresh flowers; it is elegance deluxe.

What kind of name is Beef? My reflection catches me off guard, hair wind whipped and a smear of something across my forehead. I lean into the mirror and discover its blood! While using a tissue to remove it I find its source, a small cut on my finger. I tame my windblown hair. I apply powder and lipstick, straighten my collar, and take a deep breath. In the hallway Beef is waiting.

"This way Miss Clarke," he says.

The residence is exquisite. My eyes dart right and left and even above to the ceiling, trying to take it all in. A dramatic open staircase cascades upward. A grandfather clock sits upon the first landing with an oil painting twice as large above it. Arched openings with stone sills, flank each side of the massive oil painting. I half expected royalty to stand at the sills waving to their subjects below.

On the first landing, the lavish staircase splits to form double cases going opposite ways. My urge to take pictures is quickly dismissed knowing that privacy is a priority to the Royce family.

I follow Beef to a chair in a sitting room. A gilded mirror rests on the curved marble mantle, above the fireplace. Muted floral print covers the furniture that surround a tea table topped with a vase of fresh freesia. Everything is stunning and perfect.

Beef arrives with tea service and I eagerly accept hot tea.

My eyes soak up this historical English manner. My curiosity about those who live in such grandeur is elevated but there will be no more waiting. Just as I sit my tea cup down, she enters.

Chapter 9

Beef enters followed by the woman.

"Mrs. Romulus Royce," he says.

I rise to my feet, Beef excuses himself from the room.

Mrs. Royce moves to the center of room, a stoic half smile upon her face.

"Welcome to Royce Estate, Miss. Clarke. Thank you for making the trip here to view the collection," she says nodding. Some of her long dark silky hair slips over her narrow shoulder. She presents her alabaster hand to me and I accept her gesture. She is standing too far from me to grasp hands palm to palm. We merely grip fingers.

A sensation of despair hangs heavy in the stuffy room, odd like the other peculiarities of the day.

"Thank you for offering me an opportunity," I say unable to offer anything but a standard reply.

Her presence is demanding, and her beauty mesmerizing. High cheekbones and dark smoky eyes stayed fixed on me as she waits for me to speak. I am unsure of what to do or say next, and she does nothing to rescue me from the awkwardness. Again, I am forced to find the next exchange of words.

I ask, "Is the collection in the sitting room, Mrs. Royce?"

Suddenly her semblance shifts, her expression relaxes.

"Please call me Petulah… follow me Miss Clarke," she says and leads me out of the room and down a corridor filled with sculptures and oil paintings.

Her name is unusual, more common in her homeland maybe. Her fitted garment dusts the floor, flaring around her feet. Long hair cascades to a point above a small waist.

I follow her to a library. This winter day offers little light through the windows of this two level book lovers paradise. No telling how many thousands of books are on these shelves. Silence is disturbed only by the rustling of her long garment as we make our way up the spiral staircase.

"This is the collection I am interested in selling Miss Clarke," says Petulah, "Hathaway, Mr. Bartholomew Hathaway... this is his cumulative work. Astrology from 1790-1803, seven books in all. I must attend to another matter. Examine the books, I will rejoin you. If you need assistance, here is the call button," she says. Petulah manages a partial smile, forced it seems.

"Thank you Mrs. Royce, um...Petulah," I reply as she leaves. I inspect the condition of the collection. My phone signals a few missed calls. These books are first editions. Their bindings are original. The bookplate bears the name Ancel Thomas. I am interested. Few were printed and their demand high. I will undercut the estimated value slightly with my offer to determine how motivated she is to sell the collection. My prepared form offers the description of the collection and estimated value. I only have to fill in the condition of each volume and take pictures, then add my bid. I collect my papers and browse the library. This room is filled with a vast collection. I am stunned by Mrs. Royce standing, only feet from me. Her reentry back into the room and her approach void of sound. My reaction evokes no response from her. Once again, she provides no rescue during the awkward moments before I speak.

"You startled me, Petulah, please excuse me. I was so engrossed in your massive collection," I say stammering.

The shift in her demeanor occurs again.

"Did you find the collection of interest Miss Clarke?" she asks.

"Yes, I am interested." I hand her my bid sheet for the collection. "I believe the price is fair," I say.

"I accept your offer Miss Clarke. The collection will be delivered to you after the paperwork is taken care of tomorrow. I am afraid the eye of the storm is upon us, I must insist delay leaving until the storm clears. Beef has prepared the north wing flat for you," she says.

"Oh, I'm sure if I take my time, I will be fine, thank you anyway for your kind offer."

"Suit yourself, Miss Clarke. Good day," she says and leaves.

This collection is a good purchase for me but the experience has been unusual in many ways. I will be ready to leave this place.

Before I can make my way through the inner hall, Beef appears.

"Miss Clarke, the weather is dreadful, I'm afraid, you will not be able to leave Royce Estate until morning."

"I have other appointments, I need to leave."

Beef recognizes my determination, and leads me down the hall and opens the massive oak outside door for me. It is thrust from his grasp by fiercely blowing snow.

My car is not even visible through nature's fury. Wrestling with the door for a moment, I step back inside as he struggles to shut out the violent storm. We are both windswept and freezing within moments.

"Miss Clarke, I am sure you will reconsider."

Beef made his point.

"Yes, Beef, I can't leave. When is it expected to clear?" I ask.

He says, "I will check the latest forecasts, after we get you settled. Do you need anything from your car?"

"No, thank you."

Beef signals to follow him down yet another estate corridor. The right wing flat, as they refer to it, is a continuation of the opulence.

My hesitation to stay gives way to an overwhelming desire for privacy, I am anxious to be alone with my thoughts.

"The fireplace should take some of the chill from the air. May I bring dinner for you seven, along with a weather update?"

"Oh, yes, thank you."

When Beef closes the door, I am relieved. I kick off my shoes and explore.

The apartment consists of a bedroom, living room and bathroom. This windowless room is drafty I'm hoping the fireplace will raise the temperature. Gentle flames flicker, throwing shadows and light dancing on all they can reach. A soft cashmere throw is draped over the arm of a bronze brocade sofa and an ornate mirror rests above the mantle. A sideboard holds glasses, a pitcher of ice water, various bottles of wine, a small coffee urn, a tray of fruit and cheese.

In the bedroom, a large bed crowded with fluffy pillows atop a billowy duvet is inviting. From the only window the sky is gray, giving way to dusk. Snow blown by angry wind makes viewing impossible, only the faint outline of buildings and stark branches of trees bending as winter rules. The marble floor is cold and the shiny claw foot tub, stack of white towels and clear bottles with bath salts call to me. On the back of the door hangs a guest robe and slippers.

Comfortable on the sofa with a glass of Cabernet, I take a moment to check my missed calls. Keefe Remington left a voice mail message asking me to contact him when I am available. My phone signal is weak and won't allow a call back, at least not at this time. The fire is hypnotizing. I sit in silence except the sizzling and crackling of the flames. With legs drawn up, cashmere throw warming me, sipping my wine, my lids are heavy. Relaxation melts into drowsiness and sleep.

Fleeting scenes of distant shores, unsolved conflict, and other random subconscious thoughts seize their opportunity to disturb a mind at rest. Time for hidden agendas to surface, along with schedules to keep, details to organize, and decisions to be made. North winds carry tiny diamonds of stinging ice. My lowered head looks to bare feet as I trudge forward. Bone chilling temperatures threaten to take my breath away, but ahead is stillness and warmth. The white snow rests peacefully wrapping its arms around a frozen pond. The ice lies stoic and formidable except a dancing, wind whipped veil swept one way and until nature changes her mind and sweeps it another. Each snow covered pine surrounding the pond, stands gallantly devoted. The scene is so entirely peaceful, so breath taking, so magical, time is suspended. Here and now is where my mind's gossip can stand exposed for exactly what it is. Barriers in the maze of uncertainty dissipate. Everything is clear.

Tropical fish in rainbow colors meet me at ponds edge. They are prisoners housed under the barrier of ice. I reach down and brush the dust of snow from the frozen surface with my hand, but my touch sizzles with heat, melting a spot in the frozen pond. The water becomes exposed through the small opening; it boils and bubbles, causing the colorful fish to be thrust out dead onto the ice. Beauty turned to death. I so regret my touch. I wrap my arms holding myself, and see the man.

On the far side of the pond he waits.

"Quinn, come to me," he says.

Without hesitation I begin to move in his direction, my body gliding unnaturally over the ice.

Blue eyes welcome me as I approach. At the pond's edge, he holds his hand out to guide me. The energy of his touch travels through me, our connection spiritual. Not wanting to release his hand because of the familiar I recognize. He begins to fade into transparency and my hand grows cold in the frigid air.

"Wait," I plead. "Please don't leave."

"Miss Clarke....Miss Clarke, it's Beef!"

I am jolted awake by firm knocking and my name being called at the door. A few seconds pass before I remember where I am. The fire is roaring as I rise to answer.

Beef stands at the threshold with a cart.

"Miss Clarke, dinner and your weather update. I am afraid the news is not too good. The storm is supposed to bring several inches of snow, and the wind in the 40 mph range will continue to give us these blizzard and white out conditions. You most likely will not be able to leave first thing in the morning; perhaps later in the day. If you need anything at all you may ring for assistance here," he points out the intercom.

"Thank you Beef," I reply, still trying to wake up.

I lift the domes covering several plates. A placard reads, Seafood Bisque, Spinach Salad, and Veal Marsala. A bottle of Pinot Noir and crème Brule make this meal a hearty one. I am hungry. I enjoy the seafood bisque and the pinot, but I only taste the veal and the salad, and ignore the Brule. I am occupied with thoughts of the man in the dream . . . his face appears over and over. I take a long sip of wine, and settle back to savor the fire. When Beef brought me to the north wing, the fire appeared freshly stoked, and seems so now.

This place transfixes my senses. Mrs. Royce adds more mystery to this estate instead of clarity. These strange sensations are unsettling yet I am drawn to this place. Bathing should relax me after a long day and help me sleep.

Steam rises from the hot water filling the claw foot tub. Tranquil waters soothe my muscles and the tension. My head rests on the back of the tub, the glass of pinot within easy reach. Can self-doubt be soaked from one's mind? Indulging myself, I close my eyes and rest my arms on the tubs edges. My solitude ends abruptly when I spot blood. My finger is bleeding down the walls of the white tub into the water. Terror grabs me when I realize the bathwater is nearly red. I draw my trembling hand up from the water; the surface scratch is now a deep laceration! I spring from the bath and lift the drain. A clean crisp washcloth becomes a bandage wrap. The fluffy robe tied tightly can't stop my body from shivering in this drafty room. Before I can leave the bathroom, the cloth is saturated with red blood, and a panic rises in me. I frantically wrap another around tighter and lie in bed wondering how long before I call for help. After several minutes pass, I reexamine the wound. The bleeding has stopped, and my panic subsides.

The first aid kit in the bathroom provides a large bandage and I cover the finger. Saturated white cloths lie at my feet, the bath tub is stained with blood. I rinse the tub and collect the towels and cloths, longing for sleep and the end to this day.

All of my thoughts swirl, each taking their turn to land and disturb me. My muscles tighten at the thought of being pushed from the cliff edge. Who was the mystery woman, what did she know...how did she know and why the secrecy? Who would care the message was delivered? Was I in the way of someone wanting to kill Alec? Who knew how to find us? With my mind racing, sleep will never come. I have no choice but to get up.

Dare I do a little wandering? I cross the threshold of the door, only the gentle brushing sound of slippers on the marble surface and the howling and relentless wind are heard. The area is dimly illuminated by showcase lighting glowing above each painting, and gothic lanterns hang from elaborate wrought iron hooks every fifteen feet or so.

I follow the corridor around a corner into another. Ahead on the left is a landing and a wide limestone staircase inviting me up or down. My curiosity grows around each illuminated bend. Voices freeze me in my tracks...arguing. I stand motionless, like a rabbit, listening. I rotate and step quickly back down. Scurrying down the hallway, I return to the safety of my room.

The roaring fire invites me to sit. Mesmerized by the flames I think about the voices. Tired eyes travel across the room and lock on a shadowy shape standing motionless in the bathroom doorway. I gasp and jerk simultaneously.

The figure moves forward and is illuminated, a young woman.

"I am so sorry I scared you! Beef told you are our overnight guest, and I wanted to introduce myself. I apologize again for giving you such a fright!"

She approaches and reaches her hand out to me.

"I'm Sapphire Royce," she says. Her hand shake is gentle.

She is petite and soft spoken and young, sixteen or seventeen.

"A pleasure to meet you Sapphire, I am Quinn Clarke. Your mother invited me to the estate to view a collection of books she wants to sell, and now I'm snowbound!"

"It's good to make your acquaintance, Quinn. Beef mentioned the reason for your visit. Have you been collecting books for long?" she asks plopping down on the sofa. She puts her feet up casually on the coffee table and crosses her ankles. Her jeans and tennis shoes lend to her laid back demeanor. The atmosphere lightens.

"Shop owner for only a short time, but a collector for years," I reply.

She seems interested in our conversation; her kind face peeking out from volumes of long kinky chestnut colored hair. The sincerity expressed from her jade eyes, somehow raises my spirits. For the first time at the estate I feel more at ease, secure in a way. My cell phone beeps indicating coverage once more. I turn my attention back to the young woman.

"Tell me about you," I say.

"I am the baby of the Royce family, which I am constantly reminded of, which I abhor. I am almost finished with my formal education . . . not interested in college . . . at all!" She emphasizes this by saying the last three words slowly as she tosses a portion of her thick mane over her shoulder. "Mother hates the few friends I do have, no big surprise! Sister Jexis is 25 and brother Cashton is 27. My brother will love you! He will think you are gorgeous! Are you married? Wouldn't stop him from trying anyway!"

Before I can respond she picks up my left hand.

"Nope, single! Just watch him; he is a real ladies man, irritating!"

Her talkative nature is so refreshing, but the day as been long and my yawn difficult to conceal.

Sapphire takes the hint.

"I'll let you turn in."

"Yes, I am sleepy; I enjoyed getting to know you Sapphire. Will I see you in the morning before I leave?" I ask.

"Oh, you'll be around longer than you want I am afraid. The storm system is stalled right over us, and it's doubtful you will get out of here tomorrow at all. My father may be delayed in his return home as well," she says.

"Your father?" I ask.

"Yes, he's been in England for a couple of weeks, and is home tomorrow, can't wait," she says.

"Until tomorrow, Sapphire," I say with a smile as I close the door.

Chapter Ten

The howling of a relentless winter wind wakes me. After dressing, I'm on my way to explore the Royce Estate. Dreary daylight does little to brighten the place. I pass a few closed doors before arriving at the open doors to a solarium.

Spacious, lofty and constructed of glass, the solarium is warm regardless of the storm that rages from all sides. Blowing snow piles against the transparent walls, but the invisible barrier protects the plant life. The flowers of vivid blues and reds, oranges and pinks are crowded by vines and succulent plants. The sweet floral scent combines the heady richness of black soil transporting my senses to a sundrenched spring garden. Some of the indoor trees touch the top of the domed ceiling. I stroll leisurely distracted occasionally by sounds of movement.

"May I help you?" says a low voice.

Startled, I turn to answer but no one is there.

A man leaps from towering limbs above.

Stepping back I lose my footing, the man catches my hand and brings me upright.

"I'm sorry I scared you," he says.

With his one hand on my arm and one hand around my waist, we stand face to face.

"You did surprise me," I reply.

The mesmerizing smile captivates me for a moment.

"My name is Cashton Royce. This is a passion of mine," he says gesturing to the whole solarium.

"Your exploring distracted me from my pruning; I've got a tree top view from up there."

"My name is Quinn Clarke; I'm here to about some books Mrs. Royce wants to sell. Now I'm… snowed in. I thought I would explore some of your fascinating home, I'm not trespassing am I?"

He smiles mischievously while extending his hand.

"A pleasure to meet you, Miss Clarke."

He kisses my extended hand instead of shaking it. His touch suspends me for a moment. I sense his passion and I feel transparent. I pull my hand but he grasps and pulls me closer.

"Allow me to give you a tour Miss Clarke," he says releasing his hold on me.

"Ok," I say feebly.

His affect is apparent. I behave like a star struck teenager. This reaction is uncharacteristic, unsettling and confusing.

"May I call you Quinn?"

"Please do," I say with false composure.

"Good," this is where I spend quite a bit of time. Horticulture is a hobby. We are surrounded by hundreds of plant life species. Let's move on shall we?"

Cashton's dark hair skims the collar of his white untucked shirt, he wears dark trousers and boots.

The dining room is on his tour. In the center of the elegance, sits a polished cherry wood table reflecting the room like a mirror. Above the buffet hangs a sizeable portrait of a woman with two smaller portraits on each side.

"This tower is the hallmark of Royce Estate, standing four stories with an octagonal pinnacled parapet. Follow me, Quinn."

I didn't want to mention I'd explored the night before. A series of twists brings us to the spiral staircase. Walls glow golden from flickering light casting our shadows. As if transported through time, limestone walls and wrought iron lanterns make Royce Estate every bit a castle. The higher we climb, the more narrow the tower becomes. Small windows about every ten steps show only more blowing snow and the air grows colder. At the top a barrier prevents passage to the octagonal shaped look out.

Cashton steps over and offers me assistance which I do not need but accept.

I admit I don't even realize what the bottom half of my body is doing.

"This is the view of our kingdom, as my mother likes to say. These glass panes are removed in the warm months. Unfortunately today we're shown more of the winter storm. We'll try again another time when you can see everything."

On the way down, we share small talk about White Oak and Fireside books, and his sisters Jexis and Sapphire. He isn't surprised to learn Sapphire and I have met.

"At times I think Sapphire's direction is stronger than either Jexis or myself," he admits.

"Why?" I ask.

"My mother repeats it often."

With two stories left before the main floor, Cashton pauses and pushes on a section of the winding wall. A door is camouflaged perfectly and we enter.

Cashton says, "This is where I come for privacy." he comments.

The warm space is filled with leather bound gold embossed books on two walls. Opposite the rooms entrance is the fireplace wall with a mantle of mosaic tile in brilliant reds and blues holds dozens of candles in varying heights. A carved wood frame surrounds an oil painting of white doves in flight. Cashton lights a multi colored lantern that sits on a small drop side table near a small washroom.

"Many of the books are filled with ancestors and history of the family." He says.

"Why is this room all the way up here?"

"I am not sure. My parents moved here from England, and this home is a replica of the estate we left behind. I've been told my mother was not too keen on coming to the United State, and I think this was my father's compromise and she was pleased. That was a long time ago; all of us were born on American soil." Cashton gasps as he reaches for my right hand, "You are bleeding, Quinn!"

The laceration is much worse; the cut bleeds so profusely I begin to panic. Cashton disappears into the washroom and comes out with several hand towels. He applies pressure to my gushing wound.

"How did you injure yourself?"

"I don't remember doing anything to hurt myself."

He lifts the saturated hand towel, the injury still bleeds. By this time both of us are covered in blood, then everything goes black.

I open my eyes; he cradles my head in his lap.

"What happened?" I ask.

"You fainted . . . the bleeding stopped. The finger is wrapped well enough to go down and get some first aid. Are you ready to get down from this tower?" he asks with a kind and dazzling smile.

"Yes, I think so."

I stand but am still shaky.

Cashton bends down scooping me into his arms.

"No need for this, Cashton, I'm better," I tell him.

"Quinn, hush, everything will be alright," he says, making his way effortlessly down the spiral stairs.

I surrender and lay my head against him. His scent is intoxicating.

Cashton lays me on the sofa in my room.

"Thank you."

Cashton leans close, his warm lips kiss my cheek and linger for an instant. He surprises me by his forward action, but I do not stop him. His eyes remain closed as he takes him time pulling away.

"I will get you some help for your finger, Quinn."

"Don't go," I say.

"Dr. Brazil will get you bandaged up. She is our resident physician," he tells me as he leaves. The door closes behind him.

Dr. Brazil is a kind woman. She removes the bloody bandages, revealing only a deep scratch. My puzzled expression reveals what I am thinking.

"This did not leave all the blood on your clothing. Is this your only injury?" she asks.

"Yes."

"Beef called for me in good time. The important thing is you are not bleeding anymore, and your finger is looking good. She cleans up my hand and puts a small dressing upon the scratch.

"How is it possible?"

"Did Beef bandage this?" she asks.

"No, Cashton did."

A knowing look comes over her, and she rises to leave.

"What, Dr. Brazil? What is it?" I ask.

"Cashton has a connection with nature. This isn't the first time I've witnessed his gift of healing," she says.

She leaves me with some supplies and her direct number. She

suggests I put on a robe and leave my clothes outside the door and they would be cleaned.

What happened here? I am trying to sort it all out. A handsome man gives me a tour of parts of the estate. He hypnotizes me with his charm and his touch leaves me wanting more. He is there when I awake from passing out. While out cold, he heals my finger? I allow myself to be carried, even resting my head on his shoulder. I won't soon forget his scent or the warm kiss. Lack of rest catches up with me, and I sleep deeply, his scent only a pleasant lingering memory.

Chapter Eleven

By now my messages have been received by Tera and she understands why I couldn't meet with her last night. But I've yet to receive a response.

Beef comes to the door with my laundered clothes and suggests I join the family for a late lunch in the dining room. When I arrive the room is empty, servers show me to my seat.

Sapphire's joyful spirit fills the room with light. She sends a beaming smile my way as she approaches with a quick embrace. Once seated next to me, we begin a casual conversation. A commotion among the servers cuts our chatting short.

They stop what they are doing, and stand alert as Mrs. Royce enters the dining room. Her presence creates a tense atmosphere. Unsure if I am to stand as well, I lean forward to slide my chair out but Sapphire reaches over and presses my leg down. She rolls her eyes, making light of the formalities her mother expects. So I sit stationary. Mrs. Royce waits for her chair to be pulled out, and Beef takes enjoyment in seating her formally. He places the napkin on her lap as the server pours water. Beef makes his way around the table, placing napkins for each of us. As the midday meal is being served, and the wine is being poured, Mrs. Royce's attention turns to me.

"Quinn, I pray you slept well last evening?" she asks.

"Yes, thank you," I reply.

"Dr. Brazil reports she dressed a wound for you. Are you alright now?" she asks.

"Yes, fine now, are we waiting for anyone else?" I ask.

Petulah seems only able to tolerate visitors to the estate, she does not enjoy them. She lays her fork down and takes a long drink from her wine glass. She raises her eyes and pauses for more than a few seconds.

I am immediately sorry I asked.

Sapphire and she rolls her eyes again.

Mrs. Royce says, "No, Mr. Royce is delayed in his return from

England, because of this dreadful weather."

Sapphire cannot hold her enthusiasm.

"He will be home in the morning, mother?"

"Yes, dear."

I don't remember much else from the whole mealtime. There is no mention of Cashton at all. Asking about the vacant place setting, could look like I'm fishing for information. Mentioning I already met Cashton might get somebody, including myself, in trouble with Petulah, who I would hate to see angry if this is her hospitable side. After lunch, Beef stops me in the hallway.

"The carport is clear, and passage to the main road will be cleared by morning. The weather is looking fine for your departure then," he says.

"Thank you."

My ringing phone means reception has improved.

"Quinn, this is Keefe Remington, are you still at the estate?" he asks.

"Yes, I won't be able to leave until tomorrow morning."

"One of the worst storms in quite a while," he says.

"I am not relishing the thought of hanging around here again tonight," I admit.

"Our emergency road crew cleared the highway to the west. We could pick you up around five o'clock this evening," he suggests. "We've transported a couple of doctors and a generator part to the nursing home. I took over a space heater for frozen pipes at the courthouse. No problem getting you back into town."

"Yes, I need to get back. What about my car?" I ask.

"I can send for your car later. Be ready about five."

"Thanks, Keefe I am grateful," I say.

Detective Remington is showing an interest in me or in my case, I'm not sure which yet. The day drags on. Tera and I make new plans for tonight at Bordeaux's. I 'm anxious to be on familiar ground. Tera didn't mention why she is in White Oak. I am hoping Sapphire might pop in, and am disappointed I won't see Cashton again.

Beef brings some tea to my room and I tell him I will be leaving at five.

The time arrives and I gather my things. I brace for the burst of cold air. I am surprised by Keefe Remington holding the door of a squad car for me. I didn't expect his personal escort.

"Thank you," I say.

No reply as he closes my door.

I put my seatbelt on; he does the same. When we are on our way, he radios back to the station.

There is little small talk with Keefe focused on driving the snow-covered roads. Blonde hair falls into his face when he pulls off his wool hat. The parka he wears bears the police force seal. I notice he wears no ring on his finger.

"The roads are still pretty bad."

"Yeah," he says.

"Worst storm for a few years," I say.

"Yes, it is, reminds me of Chicago."

"Is that where you and your family are from?"

"It's just me. Prior to relocating I was with Chicago PD. A gritty place when it comes to law enforcement; glad to leave."

I didn't know Keefe very well, but he seemed nervous, on edge.

"Oh," I say. He is not interested in filling in my blanks I guess.

He asks, "Once we are back in White Oak, would you mind coming into the station? I've discovered more on the amulet."

"Yes, sure."

We arrive back about six. Carolynn Langford's at the station, her impeccable image sitting in front of Dawn Bishop's desk.

"Hi Carolynn," I say.

She turns and gives me a wave.

"Quinn, hello!" I pause, as Keefe continues on to his office.

"Seems some bored youth with cabin fever broke into Bordeaux's. They took some alcohol and shattered a window. We're still taking stock of what's missing. I am concerned about the character of some of these young people in our town!" she says.

"How can you be sure young people are responsible?" I ask.

"We may know the culprits. What about the victim of the accident near your shop?" she asks.

"Well, it's a mystery still. Detective Remington isn't ruling out foul play," I say.

"Surely, not!" Carolynn smiles, while dismissing this theory. "A flair for the dramatic!"

Officer Bishop snickers.

"I will be stopping over to meet Tera at Bordeaux's later, maybe I'll run into you again," I say walking away.

"Tera and I had a grand time in St. Charles yesterday at Mason and Murdock."

Her comment stops me and I turn.

"Wish you were with us," she says.

"What?"

Carolynn repeats her announcement.

"Oh, I didn't know," I say.

"You had other plans, Tera told me," Carolynn says.

Tera and I talked about making that trip together. I am sure there is an explanation, Tera wouldn't go without me.

I take a seat in Keefe's office; he closes the door behind us. Instead of sitting opposite me at his desk, he sits on the same side as me and produces a folder with pictures of the amulet.

"This is a St. Benedict medallion or amulet, worn to protect," he explains. "There is significance to the medal. I want to take a closer look at yours, would you remove it?"

"I don't remove it."

"Are you saying you never do?" Keefe asks while raising his brows.

"I feel better when it's around my neck, so I leave it there." I dislike him thinking I'm the superstitious type.

"Where and when did you get it?" he asks.

"It is a part of me, a family heirloom. The necklace is the only link remaining to my deceased parents. I never thought much about it, I guess."

"You wore it on the day of your accident?"

"Yes I did," I say in soft tones. "I've never worn the amulet for protection. The amulet's been part of me for so long, and I have never questioned the reason. I feel better somehow, when it's there, so I just always leave it on."

"The mystery woman knew you had one. The note may suggest the amulet had something to do with your survival. I must find out more about her. I am ordering police protection," he says.

He is serious, raising my concern.

"What do you mean?" I ask. For a fleeting moment I entertain Carolynn's negative comment about Keefe, but dismiss it.

"It's no big deal, Quinn. You won't even know we're around. It is wise to keep an eye on things."

Before I can complain, he grasps my forearm gently but with strength and begins to say something, but stops when there is a knock at the door.

Without waiting for a response from Detective Remington, Officer Bishop enters.

"Detective, here is the information you wanted from the lab."

"I am in the middle of a meeting with Miss Clarke! Please allow me to finish, and I will be with you!"

"Keefe, this is urgent," she argues.

Keefe stands and in a strong voice he says, "Dawn, I will decide the urgency of the report. The door on my office is closed for a reason. Thank you, that's all."

Officer Bishop freezes for a couple of awkward moments before sulking out with a frustrated expression.

"What's her story?" I ask.

"You tell me. She is competent but wants to be the one in charge. Before we were interrupted I wanted to assure you the protection is precautionary Quinn; I don't think the woman was anything more than an eccentric character stirring up drama, and her death a tragic accident," Keefe says.

His words are comforting, but an underlying fear within me remains. Since the moment I laid eyes on the mystery woman, my life has been full of bizarre experiences and growing confusion.

Chapter Twelve

Keefe drives me to Bordeaux's to meet Tera. We both recognize Rand Jolliet's red sports car stalled on the side of the road. Keefe pulls behind his car, and Cindy Arness comes running towards the car in a panic.

She drops the phone and says, "Help me, Rand is not breathing!"

"Did you call 911?" Keefe asks.

"Yes, they're on their way."

Rand's face is so swollen; he's barely recognizable. All his features are oversized and his eyes shut.

Cindy says, "Bees attacked us, swarms of them from inside the car."

The paramedics arrive and treat him for allergy reaction without moving him. He is given an injection and oxygen. His breathing regulates within minutes, and the swelling begins to subside. He still will be taking a ride to the hospital. Red welts cover Cindy's arms.

"Cindy, are you alright?" Keefe asks her.

"A bee came out of the vent on the middle console of the car, and soon they poured out of all the vents. Rand pulled over; the bees swarmed his face . . . terrifying. I didn't know he was allergic," Cindy says.

Keefe suggests Cindy get herself checked out as well. She agrees and I help her into the ambulance while he checks out the inside of Rand's car.

Two more officers arrive at the scene and Keefe instructs them to take Rand's car back to the station to do a more thorough inspection. We continue on to Bordeaux's.

"Bees attacking in winter is not normal. Why wouldn't Rand wear a medical bracelet?" asks Keefe.

"Professor Enderlee was stung recently, I came along in time to give him an injection. He wears a bracelet but this is new for him. Can one develop a reaction later in life?" I ask.

"Damn strange, I didn't see one bee, dead or alive in Rand's car," he says.

Keefe holds the door for me and Tera spots us right away. I knew she'd be concerned when she saw me with the detective.

She rushes over to embrace me.

"Is everything alright?"

"Yes, fine Tera. This is Detective Keefe Remington. Keefe meet Tera, my best friend."

Keefe says, "It is nice to make your acquaintance, Tera."

Tera does a visual inspection, making me squirm.

"Likewise," she says drawing her words out.

Keefe leans over and whispers in my ear.

My eyes search till I find a man sitting at the bar.

Keefe leaves, Tera takes my arm and deposits me tableside.

"What's wrong, why are you shaking," she asks.

"We came across an emergency on our way over. Rand Jolliet was stung by bees and stopped breathing. The paramedics administered the antidote and oxygen. He will recover. I need a few minutes to get my bearings," I say.

Tera orders drinks for us both, and I took a moment to breath before asking her about the trip with Carolynn.

Tera orders drinks for us both, and I take a moment to breathe before asking her about the trip with Carolynn.

"Carolynn was at the station and mentioned you went to St. Charles with her to Mason & Murdock."

"Yes, I wanted you to go. I was so disappointed when Carolynn said you had plans already. I wanted to verify, and called you several times. The idea was last minute, and I declined telling her the trip was something we wanted to do as friends. Something was upsetting her, and she confided in me, the marriage is falling apart. She needed to get away, and didn't want to be alone. I crumbled when her tears came. I felt compassion for her pain. Honestly, I found the whole thing odd. Carolynn's demeanor once we were there was not that of a distraught woman. It was weird. I was... uncomfortable with her. I regret sharing the experience with her instead of you, Quinn. Carolynn pushed the trip, and I allowed myself to be manipulated by her fragile situation. My sincere apologies to you, friend. The last thing I would ever want to do is hurt you."

"I don't blame you for going. Your nurturing spirit wanted to help her. Cell reception at Royce Estate was poor. I got the strangest vibe at the station when Carolynn told me, like she enjoyed dropping a bomb."

"Something is a little off with her, and I'm not quite sure what it is," says Tera.

I kept my reservations about Carolynn to myself for now. She didn't invite me, even though she said she did. This is not the first red flag when it comes to her.

Tera says, "Spill it."

"The Royce experience, yes there's plenty to tell you." I say.

"Right!" she says with sarcasm. "I'm talking about Detective Dreamy!"

Her response makes me laugh.

"Ok…he found the mystery woman's note after I left his office," I say, raising my shoulders and clenching my teeth.

"Oh, oh…busted," Tera says, making light of it.

"I'd dumped my bag searching for my cell and must have left it. He paid me a visit and confronted me about not disclosing the information."

"Are you in trouble? What's Remington's theory?" Tera asks.

"I think I explained my way out of it. I'm not sure what his theory is yet. He asked questions about the initial investigation of my accident. Since the amulet he discovered is like the one I wear and the note from the mystery woman referred to my accident, he considers the two incidents linked. He came in the day I was headed to the Royce estate so he knew I was there, probably assumed I was snowed in. He offered to pick me up after the road cleared, and I was glad to get out of there."

"Wait a minute, Quinn," Tera says, "Are you saying Detective Remington himself, picked you up?"

I nod.

Tera asks, "What did he say?"

"Not much…at all," I answer.

Tera leans back against the soft leather of the booth and crosses her arms, staring squarely at me and pauses.

"In my opinion, Detective Dreamy is showing interest beyond the investigation."

"He didn't act interested after I got in the car."

"Preoccupied with getting you home safely, I'm sure."

"He must know more about the mystery lady, to put me under police protection."

"What?" she asks.

Carolynn arrives at our table with two glasses of wine on a tray.

"I thought you girls might enjoy a token of our appreciation, a round on the house. You two and the officer over there are the only one's who tackled the roads and came out tonight." she says.

Tera and I exchange glances.

Without missing a beat, Tera picks up her glass.

"Thank you, Carolynn, how thoughtful," she says.

"You are welcome, Tera; make sure you get some rest," she says before she leaves us.

"Best to keep the police protection to ourselves," she says in hushed tones.

Tera was reading my mind.

"Is it correct to assume he is your . . . protector?" Tera says, eyeing the man at the bar.

"I guess so."

"Securing your safety tells me Remington's theory about this whole situation involves some kind of danger for you," Tera says.

"He told me it's only precautionary and assumes the mystery woman was a lonely lady with too much time on her hands."

"We'll see."

I add, "Keefe wants to get a picture of my amulet, so I am stopping by the station tomorrow morning. Join me?"

"Sure, but why didn't he do that tonight when you were at the station?"

"No idea."

"To see you again...duh!" she says and laughs.

"What did Carolynn mean when she suggested you get some sleep?"

"I came down with something after having dinner in St. Charles last night. Was up most of the night," she says.

"Good thing you are spending the night with me tonight. You always sleep well at my house."

When Tera drives us to my house, my car sits in the driveway, already retrieved from the estate.

"That was fast," Tera says with a wink.

Before we sleep, we spend another hour talking about my bizarre experiences at Royce estate. There is only one thing I don't mention--Cashton.

I sleep deeply and awake rested the next morning, except my clock tells me it's only four thirty. I stay in bed as long as I can, listening to the howling winds, and decide to use some of my renewed energy in the kitchen. I brew some espresso and prepare several batches of Rosemary herb bread. After I put them in the oven, I take a steaming cup to Tera, then take my shower. I wrap a few loaves to take to the professor's.

His face lights up when he answers his door.

"Quinn, what a dandy surprise! Please come in out of the dreadful tempest!" he says.

"Good morning, professor, I brought you a treat. This is a loaf of my special bread for you and one to give Pony. Let me introduce my friend, Tera, from Kansas City," I say, handing him the loaves.

"Goodness, another charming and breathtaking young lady! So happy to meet you Tera," Professor Enderlee says.

"I like him already," Tera says.

The professor smiles, and with sincerity.

He says, "Oh, how thoughtful! I will take Pony's to the shop with me. He won't be in until later; he is in a spot of trouble, I am afraid, but please do come in. I have something for you."

We wait in the foyer, for him to return. The home is a classic, but the traditional décor is showing signs of neglect. Wallpaper with edges turning up, stacks of newspapers lying around, and plastic shopping bags on door handles tell the tale. The wood floors are dull and the faded window treatments are droopy. All available open space is scattered with items. I feel sadness seeing a home, and perhaps a life, in need of a lending hand.

He rounds the corner with a book and a beaming smile.

"This is one of my favorites and I would like to donate it to Fireside Books. This children's edition has been in my family for many generations. *The Little A, B, C Book, 1884.*"

"Thank you Professor Enderlee, I will put it in a place of honor. Please enjoy the bread."

Tera follows in her car. The bitter air sends us scurrying to the front door of the White Oak Police Department. A squad car speeds in right behind us and pulls around to the back.

Inside, Elliott Kenadie, along with everyone else, observes action going on in the rear of the station.

Officers escort two people into one of the offices and a gust of wind follows, tossing papers into a tailspin. The bone chilling air is shut out as the back door is closed.

Elliott Kenadie snaps photos.

Dawn Bishop says loudly, "Ok, Mr. Kenadie, that's enough. Detective Remington will provide a statement later...stay out of the way or wait outside."

While Dawn Bishop gives the stern warning, another officer hustles over to pick up a ringing phone.

Elliott Kenadie turns and walks off in a huff.

"What is going on?" I ask Kenadie.

"Confession to the brutal murder of the woman on Main Street!" he says, walking right past us and out the doors.

Tera and I stand dumbfounded for a moment before I approach Dawn Bishop's desk.

"I have an appointment with Detective Remington," I say.

The phone begins ringing again, and she pauses to answer. After a brief conversation she turns her attention back to me.

"Detective Remington's hands are full, perhaps you should come back," she says

Keefe appears at his office door and motions for us to come into his office.

Officer Bishop tends to another ringing phone.

Keefe Remington closes his door.

"Kenadie could sensationalize a dripping faucet! Someone claims to have accidently hit the mystery woman. They just came forward. We don't know the circumstances yet. I wanted you to learn about these new developments from me. Don't listen to anyone else in this town," he says.

"They?" I ask.

"Tripp Acheson and his wife. I won't be able to meet with you at this time. Perhaps we can connect later today?" he suggests.

"Yes, call me. They are good customers at Fireside Books. I met them at the grand opening."

Outside a small group of citizens is huddled and braving the fierce gusts of winter wind. Amidst them are Elliott Kenadie and Madge Botherme. Many people are talking at once.

As we pass them Elliott Kenadie points at me. Madge Botherme walks over to Tera and me. The crowd follows.

"I am Madge Botherme, City Council President of White Oak. I think we met briefly when you first moved to town and again at the Chamber meeting."

A frog logo badge is displayed on the lapel of her dusty pink suit jacket; a dated fur coat hangs from her shoulders. Her windblown, teased up hair still doesn't boost her height much past five foot. Her style is circa 1959.

"This is my friend from Kansas City, Tera Santiago."

Ms. Botherme makes a hasty nod at Tera and they exchange a quick handshake. Madge gives Tera a Reach Out Frog badge then says, "Miss Clarke, what is going on inside? Did you meet with Detective Remington? As council president, it is my duty to inform the citizens of White Oak about a potential murderer on our streets!"

"My meeting with Detective Remington was postponed. I am sure you will be informed soon," I say, heading to our cars. "Mr. Kenadie and Ms. Botherme are not helping the situation. Stop over to the bookstore before you head back to the city?" I ask.

"See you there."

Soon, after unlocking and lighting the place up, I adjust the temperature. Tera starts a fire. There is a delivery at the back door and Tera accepts it for me.

I am anxious to hear from Keefe and check my phone a few times while I water plants and feed Thomasena.

"After the professor was stung, I did some research on bees. With Rand's incident I am even more interested. Let me tell you what I discovered," I say.

"Can't wait," she says, rolling her eyes.

"It's interesting, Tera. The bee attacks are uncommon, and I wanted to find out more about them."

"What did you discover?" she asks as I sit down next to her.

"While allergic reactions are common, the location of the incidents makes them unusual. And swarming in the winter is not natural for bees. First, Professor Enderlee and now, Rand. I found no explanation for this odd behavior," I say. I show Tera the article on my phone.

She begins to read. I add a log to the crackling fire.

Tera says, "The bee holds quite a bit of symbolism in many different cultures and religions. Most believe the bee to be a sacred insect, bridging the natural world to the underworld...yikes," Tera says.

"Yes."

The jingle of the doorbells alert me to my first customer.

"Good morning, again Quinn. I brought you both a hot coffee. I sampled the bread . . . divine! Thank you for thinking of me, young lady!" the professor says with his kind smile.

"Professor, the coffee is much appreciated as well!"

"No problem at all. I need to get back to the shop. Pony won't be back for another hour or so. I am concerned about him. His bright future is now in jeopardy, I am afraid," he explains.

"Professor, anything I can do to help?" I say, touching his arm.

"The two young men being held accountable for a break-in at Bordeaux's have implicated Pony, an unfortunate setback for this young man. Pony's aptitude is only now blossoming. His aunt Carmen adopted him and has shown him a different way of life. God bless that woman! The rest of his family is in and out of jail . . . bad influences. Carmen has been his saving grace. A devout Catholic, she claims faith is the ingredient needed for a good life. Pony is interested in learning all he can about religion."

"His aunt is a licensed addiction counselor, money is tight. Pony can only manage a few hours of work with me while he is in school. Right now he is scared and confused with this false accusation. Once Pony took a different path, he severed the ties with these two young men. He hasn't been associated with them for over three years. Police brought Pony in for questioning this morning. He and his aunt should be proud of the life they are striving for. This is a setback."

Tera commented, "I think I know her-- Carmen Coldstone. Yes, my firm handled her adoption. She is quite a formidable woman. She legally adopted Pony; I remember her case."

Professor, do you think Pony might consider working here in the afternoons? I need help, and he could study during that time," I offer.

The professor's eyes light up at the idea.

"Quinn, a splendid solution! I will discuss it with him today," the professor says.

Tera chimes in, "I will talk to the firm about legal assistance, if it is needed. Pony impressed us all, my boss nudging him to consider a career in law."

"I am so grateful, ladies. Thank you so much for caring," he says.

I see a tear in his eye as he embraces me and puts his hand on Tera's shoulder. He leaves Fireside Books with a spring in his step. The wind tries to claim his Gatsby hat as he tips it while passing the window.

Tera says, "White Oak is not as sleepy as it seems."

"I am thinking the same thing."

"Professor Enderlee is a sweet soul."

"He can use a friend, and someone to watch out for him. I guess we all do," I say. "You are important to me. I cherish our friendship, Tera."

We sit down in front of the fireplace to savor our Mocha Joe's brew.

"Before you head back to the city, I want to tell you about my plan!" I say. "I wonder if Professor Enderlee would be offended if I offered to help out a little in his home."

"I doubt it Quinn. He would appreciate it. I can offer you a hand when I am in White Oak. Now . . . when is Detective Dreamy going to call? The suspense is killing me!"

"I am surprised about the Atchisons. Why stay silent for this entire time if the tragedy was only an accident? Perhaps I can forget about needing protection," I say, closing my eyes and taking a deep breath.

Thomasena purrs as she curls up next to me.

Tera takes a long sip on her coffee before responding.

"Not necessarily," she says. "It still doesn't explain the note, the amulet, or why the mystery woman can't be identified."

"When are you going to fill me in on this new man in your life?" I ask.

"Yes, I did meet a man, last week at Bordeaux's. He still was wearing a name badge from a meeting. A quirky frog on it caught my attention. His name is Chamous McCoy. He's only been in White Oak a year or so. He works with teenagers at Trinity…he's an ordained minister."

"What?" I exclaim.

"He is on the staff at Trinity. The congregation, like many in town, is dwindling. He was hired to turn things around."

Before I can respond, Mr. Edison arrives to do the repairs to the windows. He gets straight to his work and we go back to our conversation.

"You went to church with him?" I ask.

"I did! I wanted to hear Chamous speak. He's good, but the pews were less than half full. He is a good man, and I hope to see more of him. He is not like any man I have ever known," she says.

"I extend a dinner invitation to you both for this weekend. I would enjoy meeting him."

"Ok," she smiles, "I have to leave, but I'll be in suspense, waiting to hear what Keefe tells you about the Tripps.

Chapter Thirteen

It is late afternoon when Keefe calls me. He asks if he can stop over to photograph my amulet and fill me in on the Atchison developments. I am anxious to get to the bottom of this mystery.

I browse headlines of the White Oak Advocate.

"Birds Fall from the Sky" by Elliott Kenadie

"Construction of Fire Hall" by Morgan Epps,

"Churches Taking Their Last Breath?" by Elliott Kenadie.

"Identity Sought in Hit and Run Accident" By Elliott Kenadie.

Something interesting catches my eye . . .

Black Tie Dinner & Symphony Concert Benefit, Royce Estate

Kansas City Symphony's Spring Concert

April 5

Featuring Soprano Moriah Jones and Violinist Herschel Montgomery

Tickets sold in advance-$250. Table $500. For Reserved seat

5:00 PM cocktail reception in the Parterre Gardens, 6:30

Dinner in the Rose Garden

Chef Alfonso Giovanni of the Plazadom

Hosted by Jexis Royce

PROCEEDS FROM THE BENEFIT CONCERT SUPPORT THE

KANSAS CITY SYMPHONY YEAR -ROUND EDUCATION PROGRAMS.

Keefe's arrival is signaled by the bells on the shop door.

"Tough day, Detective Remington?"

"Eventful," he responds, "I can't stay long. May I see the amulet?" He snaps a couple of photos.

"Quinn, you will no longer require police protection, at least for the time being. Based on what Tripp Atchison has told us." His phone rings, and he checks the number but continues. "It seems Mr. Atchison takes a drug for insomnia with dangerous side effects, one of which is unconscious actions. His wife noticed the damage on the car, and when asking him questions, they realized the gravity of things."

"How awful and senseless!" I say.

"Tripp's confession still doesn't explain the mystery woman's warning. The case is active, but for now I think you are out of danger."

I sense some relief in his tone, or at least I think so. He apologizes when he takes another phone call.

Keefe is attractive. I try to imagine how he looked as a boy. Leniency is given to little boys with messy hair and to good looking detectives. His long layers of hair are sun kissed, golden and untamed. Keefe's appearance is professional, but this image follows his own set of rules. His quiet and unassuming demeanor is appealing.

I take a deep breath and say, "Thank you Keefe, this is good news. I feel like celebrating! I'm free around eight, would you join me for a cocktail?" An awkward few moments of silence follow.

With a captivating smile he says, "Ok, Quinn."

"We can meet at Bordeaux's and feed the gossip mill, or you can come over to my place," I say, praying my offer doesn't sound too forward.

He gathers his camera and notebook.

"Your place later then."

In the evening, the fierce gusts of wind make the walk up to White Oak High School challenging. I set up a booth amidst dozens of others. Cindy approaches me with her clipboard.

"Thank you so much for coming, Quinn."

"How is Rand?" I ask.

"He is doing fine now, wearing a bracelet for the first time. No signs of a nest in his car but after the episode, I suggest we take my car! Let me know if you need anything," she says. She makes her way around, speaking to the participants at each booth.

The doors open again, and cold gusts intrude, along with Madge Botherme. She and about six women carry signs with frogs, poster board with frogs, a large basket of badges, etc. Mrs. Botherme begins spouting orders and her little troop sets up a booth. Despite the wind, Madge has not a hair out of place. She takes the first space by the front door. This seems to create a little stir with Cindy.

Soon students begin filling the evening with questions and writing down responses given. It's obvious they are completing a required assignment by attending. Many stop by to ask questions about owning a business.

The event thins out and an agitated Cindy stops by my booth.

"Did you see Madge wheedle into the first booth? She was supposed to be speaking at the Business Women's monthly meeting, I checked!" Cindy says.

"What did you say to her?"

Cindy says, "Nothing, I mean what is the point? I don't care if she is here, but I dislike her lack of respect and her total disregard for any leadership other than her own."

Madge approaches my booth and addresses Cindy with a mischievous smirk.

"This is a decent turnout, Cindy. Where is the frog banner and badges we sent to you?" Before anyone can answer she says, "Cindy, you look delightful tonight, but has anyone told you, your skirt is nearly transparent? With the light coming full force through the big front windows, it is like you are wearing nothing at all!"

This comment sends Cindy straight to the ladies room.

As soon as she is gone, Madge takes charge and addresses those remaining.

"Leaders, thank you so much for attending. It is so important to REACH OUT to all industries and institutions in our city, and what a grand way to do it! Please leave your surveys with me, and travel safely, it's still quite windy out there."

Her little posse packs the booth up and she leads them out. Everybody is gone before Cindy comes out of the ladies room and with a disappointed tone says, "It's over?"

"I'm afraid so, Cindy. Madge thanked everyone and concluded the event," I say.

"Well, I guess I'm glad she did. I couldn't have," Cindy says.

"Cindy, your skirt was not a problem. Madge manipulated things for control of the evening."

"She is horrible," Cindy says. "Thanks for your support anyway, Quinn."

I leave the school. I remember what Carolynn said about Cindy's past; must be only a rumor. I press my keychain to unlock my car, disturbing dozens of white birds perched upon the few cars remaining in the parking lot. They take flight with strength through the bitter winter winds. In this driving wind, I need both hands firmly on the wheel, and I'm glad to get home. I freshen up and light the fireplace as the doorbell rings. Keefe arrives and I usher him out of the miserable bluster.

"Your place is nice, Quinn. I brought a bottle of wine," he says. His demeanor is quite different than when he picked me up at the Royce Estate.

"Thank you."

I lead him into the kitchen. We make small talk about my house as I open the wine and pour us each a glass. I slice some of the Rosemary herb bread and Jarlsberg to go with our cabernet and he follows me to the living room.

"What happened with the little mob at the station?" I ask.

"Botherme and Kenadie got them riled up. Botherme is making her concern over city utilities public."

I narrowed my eyes, not understanding.

Keefe explains, "Some citizens are getting sick and blaming the tap water. The source water and the treated water checks out safe and the distribution lines and cross connection lines all check out ok. Yet some homes are still having problems. The problem comes and goes, and oddly, the water might test safe in one part of a dwelling, but not another. Botherme got involved when the nearly defunct LEPC was summoned to assist. Mayor Welsh dropped the ball and the LEPC is pretty much non-existent."

"LEPC?"

"Local Emergency Planning Committee. She wants to be mayor of White Oak so she can revamp it. She ran for the office once before, with dismal results. It wouldn't take too much effort to outshine Welsh. But, I don't think Botherme is right for the position. She seems out of touch with the voices of the citizens. She is not a good listener, making becoming elected pretty hard, I would think," he says.

"Cindy Arness is going to manage Rand Jolliet's campaign for mayor. This evening Madge attended the Occupation Fair uninvited and took over."

He smiles and raises his eyebrows.

"She gets around. Nobody showed for the Women's Business meeting at the station tonight and she hot-footed it to the school."

I say, "Goodness, Cindy wondered why she was at the high school."

"And Elliott Kenadie, he is another matter entirely!" Keefe says. "Since I took over as chief, he is in my face with a host of issues."

"Chief?"

"Yes, appointed as chief by Mayor Welsh to finish Dow's term, so I left Chicago. A few months remain in the term now. I was told nothing ever happens around here!" Keefe says, chuckling.

"Me too.... what issues is Kenadie bringing to you?" I ask.

Before Keefe can answer me, his phone rings. He checks the number and takes the call.

The chill is gone, but I add a log to the fire. I pour more wine and wait for Keefe to finish.

Keefe says, "Oh, yes...Kenadie is concerned with the recent bird kill, incidents when birds littered the ground. He is trying to link that to dead fish washing up on the shoreline. He is excellent at stirring up confusion and suspicion,"

"He does always seem to sensationalize a story," I admit.

"Yes, I agree. But there is some validity in what he's saying about White Oak's environment. With the water and the fish and bird kills, it's odd. However, no proof any of the occurrences are related, according to conservation testing. He would like to tie everything together with a big bow, and a juicy story, but it can't be done. When Botherme and Kenadie hooked up, the pressure in White Oak started to rise."

"Are you at liberty to discuss Tripp Atchison?" I ask.

"Tripp was suffering from the possible side effects of a prescribed drug. The Atchisons are devastated by this tragedy. We are still trying to identify the victim," says Keefe.

We were quiet for a moment watching the fire and I remembered the situation with Pony.

"Professor Enderlee mentioned his employee, Pony Coldstone, is in some trouble."

Keefe sipped his wine and set his glass down.

"Yes, he's a suspect in vandalism and theft at Langford's Winery."

"I have met the young man, I offered him some hours at Fireside Books in the afternoons," I say.

"Yes, he's a good kid. I hope he can vindicate himself. He claims he was home, but has no one to corroborate his claim. The two other young men have changed their story a couple of times now. They have some kind of vendetta against this kid. The winery owners are pushing it, even though the damage consisted of only a bent door frame and some stolen alcohol," Keefe says.

"The Langfords are pushing it?" I ask.

Keefe smiled and reminded me he is not at liberty to discuss all the details.

I am embarrassed and look down at my glass of wine.

"Of course you are right, sorry," I say.

"Not a problem, Quinn. But it's getting late," he says as he stands.

"Yes, I am tired," I announce.

"Thanks Quinn, I'll be in touch," he says as he goes through the front door. "Good night."

"Good night, Keefe," I say, closing and locking the door.

Keefe is hard to read. Is he interested in friendship only? I need sleep, but my thoughts turn to the birds, the fish and the water. Tripp Atchison caused the death of an innocent woman. I am intrigued by the Royce family, Keefe is on my mind. My body is tired, but my mind is occupied. Most likely the howling wind won't be much help either. I need some rest, so I take a sleep aid.

After tending to the fire, and turning off lights, I climb the stairs to bed. There is light coming from my bedroom. It would be unusual for me to leave it on. All is fine in my room, until I see night clothes on my bed. Laid out neatly are my satin pajamas and robe. Slippers lie positioned on the floor below. I recognize this as a sweet gesture from Tera. She is always thinking of me and, must have done it this morning before we left. I send her a quick text;

"I haven't worn my satin pajamas forever!"

I ready myself for sleep and slip into the satiny softness and already feel relaxed when I turn out the light. I am almost sleeping when I receive a text back from Tera.

"What are you talking about, satin P.J.'s?"

"Never mind, talk tomorrow, night." I text back.

I'm confused but I'm not ready to sound the alarm bells. I'm lying in bed, in the dark, listening to the relentless winter wind. In my rush to get ready for Keefe did I lay items out myself while being absorbed in something else? Yet, I'm certain I did not set out the clothing. Which means someone was in my house. I shudder at the thought and want to call Keefe, but what will I say? I will certainly sound unstable. I can't remember my next thought. The sleep aid snuffs out the turmoil and I am asleep.

Chapter Fourteen

I receive a text from Carolynn Langford asking me to stop by the winery on my way to Fireside Books. She plans to share the contact information for the Merchant event she'd promised from the wine tasting. My cell phone signals a call from Professor Enderlee.

"Can Pony drop by after lunch to speak with you?" he asks.

"Sure professor, Tera and her friend are coming for dinner 7:30 Friday night. Please join us?"

"Quinn, I would love to," he says, sounding happy to be invited.

I stop at the winery and Carolynn is seated at a paper-scattered booth, a large, steaming mug in front of her.

"Would you like some coffee, Quinn?" she asks politely.

"Yes, thank you."

A server brings a carafe and a small tray of fruit and breads.

"Quinn, I want to go over the information for the Merchant's night, to make things easier for you. This year the Chamber has named the event Moonlight & Merchants. Here is the flyer showing what we did previously. The evening was well-supported by the community. All you need to do is make sure the list of participating merchants gets all the details, including what they plan to offer patrons in the form of discounts, coupons, etc. The live music in the square was one of the highlights last year. Here is the contact information for the musicians we used. They never responded to my email, so phone contact is best. The magician, a surprise hit of the event, did a fine job and here is his number."

As Carolynn goes over her notes, I realize how helpful they will be and how much time this will save for me.

Carolynn says, "This year we are offering a costume contest for any patrons wanting to take the theme further. They must register by a certain date to be included on the ballot. Our voting box will be in the square and shoppers can drop their votes in. Call me if you have any questions at all."

Carolynn stifles a yawn.

"Not enough sleep?" I ask.

"Exactly right. I'll come around after another cup of coffee. We missed you on our little road trip."

"You didn't ask me to come," I say, not mincing words.

Carolynn removes reading glasses, her stunned expression turns to confusion.

"Oh Quinn, yes I did. You remember, at the bookstore . . . after the wine tasting event. We both checked our calendars; you weren't free. Tera had left and it was right before Adam called," she says. "The conversation wasn't that long ago, Quinn."

Her comment puts me on the defensive. She is so matter-of-fact, so confident. I didn't want to give the impression I didn't remember, so I nod in affirmation. Could this be another oversight in my recollection?

"Our visit covered many subjects. You're right, I remember now. Thank you for the coffee and your notes. . . and also for the bracelet, very thoughtful," I say, as I slide out of the booth to leave.

"Wear the quartz daily and find improvements in all areas of your life," she tells me.

Her comment lacks enthusiasm, like she is forcing herself. Her demeanor is different in some way, loss of sleep or marital issues possibly, and hopefully, not substance abuse. The comment about the quartz is curious, coming from her pragmatic personality.

The events of the morning temporarily mask my growing concern over my ability to remember. Staying busy will not make these concerns go away, but I wish it could. The only logical explanation would be that I laid the clothes out myself. Could my thoughts be so distracted I didn't even realize what my hands were doing? Did the anxiety about Keefe coming into my home, into my life, cause my lapse in memory?

Madge Botherme walks through the door in a powder blue suit with patch pockets and her trademark faux fur around her shoulders. Her heady fragrance arrives before she does.

"Miss Clarke," she says as she thrusts her hand across the counter for a handshake. "May I request a moment of your time?"

"Certainly."

"As city council president, I must gather support for a complete and widespread campaign to get to the bottom of this water problem," she says with conviction. "Are you aware of our dangerous drinking water?"

Before I can respond she keeps right on going.

"White Oak is on the verge of destruction. Mayor Welsh is asleep at the wheel I'm afraid. Business owners must unite under this cause. Change in our leadership is needed. An emergency town hall meeting is set for Friday evening. Can I count you in?"

"I would like to understand the issues, so yes, I will attend."

As soon as she hears my affirmation, she is already headed toward the door.

"Now, that's the spirit! Good day, Miss Clarke."

Madge seems pleased with herself as she leaves.

Pony Coldstone arrives. He is eager to earn a little more. Having him here will give me more flexibility. My sales are increasing each month since opening the bookstore, an indicator I can justify the hire. He tells me he can begin right away and I show him the newly arrived box of books. He rolls up his sleeves and goes to work.

One customer needs help finding an author, and another wants to discuss current affairs. I answer a couple of phone calls and remember the deadline on the symphony event to be held at the Royce estate. If I plan on attending, I need to start a list of people who would join my table.

"I'm finished Quinn," Pony says.

"Oh, wonderful! How are your studies going?"

"Better than last semester." He pushes dark waves of hair away from his eyes. His brown eyes are not smiling as they were when I first met him.

"What do you like to do when you are not studying?" I ask.

"When would that be?" he says sarcastically.

"Oh, I understand."

Pony grins, lowering his eyes. He is shy in his youthfulness. He puts both hands into his jean pockets.

"I enjoy learning about subjects of my choice," he says.

"Ok, what interests you?"

Pony lights up at the question.

"I am interested in theology." His response surprises me. Pony says, "My aunt believes her faith changed her destiny. I never understood what she meant, but I am beginning to. She is showing me a better life is possible, and I want to learn more."

"Professor Enderlee tells me your Aunt Carmen is setting an excellent example to follow."

"Professor E., he's a good one too," Pony says.

"I love that man. A gentle soul. But I do worry about him."

"Yeah, I know what you mean. His house is a mess."

"Yes, I am hoping he won't be too offended if I offer to help him out."

Pony says, "He could use a hand. Been rough since the loss of his daughter, Rose."

"Rose? He referred to her as his assistant."

"Rose was both his assistant and his daughter. Her illness and death happened fast. Rose was cool. She was writing a book on the history of White Oak. He always tells people his assistant Rose graduated or something. I guess that explanation is easier. Her pictures are all over his house."

I say, "Yes I saw a picture. How sad! I will find a way to help him, a way to get all the clutter out."

Pony scuffs at a spot on the floor with his shoe.

"He sure doesn't need any more grief, and I am giving him some right now," he says.

Although I know the situation, I remain silent, hoping he will continue.

"These two guys, Marcus and Kent, broke into Bordeaux's and told the cops I helped. I was nowhere near the winery that night." Pony's innocent looking brown eyes are sincere.

"Why do you think they implicated you?"

Pony is stone-faced and his gaze never leaves me.

Lowering his voice he says, "I know something about them." His eyes give away his fear. He moves a dark lock away from his face with his hand again. He turns his back to me. I assume he is hiding his emotions during the awkward silence. I'm not sure what to do.

"I have to talk to someone."

"Pony what about me?" I venture.

"No, I can't involve anyone," he says, his face still turned away.

I move around and face him.

He lowers his head, embarrassed by his emotion.

"Pony, if this is serious, all the more reason. I will not judge you. I would only like to be your friend. Come and sit."

I lead him to the chairs in front of the fireplace. I pour us each a cup of coffee and bring him a tissue.

He accepts both.

The cat jumps on him and when he pets her she makes her nest next to him.

"Pony, meet Thomasena, my first friend in White Oak." I say.

"She's awesome," he says. After a long pause he confides in me. "I am in a study group at school with a girl named Jessie. She invited me to her church when she found out about my interest in theology. She called her church the River Family. I like Jessie, so I figured, why not?

"She drove us towards the river, and I remember thinking this church was a long way from town. She turned onto a gravel road running alongside the river. She told me about White Oak and school. I asked her how the church got its start. She told me a weird story about a miracle. This church was created from a woman's love for a man. This dark and evil man was undeserving, but she would find something in this man. She told no one, knowing she'd be an outcast. Her love for him stayed a secret, even after his death. Her teardrops for him is the miracle, the seed starting this church. Weird huh?"

"Yes, weird."

Pony takes a deep breath and continues.

"When we came to the end of the road where the snow was plowed into heaps, making road blocks, a portion in the wall of snow swung open, like it had been piled on a flatbed, and we kept going as the portion of the wall swung back, making the wall once more. She parked further up towards the river in a clearing and got out of the car. A strong feeling gripped me . . . I was in danger. She told me the church had many followers and they worshiped surrounded by nature. Street clothes were not permitted. She put a dark robe thing over her clothes and tossed one to me. We looked like monks."

Pony sips his coffee, and then continues.

"Smoke was in the air as we walked through a thick forest. Then again, I felt this strong urging to turn around and go back. Daylight was going fast, making it hard to see. We walked past a bunch of cars in the trees on our way to the river's edge. Jessie stopped and lifted up the hood of her robe and helped me to do the same, hiding our faces. Others came out from all around us. This is going to sound crazy, but someone grabbed my arm and pulled me back. When I turned, no one was there!"

My cell phone interrupts his story. I answer a question for a customer and when I'm finished, Pony continues.

I recognized Kent and Marcus's voices as they talked with Jessie, but I don't think they recognized me. I heard the robed figure saying, 'Show the mark.' Each one who passed was examined for it. I would be singled out for not having this mark. I figured I would be granted access as a visitor, but my instincts told me a visitor might be more like a victim. As the line moved I let others pass me by. Before Jessie was through, I faded into blackness, then caught back up alongside Marcus after he was through. Jessie joined us once she was through. She never knew the difference. As we made our way to a gathering and a roaring fire, I heard a voice whisper, 'Get away'. I decided I wanted to get away but I didn't know for sure how."

"Sounds terrifying," I say.

Pony continues, "We became part of the big group and one figure began some weird chanting. Other robed figures walked out of the forest, and the numbers doubled in size. From the moment we arrived, I was pretty sure I didn't want to be part of this church. Three men came out of nowhere. They wore similar robes, but large round medallions of some kind around their necks. There was a huge bonfire.

"An older sounding voice said, 'River People! Who presents new followers tonight? Bring them forward.'

"Jessie began to move but I grabbed her arm, preventing her from moving. Other sets of robed figures made their way to the front of the fire. Another in the trio spoke loud enough for all to hear.

"'Welcome souls of Nadellawick! We unite under the supreme

rule of the dark angel. Our allegiance is to him. The growth of the empire is the responsibility of every soul who worships here tonight. Begin the cleansing process.'

"The whole crowd stepped back to make a circle larger. The trio surrounded a large tree stump, as round as a table top. A robed figure brought a guy to the front. Another leader lifted the medallion from around his neck up to the moon and said some words. He lowered his arms and placed the medallion on the new member's neck.

"The chanting continued and the victim collapsed on to the stump-like table! The three surrounded him and one of the robed figures took out a knife and cut the victim's finger. Drops of blood fell onto the medallion below, sizzling each time a drop hit its surface. I will never forget the smell of burning blood. One of the trio was commanded to confirm the mark. They pulled the poor victim's bottom lip out and looked at it.

"Then he said, 'The dark lord's region grows!' or something crazy like that.

"All began to chant together and the victim was taken away. The same thing happened to another guy, but he struggled and I was starting to freak out. I saw this as my last chance to escape. I kept stepping back slowly until I was in the shadows of the thick tree line. I heard a scream and began to run deeper into the night. From a secluded spot I witnessed more. There was a lot of blood. A commotion ensued . . . members of the group began searching. They spread out and came towards me. They were looking for me! I kept running until I was in White Oak."

"Pony, I am shocked this is going on in White Oak!" I say.

He says, "I am not sure if Jessie would expose my identity. But I never saw her again. Now I am being implicated in the break-in. No one will believe the wild story of what I saw, especially when my reputation is being questioned. I need to get out of town, fast!"

I am speechless by what Pony is telling me. I didn't want to appear as unnerved; he is scared enough.

He pushes his hair back again and tears up a little.

"My Aunt Carmen doesn't deserve this. The people by the river are evil. I don't know what they will do to me, or to my Aunt. I'm being watched by them. I think the best thing to do is leave."

He stands and Thomasena leaps to the floor.

"Wait, Pony!" I say. "Let's think this through. You need to understand what is happening and what the actual threat is. You need to know all your options. Acting in haste could make things worse. A decision as important as this takes clear thinking. Your future may depend on it! Sit back down and let's talk this through."

Pony flops back down on the chair.

"It's possible Jessie did not tell them who you are," I say.

"She wasn't too worried about throwing me to the wolves in the first place. They gotta know it was me."

"I want to help you." I tell him.

"Why, why would you want to be dragged into this?"

I lock on Pony's eyes.

"Pony, I have been at the lowest point. I lost my best friend, the man I was to marry, in a tragic accident and I nearly lost my own life. I am growing in my suspicion I might be in danger myself. I can no longer dismiss all the red flags. Everything in this town is being affected. My fear seems to grow daily. Maybe you can help me too."

Pony says, "How?"

"You won't talk because you might be labeled as a liar, and if I do I might be labeled unstable. I accept and believe in your innocence and if you accept and believe in my stability, it's a good basis for a friendship, don't you agree?"

Pony smiles and seems to relax a little.

I say, "We need to first deal with the legal issues in front of you, Pony. What were you doing on the night of the break in?"

Pony looks panicked again.

"That night Carmen was in the city and I was at home."

"Tell me what you did, don't leave anything out."

Pony stands and begins walking around the shop. He rubs the palms of his hands on his jeans.

I walk over to him.

"It's ok; I have no reason to tell anyone," I say.

"I wasn't alone that night. Jessie was with me."

Pony turns away and paces.

"Jessie? The girl who took you to the river?"

"Yes…I will lose the trust of my Aunt. I can't tell her. Jessie couldn't stop talking about these River people. Her experience with depression, her unmet expectations, all her turmoil have taken a toll on her life. Since joining this church she accepts her imperfections. The River People helped her through some very bad times. She made the church sound great. She never said anything about the things I saw. Do you see now why I need to get out of here? I want to draw the danger away from my aunt."

"Running will only make you look guilty. We will find out all we can about the River People." I take his arm. "Pony you must trust the authorities. Otherwise, we are giving the River People all the power. They must be exposed."

Pony turns his shoulders squarely towards me.

"Quinn, if I go to the police, my future is sealed for sure. They are being fed so many lies, I won't ever get justice."

"Pony, you need to trust me. I have a source, a friend in the department. He will listen. Without his help you have no future. This is your best chance, please Pony."

He lowers his head and tears come again; such pressure on this young man.

I call Keefe and ask him to meet us at Mocha Joe's as soon as he can.

The professor greets us when we arrive. He does his best to show an enthusiastic smile, but it doesn't conceal his concern.

"I think we can find a booth or two left. The Writers Club Rose once belonged to is meeting today."

I catch a glimpse of Elliott Kenadie and ignore him in the hopes he won't come over and pry.

Professor Enderlee brings coffee and joins us when Keefe gets to the coffee shop.

Pony is shaken as he grips the mug with both hands. He repeats his experience again for Keefe.

Keefe confirms his knowledge of the River People and the strange rituals.

He says, "They never meet in the same place twice, slowing down our investigation. This is a real threat to White Oak. Would you please excuse me, I need to make a phone call."

During his absence, Professor Enderlee praises Pony for his decision and courage.

Keefe rejoins us. With compassion he puts his hand on Pony's shoulder.

"Pony, you are brave, you did the right thing. There's a development . . . the body of a young woman has been found near the river, identified as Jessie Milsap. She was strangled."

"Huh? Oh no! She wasn't a bad person. She didn't deserve to lose her life. They are going to come after me next!" Pony says in a panic.

"Even though Pony barely knew this girl, these hooligans could point the finger at Pony, since she intended to initiate him into this church," the professor says.

"The approximate time of death is mid-morning yesterday. Pony was at the station all morning, so he can't be implicated. Pony, protection will be provided right away. I think we can help you. Follow me."

He follows Keefe and another officer waits to escort Pony to a squad car.

As Keefe is leaving I grab his arm and stop him. I am so grateful for what he has done for Pony, I give him an embrace.

"Thank you," I say. I think I caught him off guard. I look into his eyes to repeat myself but I'm interrupted when his lips meet mine. The kiss is brief.

Then, as if he put coins in a parking meter, he turns and walks out.

Chapter Fifteen

My day starts with a phone conversation catching Tera up on what's been discovered about the mystery woman's accident. The professor will be attending dinner and Tera confirms she and Chamous will be over too.

A gentleman wearing a suit and tie is the first through the door of Fireside Books this day. He secures my signature for a delivery from P. Royce, the book collection. I open the box, seven volumes in all, but I count only six. I run out to catch the courier; perhaps this is one of two boxes, but he is speeding off to his next delivery. Back inside I review the invoice: seven books listed/Author B. Hathaway. I am not quite sure what to do. An oversight seems unlikely, with the collection being so special. I prepare to give the estate a call when I am surprised by the door signaling Elliott Kenadie's arrival.

"Good morning Miss Clarke," he says. "I pray you'll be joining us at the Town Hall meeting tonight?"

"I wouldn't miss it!"

"Grand, just grand!" he says. He approaches the counter and gives a good look around Fireside Books. His pointed nose is even more prominent as his profile turns from side to side. "How's business?"

"Excellent!"

He whips around dead center to face me.

"Really!" he says, drawing the word out slowly into sarcasm. What is this gent's problem?

"What can I do for you Mr. Kenadie?"

He takes out his notebook and pen and prepares for battle.

"Are you aware the mystery woman is from Royce estate?" he asks. Did he say mystery woman and Royce Estate in the same sentence?

I ask, "She's been identified?"

"Oh, yes Miss Clarke," he says as he scribbles on his pad, "oh yes, indeed. Mrs. Murphy, from the public library, knew the woman! She offered a description matching the deceased to a tee! Can you add additional information seeing how . . . connected you are to the police force?"

"I beg your pardon," I say.

"Miss Clark, in the world of journalism, a good reporter instinctively digs deeper. The mystery woman was Calista Twinning, a tutor at the Royce Estate for many years, and a regular patron of the city library."

I am speechless. I think he is waiting for my reaction to his statement. Perhaps he is trying to verify his information. But, my silence is interpreted as indignation.

He turns his body, causing his trench coat to make a flapping sound against his legs, on his way out the door.

He says, "Good day!"

The shop fills with winter chill upon his exit. I sit in front of the fire with my coffee and my phone. I am using self-talk again to remain calm. This connection to the mystery woman and the Royce estate sheds different light on her visit to Fireside Books. I expect I will be hearing from Keefe soon. A tutor would be a credible person, perhaps. Did she have a vendetta or too much time on her hands? But why so much secrecy?

The afternoon comes and goes with no phone call from Keefe. While looking through the mail I come across an envelope with no return address. I open it quickly, a note from Sapphire Royce. It reads,

"Quinn, how are you? I wanted to explain something about the collection of books you purchased, before you receive the delivery and call my mother! I prepared the package and took out book #7 to give you a reason to come back up to the estate!!! Don't be mad at me. Hope we don't get snow! Ha! My mother is so psychotic when it comes to anyone coming to the estate. She will be in England for two weeks starting on Saturday. Come up and visit me? Text me~907-587-0003. Sapphire"

How interesting! I wonder why she didn't call Fireside Books or my cell. I do want to see Sapphire, visit Royce Estate again and perhaps see Cashton. And I need the book.

I send a text to Sapphire, "You are holding my book hostage! Yes, to coming up, perhaps on Sat. or Sun. Will let you know."

* * * * *

A stage area with long table for speakers and podium sits in front of a stuffy town hall filled with about fifty people. I find an empty seat next to Cindy Arness.

Professor Enderlee waves at me from the far right side, near the back.

"Hello, Cindy, this spot taken?" I ask.

"No, Quinn, please sit," she says.

"I am hoping the meeting isn't long."

"My same hope!" she says, leaning closer to my ear. Then in a whisper she says, "Are you aware of the controversy surrounding the former police chief of White Oak?"

"No."

"Chief Dow had information about several prominent people of White Oak belonging to some kind of secret society referred to as Wyvern."

"Secret society?"

"Information damaging to those involved. Chief Dow planned to expose some citizens, but never told Rand anything except he was consulting with a historian and gaining the last needed pieces to a puzzle he believed might bring an end to some dark entity in White Oak. His secrets died with him; he kept his theories and proof to himself."

"Chief Dow told Rand anyone in the Wyvern would have a mark." Cindy continues, still whispering.

"What is the mark?" I ask.

"Inside the lip! Rand even wanted to make sure I didn't have the mark." Cindy's expression was serious.

My expression displays my astonishment at what Cindy is telling me.

Our conversation comes to an abrupt end when a man approaches the podium.

The town hall meeting is called to order by a stout man with a bow tie and bushy eyebrows. He announces himself as Herald Moody. He introduces panel members seated at the head table.

Mayor Welsh sits among city council members, including Madge Botherme, and a few people from the water department. Keefe is seated next to the mayor, and next to him is policewoman Dawn Bishop. Mayor Welsh addresses the meeting first.

"The city of White Oak faces many challenges in recent weeks. Incorrect information always causes confusion. Tom Dorsey from the water department is here this evening to give us the most updated information about White Oak's water supply. Tom?"

A tall, thin man approaches the podium and clears his throat.

"Good evening. Recently a series of tests was conducted on White Oak's water supply. Water taken from our source water, treated water and stored water, including the cross connection lines, was tested. All met normal standards. Results of the testing on four different occasions are in your meeting notes. We did discover some below standard results from certain taps of the individuals who fell ill. In all cases, these slightly below standard numbers are not enough to cause illness."

"Tell my wife, who spent a night in the hospital!" a man from the crowd shouts.

Tom Dorsey replies calmly, "I don't doubt your wife's illness; the water didn't cause it."

Tom Dorsey takes his seat with the others up front. Mike Clemmons from the conservation department is next to address the meeting.

I catch a glimpse of Elliott Kenadie, shuffling notes. He is recording the meeting.

Mike Clemmons says, "Reports of the bird kill in our county prompted autopsy of the birds and nothing out of the ordinary was found. Bird kill has occurred in other places in the United States, indicating it is not exclusive to our community. Since parasites and virus have been ruled out, we believe the deaths resulted from fireworks on that particular date. Those beautiful and seemingly innocent celebratory explosions we love to watch displayed in the skies can be lethal to flocks of birds. The fish kill on the Missouri in the past has been linked to severe or extreme weather. This is not unusual in other parts of the U.S. as well. I want to emphasize we do not consider the birds and the fish connected in any way. Thank you." Mr. Clemmons takes his seat.

In between speakers, the volume in the room grows. Mr. Moody asks for order and tells the crowd to quiet down. At this time the floor is opened for questions. Edith Craven escorts an elderly lady to the microphone.

In a very soft voice she says, "My name is Edna Carlton. My bread is not rising. I blame the water. I've baked the bread the same way for sixty five years. I bake prize winning bread, and something is wrong, sirs. That is all." Edith and Edna Carlton take their seats.

Mr. Moody is rattled as he replies, "Dear Mrs. Carlton. I thank you for your comments to this meeting. Everyone knows your bread is the best in the county, but could we please keep our questions to a more general nature?"

Another citizen approaches the microphone to speak.

"My name is Gordon Fletcher, uncle to Dominic Bump over there." Fletcher points to his nephew. "With all due respect, I think the baloney you are dishing out is starting to stink up this whole damn hall!"

He has everyone's attention. His comment ignites the opinions and the murmuring grows.

Gordon Fletcher continues, "If you think the discolored water coming from our faucets every now and then is acceptable, I would like to offer you a glass of it right now!"

This statement evokes a few cheers of support from the crowd and a couple of men rise to their feet in support as Mr. Fletcher delivers his last comments.

"And you must think we are stupid if something as basic as water is not connected to the bird and fish kills. Now, I am not a highly educated man, but do I need to draw you a picture of the hydrologic circle . . . connect the dots for you folks up there? If you ask me, this meeting is to stifle concern, not address it! Damn liberals!" Fletcher takes his seat to a round of applause.

Many people approach the microphone and the room is louder than ever.

"Everyone simmer down and take your turn!" Mr. Moody shouts.

Madge Botherme rises from the panel table and approaches the podium. She bullies Mr. Moody right out of her way. The teal blouse does nothing to enhance her lime green polyester suit. For this occasion Madge wears a dressy wide pillbox hat to match her trademark white pumps.

She speaks into the microphone, "Good citizens of White Oak, we are in peril! We must unite. Mayor Welsh has failed in organizing the LEPC. This committee is needed to address these types of emergency situations. Mayor Welsh . . . "

"Madge you are out of line! Everybody knows we don't need a committee to address these issues that are few and far between. Your personal ambition for taking over my position, and your dramatics, are hurting, not helping this town. Why don't you sit your ass down?" Mayor Welsh says in a booming voice.

Mrs. Botherme takes offense at his comments, and storms away from the podium, right toward Mayor Welsh. She shakes her finger so violently her hat falls from her head as she lunges toward the mayor.

Simultaneously, Elliott Kenadie starts snapping pictures, as Dawn Bishop overreacts by rushing and tackling Mrs. Botherme.

Keefe jumps up to assist Mrs. Botherme.

The remaining panel members abandon the head table.

Amidst the commotion, Mr. Moody announces the meeting is adjourned.

Citizens are pointing and shouting passionate points of view.

I duck out and head home, taking pleasure in the solitude my car provides away from the chaos. My thoughts turn to the conversation with Cindy Arness. Keefe didn't mention any suspicion surrounding Chief Dow's death.

I arrive home in time to prepare dinner for my guests. I assembled most of the simple meal yesterday--clam dip alongside roasted cloves of fresh garlic to serve with savory crackers as our appetizer. I prepare both the fettuccine piccata and a salad of mixed greens with poppyseed dressing.

Tera bypasses the doorbell and lets herself in, Chamous McCoy on her arm. After a hug from Tera, she introduces me to the man with a wide, genuine smile. Chamous takes my hand.

Tera opens a bottle of wine when the doorbell rings.

Professor Enderlee greets me with an embrace and I lead him back to the kitchen. Chamous is introduced to the professor and Tera offers to start a fire. With everyone gathered in the living room, I bring out the clam dip during the professor's lively recounting of the Town Hall meeting.

"I might catch the next one!" Tera says laughing.

Our conversation takes on a more serious nature.

"There are matters needing attention in this town," Chamous says. "We're seeing widespread deterioration of a religious community, not only one denomination, but all of them. Pastors are preaching to near empty congregations. A poor economy sends people to the church doors, and even with that, nothing. The loss of optimism in the community is overwhelming. We are attempting to reach out to people in every way we can. But membership is not our only challenge. Our structure itself seems to be falling apart. Our stubborn plumbing problems are costing our parish thousands in repairs and still the problem is not fixed. The odor in the church is unpleasant, to say the least. At times I don't want to be there myself!"

Chamous is over six feet, and the belt laced through his jeans is accented with a large, eye catching buckle. The sleeves of his western shirt are turned up and he uses his big hands to communicate his point. Well groomed light hair and mustache and rugged good looks pale in comparison to his passion. This man is easy to like. He will be good for Tera. Tera watches him with adoring eyes.

Once Professor Enderlee asks Chamous a few questions about his life, we are all intrigued by him. Chamous is a humble man, and it takes some coaxing for him to open up about the past.

"Law enforcement was my life, following in my father's footsteps. Seeing lives in crisis was a unique window to the world, and opened my mind to serving people in a different way. Four years ago I became an ordained minister and I enjoy working with younger people, teenagers."

Tera hangs on his every word.

"Satanic worship is a growing concern in our society, even here in Missouri. Our church built The Barn, giving our youth a place to hang out and us a place to provide choices for them. That is how I met Keefe. He spoke to our youth on the subject of violence, having moved in recently from Chicago, and shared some of his experiences as a detective there," Chamous says.

"Oh, I wasn't aware you knew him," Quinn says.

"He was effective with those kids, really got the conversation rolling. Kids talk plenty," Chamous says, "and the word on the street is all about a new Caesar."

Professor Enderlee asks, "New Caesar?"

"Yup," says Chamous, "that's what they call the leader of this church or group of river people. We've discovered little about them. But, concern is growing, with so many churches dwindling. I pray we are not losing souls to this darkness."

My phone signals a text from Keefe.

"Pony is safe-call you later."

I can't help adding what we've learned from Chamous to the list of problems facing this town. Is Elliott Kenadie correct in his theory that something, one thing, is affecting everything? This subject puts a damper on our conversation. I announce dinner is ready and we move to the dining room and enjoy the meal. Professor Enderlee comments on the house.

"Quinn, your home is lovely. I like your style. My home needs work," Professor Enderlee says.

This is my chance to offer help to the professor.

"I would love to lend a hand or even spearhead the project! It would be enjoyable for me."

"You are much too busy Quinn!"

"One can't work all the time. Please allow me to indulge myself! If Pony helps in the afternoons I have even more flexibility," I remind him.

"Well, sure, I don't see why not," the professor says with enthusiasm.

"It's all settled. I want to get started as soon as possible." I tell him, and then wink at Tera.

As we are clearing the dishes from the table, Tera asks me about Pony. I answer, "Keefe is calling me later, and I am hoping for some word on the next step for Pony."

Chapter Sixteen

The next few days are filled with busy work as I prepare for the Moonlight & Merchants event. I am grateful Tera will be helping me out. I asked her to arrive about an hour before. This will be good for Fireside Books. There is still no sign of Tera, so I send her a text.

Things are not running smoothly in the square. Chamber members are trying to arrange seating for the mayor's address. The musicians are thirty minutes late. The kick off begins with a musical number and the mayor's welcome, after which patrons can visit the various businesses. At 5:30 the band had still not arrived. I attempt to call them. After the fifth ring, I get an answer.

"Morris? This is Quinn Clarke from the Chamber of Commerce," I say with as much control as possible.

"Yes, this is him. Oh, Ms. Clarke I am glad you called. I wanted to know where the power outlet is, we can't find it anywhere," Morris says.

"What do you mean? Where are you?" I ask, afraid of what the answer might be.

"We are at the county fairgrounds. We are the first ones here. Where do we hook to the power source? Don't worry, we can still be ready by seven," he says.

"WHAT? Starting time is not seven and the location is not at the fairgrounds!"

"What do you mean, Miss Clarke?"

"The event is not at the county fairgrounds, it is in the town square! That is what I told you on the phone, and in all the correspondence you received regarding all the details!"

"Umm…hang on."

"Miss Clarke, we are not sure how this happened. I am sorry. We are packing up and heading to the square."

Tera is running late, and music will be missing when the event kicks off. Madge Botherme does her best to arrange everyone, despite my efforts to do the same.

"Where are the musicians? The mayor needs to start his address in three minutes!" Madge says excitedly. Before I can respond, Madge is off to talk to the mayor.

I turn around to a costume-clad pair standing in front of me. A few moments pass before I recognize the couple as the Atchisons, hard to identify them in their horrific costumes.

"Good evening, I was sorry to hear of the accident Tripp, how are you doing?"

"Coming along now. Hailey thought getting out would be good for us," he says.

"You're getting into the theme, that's for sure."

Both are stone faced and dressed in Amish looking garb. Tripp is bloody and Hailey pale and dead looking with black shadows around her eyes.

Hailey says, "Don't you recognize us? We are the famous puritans, Giles and Martha Corey, victims of the Salem Witch Hunt. Giles was pressed to death and I was hung." Hailey seemed quite proud.

It is ghastly and I struggle for a comment.

"Very...historical," I say.

Elliott Kenadie startles us with the flash of his camera.

The mayor begins his address and people who are on the street gather around. Music or no music, the evening is ready to begin. The president of the Chamber, Delmont Smith, introduces Mayor Welsh.

"Patrons of White Oak, thank you for supporting our Moonlight & Merchants Chamber event. Time now for a hearty rendition of The Missouri Waltz and then a message from our mayor. To introduce our musicians is our coordinator, Quinn Clarke of Fireside Books."

The small group offers some applause.

I say, "Thank you Delmont. Welcome! Please enjoy yourselves tonight. All the merchants participating burn green lights in their lampposts. Each of these businesses will be offering coupons and specials. Remember, our magician performs in thirty minutes. Everyone take a ballot before you leave and vote for the best costume. We will close the voting at nine. I take responsibility for the musicians being late. Thank you."

Mayor Welsh says, "Our music is absent, but we hope you still have a good time."

You couldn't call the group gathered a crowd, but it is still early. I anticipate Tera is at Fireside Books stoking the fire and ready to lend a hand. I can use the support.

Fireside Books is lit up but Tera is not there. I check my phone, still no word from her, but Chamous texts me. Tera is running late. Why hasn't she responded? Pony is helping out at Mocha Joe's but comes over so I can run back over to the square to make sure the magician is ready to perform. The musicians are having difficulty with their power source. A few chamber members are trying to help them. I am still waiting for the magician. Despite my best efforts, this event is doing nothing for my image as coordinator.

"HEY, QUINN!" says a loud Tera.

Arriving at the square are Tera, Carolynn and a tuxedo-clad man, unsteady on his feet.

"Quinn, dear, we are a little late," slurs Tera as she tries to conceal a hiccup. "Quick Jeffery, we got some faces angry." Tera laughs at her word mix up. "Carolynn, did you hear what I said? Faces angry? It's hilarious," Tera says as she swats Carolynn's arm.

It's clear the magician and Tera are intoxicated.

I await Carolynn's response. Will she also be under the influence of alcohol?

"Jeffery and Tera both stopped at the winery, and we shared dinner and a little wine," Carolynn says, without any signs of intoxication. "Jeffery, please set up. Why are the musicians not playing, Quinn?"

"Logistic problems . . . but they are now ready to start," I say, trying to control my emotions.

"Tera, can you run over and take over at the shop. I will be right there," I say, while keeping my cool.

Tera didn't even respond. She staggers her way across the street to Fireside Books.

The magician is in no shape to perform, but it does not stop him from trying.

Jeffery says, "Hello fine citizens of White Oak. Where is everybody? Skeleton crew tonight, eh?"

Garbled words tip off the small crowd that he is under the influence of something. He raises his arm and one white gloved finger points skyward.

"My first amazing trick will require help from my beautiful

girlfriend. I am going to make her disappear."

The young woman is concealed behind the curtain of a closet-like box.

"The truth is, fine citizens of White Oak, I do want her to disappear! She's such a witch sometimes. Why put up with it, when there are so many to choose from?" he says, winking at a woman in the small audience. "Once she's gone, please see me after to fill her position!" Jeffery laughs. He is the only one doing so. He says his magic words and draws the curtain open, revealing his upset girlfriend.

She stands with her arms crossed.

"You, bastard!" she screams and slaps him hard across the face before storming off.

Carolynn breaks in and says, "Jeffery is not...well enough to do his act. Please visit all the shops participating to enter the drawing."

She offers no explanation or apology as the small audience dissipates. I walk back to my shop and Carolynn catches up with me.

"Quinn, things are off to a rocky start," she remarks.

"You think?" I say sarcastically, "The turnout is even weak! Where were you three?"

"Tera joined me for dinner at the winery. Jeffery was at the bar with a friend. When I saw they both had overindulged, I couldn't let them drive. It is very unfortunate. I need to help Adam serve wine at the Chamber, I will check back in with you," Carolynn says and hurries away.

Back at Fireside Books, Tera is passed out on the sofa.

I send a quick text to Chamous asking him to come and pick her up. He lets me know he will be there as soon as he can.

Pony is going between Mocha Joe's and Fireside Books with lots of questions.

"What happened to Tera? Is she sick?" he asks.

"Too much wine, and she is passed out right now... don't ask," I say.

Pony gives me a salute before he goes back to help the professor.

I need to get her out of the shop. The jingle of the bells on the door signals my first patrons. It is several people at once.

"Please come in. Relax and browse," I say with enthusiasm,

hoping they won't notice my girlfriend passed out on the sofa. After about ten minutes and without anyone else coming through the door, I offer them some refreshments.

Tera becomes restless and leans over the side of sofa.

She says with impending doom, "Quinn, I feel sick."

I rush to her aid, and help her into the bathroom. I rinse a cloth for her head, as she sits upon the padded bench.

"I think I am ok, Quinn. Go to your customers."

I race back out to find them leaving. I try offering refreshments to them, but they file hastily out of Fireside Books.

"I'm much better," Tera says with a weak smile as she emerges from the back.

"Lie down Tera, everything will be alright," I say, while I wonder what happened to my friend.

Tera does not drink to extreme. With the green light in my lamppost switched off, and the front door locked, I look forward to this night being over.

Tera sits up and I offer her some tea and let her absorb the warmth from the relaxing fire.

While she rests, I put the refreshments away and deal with some paperwork. She wakes after sleeping for half an hour.

"How are you feeling, Tera?"

"Better now," she replies, taking more tea.

"This isn't your style, what happened?"

Tera holds her cup of tea with both hands and stares at the fire.

"Tell me about it! If you sent Chamous a message, I don't understand why he hasn't come yet. The night began when I stopped at Bordeaux's to drop off information on a private estate sale Carolynn said she wanted. She suggested a quick dinner, and we had wine. I had two glasses but it feels like six!" Tera says, looking puzzled. She sets her tea down, and begins to gather up her mane of dark hair into a ponytail and puts a band around it.

"How did you hook up with the magician?" I ask.

"The guy wearing the tuxedo sat at the bar, no idea what his story is. But I knew I couldn't drive, so Carolynn offered to bring us both. I am so sorry Quinn. I ruined the night for you," she says remorsefully.

"Something is very strange about this whole situation," I say.

Chamous arrives, and I send Tera on her way. The event was a complete disaster. Random thoughts run through my mind. How could Tera be intoxicated with only having two glasses of wine? And, didn't Carolynn say they had dinner together, the three of them? It seems coincidental the magician was at Bordeaux's too. When did Tera have time to visit with Carolynn about a private estate sale? I guess they are communicating. What about the musicians? I am not sure how they showed up at the wrong location. I am being undermined. Looks like Carolynn is not a friend but a foe. I am startled by a brisk knock at the door. It's Carolynn.

"Quinn, I am so glad you are here. I want to offer you a possible explanation." Carolynn is breathless and her hand quivers slightly and her eyes are misty." I received a call from the winery. Someone in our kitchen confessed to tampering with open bottles of wine! Jeffery and Tera are one of three victims. Is Tera ok? This is a serious offense; we can lose our license over this. I just wanted you to know."

"Oh, no Carolynn, this is terrible, but weren't all three of you were having dinner?" I ask.

"Oh, no," she responds, "Jeffery comes into Bordeaux's quite often. I was having dinner when Tera stopped by, and I offered her a quick bite."

"I thought you said before, you three were having dinner," I say.

"No Quinn, you are mistaken, only Tera and I…and it's not the worst of it Quinn. Our employee dropped a few pills into wine bottles, used a prescription drug with my name on it. I can't believe any of my employees would do that. It's a mystery to me. I promised Adam all the pills were destroyed. He will never forgive me. I have to go." she says as she closes the door behind her.

As I drive home, exhausted, I have to consider I may have jumped to conclusions about Carolynn.

Chapter Seventeen

Yˮou mean someone at Bordeaux's drugged me?" Tera asks the next day.

"It appears so," I respond, telling her the bombshell Carolynn delivered. "You were put in danger; the sooner you file your statement at the station the better."

"The inside of the police department is a place I would like to avoid, yet will be visiting, again," she says with a sigh.

The shop business is slow due to more blowing snow. I receive a call at the end of the day.

"Quinn, this is Keefe. I want to show you something. Can I stop by Fireside Books in the morning?" he asks.

"Is everything ok?"

"Yes, we've made some progress."

"I'll have a coffee ready."

The next morning, I pick up some freshly brewed Italian Roast at Mocha Joe's, one for Keefe too. This morning is frigid and I hustle to warm things up. The fire roars, inviting Thomasena to come out from hiding to warm herself. I text Sapphire and let her know I can come for a visit this afternoon after I close.

She responds with a "Yippee!"

Keefe arrives within minutes, cell phone ringing as he comes through the door. He gives me a wave hello, while he takes the call. Once his conversation ends, his phone rings again but he ignores it.

"Quinn, I want to show you something," he says, pulling me around to the window. Without pointing a finger he says, "Red car in front of the barber shop . . . woman with the shopping bags, see them? They are not what they seem."

"What do you mean?"

"Pony's protection, due mostly to Chamous McCoy," he says.

"Now I am lost. What's his involvement?" I ask, trying to put the pieces together.

"Quinn, Chamous is uniquely qualified. He is a former special weapon and tactics officer," Keefe explains.

"S.W.AT.? Are you serious? He mentioned his background in law enforcement."

"Did he mention he is decorated with commendations? We are fortunate the way this is working out. Pony will live in Chamous's apartment. Chamous will bring Pony to work and pick him up. His protection is transparent. Pony agreed to help us solve the Milsap murder. When we find her killers, maybe we can expose these River People," Keefe says.

I offer Keefe the coffee.

"Thanks, Quinn," he says with smile and a wink. "Jessie Milsap had a black insect inside her mouth."

He takes another drink and studies my reaction.

"What? What do you mean?"

"A small black beetle inside her lower bottom lip . . . embedded."

"Keefe, my goodness, what in the world are we talking about here?"

"It's the most bizarre detail in my police experience. Pony told us how they checked for a mark inside the mouth of each victim," he explains.

"This sounds dangerous, being a witness to the ritual. Perhaps he . . ."

"His choices are limited, Quinn. Helping us is the best way to clear his name. Under Chamous's watchful eye is the most secure place for Pony to be right now."

"What about Tera?"

"She was giving her statement to Dawn Bishop, I didn't talk to her."

I take a seat and Keefe joins me.

"The identity of the mystery woman may be Calista Twinning."

"Yes, the information was shared by the trenchcoat reporter!" I say, shaking my head.

"I'm not surprised. Things going on at the station become town topics before they can be verified! Twinning was employed by the Royce family as a tutor. Mrs. Murphy, from the library claims she knew Calista Twinning during this time. As a precaution I'm considering police protection once more for you," Keefe announces nonchalantly.

I stare down at my hands. I somehow knew this might be discussed. As much as I would like to deny my life is free of fear, confusion and mystery, I cannot. Keefe needs to know what occurred with the nightclothes and won't be pleased I waited to tell him. My coffee is cold.

I say, "After you left my house, I took a sleep aid before I turned in for the night. Someone laid out my bedclothes and slippers. Tera stayed with me the night before so I assumed it was a thoughtful gesture. I sent her a quick text referring to it, put on my satin nightclothes and crawled in bed. I received her reply indicating she had no idea what I was talking about. I felt helpless lying there, and considered calling you but . . . "

Keefe's eyes narrow and he asks, "Are you sure Tera didn't lay the clothes out?"

"She says no, and why would she deny it?"

I pause for a moment, knowing what he might be thinking. I begin to fiddle with the gold bangle bracelet touching the smooth topaz stone, all the random questions about my memory circulating. I am miles away.

"What is it Quinn? Talk to me," Keefe says, those blue eyes filled with compassion.

"My memory, what if it is me?"

"Do you mean a result of your head injury?" he asks, and continues, "Hell no, Quinn. You can't keep second-guessing yourself. With the number of cases I have open currently, the strange things happening, I would not worry about your memory at all. You are fine. A serious injury it was, but we can't dismiss it away and gamble with your safety."

"What kind of threat is this? What could it mean?" I ask, relieved he knows.

Keefe's phone rings again and he takes it out to check the number.

"Well Quinn, first of all, if you were the target of violence, the opportunity to harm you was not taken. Sounds like intimidation tactics to me. A car will be placed outside your address to keep an eye on things. Any ideas of who would want to intimidate you?" he asks.

"No idea, Keefe."

"Try not to worry about it. At this time, there is no in imminent danger; just taking precautions. We are tapping into county law enforcement resources, since the investigation surrounding Jessie Millsap's murder was near the river."

I could tell by the information Keefe shared with me, there must be more to know. But he either is not at liberty to tell me, or he is keeping things easier for me.

"Thanks, Keefe. I am beginning to form a negative opinion about the character of White Oak. What about the town hall meeting?" I say, tongue in cheek.

"A disaster and complete waste of time," Keefe says, rising to leave. "Botherme broke her nose and is threatening a lawsuit against the department." He tosses his cup in the trash. Keefe rests his hand on the door knob and adds, "Mayor Welsh wants Botherme out of the city council, and is considering action against her for slander."

"And what about Officer Bishop's tackling of Madge?" I ask. I chuckle, replaying her dramatics in my head.

Keefe rubs his forehead for a second. He sighs and shakes his head.

"I am not sure what went through her mind. What did she think Botherme would do? She made a bad situation worse and the police department appears foolish. Today she had the gall to suggest a letter of commendation for bravery. I thought she was kidding and laughed out loud! She stormed out of my office and left for the day. She somehow wanted to impress everyone. Everyone is aware of her hopes to be selected for a special training program occasionally offered by the state. Last week she brought a "terrorist kit" she ordered to the station to show everyone--the gas mask, gloves, boots, and chemical tape! What is she thinking?" Keefe shakes his head. "But, Bishop is the very least of my worries."

He turns to leave but swings back around.

"Quinn," he said, "what is your schedule for the rest of the day or tomorrow?"

I thought for a moment he was going to invite me to dinner.

I say, "I am going up to Royce Estate after Pony gets here. I got a note from Sapphire Royce inviting me to the estate. Her mother left for Europe this morning for a couple of weeks, and I need to collect a book omitted from my order. Tomorrow I am going to spend a few hours at the Professor's helping him out, otherwise I will be home."

"Royce Estate, hmmm," he says, "and you will be at the professor's on Sunday?"

"Yes, I plan to be there in the afternoon."

"Is there more Rosemarie bread?" he asks in a serious tone.

His question makes me laugh a little.

"Oh, you mean Rosemary herb bread ...yes, why?"

"I would like some."

"Oh . . . sure, I can get you a loaf; there's one more in the freezer I think."

"I'd like to share it with you. See you around four tomorrow." Keefe is gone. Guess I have a date.

Pony is dropped off by Chamous, and he is a different young man, the weight of the world lifted from his shoulders.

"Hey Quinn! What do you want me to do today?"

"Hi Pony! Keefe explained... about things. First day with Chamous go ok?"

"Yup, just fine, he's cool," he says, taking off his coat.

"I am glad for your protection. This will all be over soon," I remind him.

"I am sad about Jessie. She was a strange girl, but she didn't deserve to die. Those people must be stopped," he says, shaking his head.

"They will be, I am confident," I say as I mess his hair. "Pony, I need to get going, let me show you what I need, ok? Replace the shelves in the corner. The new one is in the box, to be assembled. Transfer books from old to the new shelf. Can you break down the old one too?"

"Sure, Quinn."

"Thanks Pony. Chamous is coming at four?"

"Yup," he replies, taking out the pieces for the new shelving display.

I show him how to lock up.

"Call me with any questions; otherwise I will see you on Monday afternoon."

He picks up a piece of the shelving and pauses.

"Thanks, Quinn. I was… lost, thanks."

"No problem, Pony."

Chapter Eighteen

Weather is not a concern on this trip to Royce Estate and after my journey last time, I have a tinge of concern until I see the main entrance. The massive gate is open and waiting. As soon as I pass through, a sense of happiness and purity I cannot explain comes over me. This time the whole sprawling estate can be seen. The overcast skies break for an instant, and sun illuminates this epic setting just for my viewing, it seems. Manicured grounds are picturesque, despite the lack of summer green. The outer perimeters of the estate are thick with leafless trees. The estate is a formidable fortress, constructed from limestone blocks. The outline is reminiscent of a castle. Two massive martial towers are connected by living quarters. This is a gothic country manor built for influence and appearance more than for defense, as castles of long ago. The structure is masculine and powerful, yet romantic and timeless. The main portion of the structure is flanked by a statuesque tower, oftentimes the subject in tales spun by curious folk. Why this sky-high lookout? So Mrs. Royce can view her kingdom, is what Cashton told me. I am relieved she is out of town. I park under the carriage structure, as I did before.

My phone signals a text from Keefe telling me the security at my home is being checked. The message makes me feel good.

No Beef at my window giving me a fright like before, I grab my purse and head towards the door. My eyes are drawn to the tower. The sound from the closing car door sends scores of white doves to take flight. Multitudes spread their wings and soar effortlessly upward. With face to the skies, I lose my hat while savoring the majestic scene. A winter breeze more kind than most twirls my hair heavenward too. The birds are graceful, strong and snowy white against the slices of blue sky peeking from grey clouds. I can't take my eyes off them as they glide on crisp winds, becoming smaller as they travel to unknown destinations.

"Welcome, Miss Clarke," Beef says, interrupting my solitude.

"Hello, Beef."

"Please come in," he says, holding the door open for me.

"Thank you."

"Sapphire is expecting you. This way," Beef says as he leads me down the corridor to the south wing.

Beef asks me to excuse him for a brief moment while he checks on something.

I peer into the opened door of a room while waiting. What a stunning room! Silk pastel pillows sit casually on the ample ivory leather sofa, inviting me inward. A marble coffee table supports a heavy urn overflowing with butter colored roses. Against the back of the spacious room, a tremendous arched oak double door stands open. Light comes flooding through the lead glass behind them. Fabric panels of ivory satin charmeuse frame the view of the courtyard and gardens.

Beef's voice trails in. He rounds the corner, and a beautiful woman wearing lace trimmed silk shorts and camisole follows.

"Beef, I reminded you yesterday," says the woman, who sounds annoyed. "And who do we have here?" she asks, not the least bit modest about her lack of clothing.

"May I introduce Miss Clarke, Sapphire's friend? This is Sapphire's older sister Jexis," he says.

This glamorous woman steps in front of Beef and says, "I am pleased to make your acquaintance Miss Clarke. Take a seat for a moment? I meet all of Sapphire's friends. Beef, that is all."

Beef tries to explain, "Sapphire is waiting for her and . . ."

"I will take her to Sapphire in a couple of minutes," Jexis says as Beef retreats.

Jexis leads me to the sofa and sits. She pats next to her, inviting me to sit too. She still does not excuse herself to put on a robe. This woman is striking. Long golden tresses, some pinned up, leave many other tendrils surrounding her ivory skin. Her perfect figure is clad in periwinkle satin-trimmed shorts and matching camisole. Numerous diamonds and white gold rings adorn her slender French manicured fingers. She is barefoot, exposing her well groomed feet and polished toes. I am unsure how this conversation will unfold.

"Miss Clarke, may I call you by your first name, which is?" she asks.

"It's Quinn."

Her satisfied smile lights up the room. Beautiful, flawless skin and expressive, round blue eyes are dramatic.

"Good, Quinn it is. When did you meet?" she asks.

"Last week I was invited by your mother to view a collection she was selling."

"Ah, Petulah!" she responds. "Yes, she is out of the country right now. We all get a bit of a break. She's....intense, if you follow."

I say nothing and smile as Jexis puts her feet up on the coffee table amid the petals fallen from the roses. She reaches under one of the silk pillows and produces a gold foil box complete with large pink bow and removes the lid.

"Chocolate brandy truffles," she says, as she swishes the chocolates under my nose once and continues. "They are sinfully delicious; you must try one." I pluck one for myself. From the first taste I understand why she is a fan.

"Delivered this morning from someone I met last night," she clears her throat and reads the card, 'Thank you for the best night of my life.'" She throws the card in the air. "A poor dancer and an even worse kisser!" Jexis says as she enjoys her truffle. "He can't call me because I gave him the number of the city morgue in Little Rock, Arkansas! What a dope! Of course I can't stop the deliveries. Everyone knows where we live."

I am speechless, but I manage to ask the obvious, "You know the phone number of the morgue in Little Rock, Arkansas?"

"Hell, no," she replies. "It's printed on the cards I give out to dopes. When I like the guy, he gets the real card," she explains, as if this is a scam every girl practices.

"Oh," I reply.

"Where are you from, Quinn?"

"I'm from White Oak; I own a book store."

"Cool," she says. "I am hosting a big shindig here in April, a symphony benefit dinner and concert. You should come! My parents think I'm an accident waiting to happen and they're scared stiff I am going to make a fool of myself and this whole family. But, they are giving me a chance. This is a big opportunity for me, to prove I am ready for responsibility," she says the word with a mocking tone. "My mother is grooming me for something big, she says, and this event is part of the process. I may not seem like a Royce, but wait till I'm in action. You won't even believe it." She pops another truffle and while she is enjoying it, Sapphire comes into the room.

"Hey, Quinn, I see my sister is detaining you."

"We are getting acquainted," I reply.

"Jexis, don't you have another date?" Sapphire reminds her.

"What time is it?" she asks, sounding garbled with a mouthful of truffle, while locating her cell phone to confirm the time.

"Nearly three, sister!" says Sapphire.

"Damn! Nice meeting you Quinn. I hope to see you again soon, and don't forget about the benefit."

She rises from the sofa and moves out of the room but circles back for the truffles.

Sapphire shakes her head, and motions for me to follow. She leads me down the hall to her room. We enter and she closes the towering oak panel doors behind us, revealing royal elegance. The focal point of the suite is the ebony French style bed. The hand engraved headboard sweeps up to a magnificent carved oval at the apex with the capitol letter "R" inside. The ceiling is grand, the only word to describe it. Stone pillars support lofty domes. All four domes are covered with plaster fashioned like folded and gathered fabric. Tapestry cascades from lofty heights, pooling on the floor and creating a wall of distinction behind the opulent headboard. As in Jexis's room, colossal arched double doors open to a courtyard. The entire room is bathed in a golden softness of filtered light through sheer panels covering her windows.

Sapphire breaks the spell this room casts on me. "Quinn, here is the book you are missing," she says.

I put the package in my bag. "Thank you, Sapphire."

She smiles with her whole face.

"I can't explain, Quinn, but I liked you from the moment we met. You are kind and your spirit is… so pure." She studies my expression.

I'm not sure how to respond. Not the kind of comment you get every day.

"That is a nice compliment, thank you Sapphire."

"My instincts are one of my commissions," she replies. What an odd choice of words, I think to myself. "My mother is uptight about visitors, so life is different when she is away. I hate saying that." She peers down at the floor and pauses for a moment.

"Jexis calls her intense."

"Yeah, that's the word. She always says she's grooming us for something big," Sapphire says, rolling her eyes.

I laugh at her expression, and remind her it is a mother's job to do just that.

"I know," she says, as she takes both of her hands and begins to lift her thick main of wavy chestnut hair and puts it up in a looped pony tail. "So what did you think of my sister? She's a trip, huh?"

I laugh at her straightforward nature.

"She's delightful, Sapphire. What kinds of things do you enjoy?"

Her eyes light up. "I paint every day."

"Sapphire, you paint, how wonderful! Show me… is this hobby new?"

"No, I've been painting forever. Sure I can show you."

She leads me to a studio in the fourth arched area of her suite. An easel stands in front of a window, its back facing us. Other canvases stretched over frames are stacked around. She brings me around to view the canvas on the easel. The painting is a nature scene. A river rushes out of control. Along the abused banks, trees bow to powerful whipping winds. The tumultuous sky is threatening and gray.

"Sapphire, how wonderful! Is this a scene from your property?"

"No, I paint from my mind's eye," she says.

"Your imagination is remarkable."

I begin to rummage through the stacked frames of many stunning scenes. One scene takes my breath away. A rock ledge viewed from the stone floor below. The sun is brilliant and the sky blue with billowy white clouds. This is my accident scene. My heart beats faster, my face is hot. My eyes study to discount the likeness, but I cannot. Sapphire does not seem to notice my pause, but I manage to comment.

"Sapphire, this is beautiful too!" I struggle to say in a normal tone.

"Thanks," she says proudly.

"Can I use your ladies room?"

"Sure Quinn, it's the second door over there," she says.

I escape to the ladies room. Alone for a moment, I sink to a chair. What is happening to me and around me? Somehow I am connected to her... this place. What is challenging my sanity, my security? Her painted scene is the exact accident scene to the detail. I am so tired of being afraid and of feeling threatened. I have been timid and quiet about these fears but I am weary of being a victim. Standing at the mirror I make a decision. I am ready to face my fears, fight my demons and trust that I will emerge with a mission of intent, new courage and a new conviction.

Sapphire sets a tray of refreshments on a table. She pours hot tea, which I accept. I pluck a cookie.

"Sapphire, why wait until your Mother is out of town to invite me over?"

Sapphire looks up from her lifted tea cup at me with her emerald eyes. She kicks off her sneakers, draws her legs up and wraps her arms around them. She rests her chin on top of her forearms.

"My mother is distrustful of anyone. Everything I do is held under a microscope for examination. Everything's easier when she is away."

"I see."

"To be honest, she did not seem to like you too much, Quinn," she offers a confused smile.

"I sensed it too. Why she even asked me here in the first place is a mystery," I say.

"I don't know either," Sapphire remarks and adds, "I don't understand the woman! Remember she doesn't like any of my friends. She is ruthless with the staff here. I'm not even sure she likes my Dad!" Sapphire laughs at her own remark, but is quiet again.

"What do you mean?" I ask as I sip my tea.

"They spend no time together, are opposite personalities, and always seem like they are barely tolerating each other," Sapphire reveals.

"I am sorry, Sapphire. Opposite personalities are quite common in marriages. I think God knows our weaknesses, and fills them with partners we need."

"I don't think that applies to my parents. She doesn't have very many good qualities. My father is kind, strong and generous. His love is unconditional. My mother is self-centered, critical and even hurtful at times. Her love comes with a price tag. She always is pushing us to do things that will prove to others we are worthy. She is preoccupied with her family in England, and their acceptance of us. She is fixated on their opinions and beliefs."

"Well, it would be natural for your mother to want acceptance for her children," I say.

"Do you want to know the weird thing? I have never met my mother's family."

Sapphire nods while I try to absorb her comment.

"What do you mean?" I ask.

"We all three were born in the United States. She talks about her family in England, but I have never met one of them. No one from her side of the family ever comes to visit us or her. When we go to England, we spend time with all of father's family. There is never any explanation except that her family members are much too busy to travel, illness, some crisis prevents it. It has been this way for so long none of us even questions it. At least four times a year she travels alone to England to visit them."

"Yes, that is unusual. I am sure a reason exists…it doesn't make her a poor mother," I say.

"I know, but it does make her a weird one!"

We both laugh. She seems accepting of the situation

"May I ask you about Calista Twinning?"

"Yes! I haven't heard Miss Twinning's name in a while. Did you know her?"

"No, the librarian in White Oak did," I say.

"She served as our tutor, she was from England too, but lived here at the estate for many years. An excellent teacher, despite her health challenges. She was kind of quirky. I have a photograph of her."

Sapphire produces a picture of Calista Twinning.

It is the mystery woman, no question. She is seated at a desk, looking studious. She wears those green eyeglasses, and her hair is bright red. Her smile is charming, hands poised to write on the notebook pictured in front of her. It is the same woman.

Sapphire says, "She did not get along with mother, big surprise! She didn't keep her dislike of Mother a secret either. Mother would always tell us to keep our doors locked, because she thought Miss Twinning to be... snoopy. Mother wanted to dismiss her but father liked her. He believed she was good for us. Mother made peace with her through the years. She was always dashing about the estate, creating fun ways to learn. I attribute my love of art to her. She was artistic, and encouraged us in the arts. We all were devastated when she began to lose her eyesight as a result of her diabetes. She took to wearing funky kinds of eyewear. She planned to return to England to study Braille and other ways to adapt to the change. Days before she was to leave, she fell down a flight of stairs in the library and never regained consciousness, horrible! As a young girl, I took it hard."

Once again I'm reeling from the words coming out of Sapphire. Calista Twinning is dead? She has been dead for four years? This is impossible.

"Would you like to meet Father?" Sapphire asks. "He is home now; he would love to meet you."

I can hear what she is saying to me, but I can hardly respond. I am struggling to make sense of this.

"Alright, Sapphire."

I follow Sapphire to the opposite end of the estate. We emerge outside, and the cool air refreshes me. The gardens are beautiful, even in winter, with their manicured beds, topiaries and stone path leading to other buildings. We pass two men tending to the grounds.

"My father is riding today," she says.

The red brick stable and coach house lie in a u-shape design. A small dome tower with a functional clock and with a lookout rises above the carriage doors. Sapphire steps inside the stable and calls out for her father. We walk out the other side of the stables and follow the stone path leading to the forest.

"Father, over here!"

Her father turns at the sound of her voice and rides over to us. He is gallant as he approaches on the back of a silver stallion. Towering above us, he gives Sapphire a big smile and a wink. He dismounts his horse and gathers the reins.

Sapphire runs to him. After they embrace, he kisses her forehead and puts his arm around her and they turn their attention to me.

Chapter Nineteen

Father, this is Quinn Clarke. She purchased some books from our collection. She owns a bookstore in White Oak. Quinn, this is my father, Romulus Royce," Sapphire says.

As if he were caught off guard, Sapphire's father stands stone-faced. He studies me before his gentle and kind eyes greet me with expressive sincerity. His smile is relaxed as he nods in my direction. Dark hair flows forward, reaching the broad shoulders of his tailored dark riding jacket. His face is valiant with high cheekbones and square jaw. His chestnut hair color is accented by silver within his trimmed mustache and beard. He extends his hand to grasp mine.

"It is nice to make your acquaintance, Miss Clark." His touch passes energy to me.

I manage a limp smile. "Me as well."

He releases my hand and turns back to Sapphire, but my eyes never leave him.

"Sapphire, you should invite Quinn to stay for dinner."

"Oh, I don't want to impose."

Sapphire says "Nonsense, we would be delighted. I will let Beef know."

She leads me back to the house.

The atmosphere of the dining room is different from the last time I dined here. The meal is delicious, creamy chicken with almonds, roasted potatoes with carrots, fried onions, and a semi-sweet Riesling. Everyone, even the staff, is more relaxed. Romulus Royce is a charming and handsome man. His devotion shows when he asks about Sapphire's friends and her painting. He reminds her of their riding date tomorrow, and invites me back to the estate to join them. I am tempted but decline and thank him for his invite. Romulus also asks me about Fireside Books, my interest in collecting, and about my life in White Oak. His demeanor is calming, genuine and warm. He smiles often and laughs even more. He talks with pride about his homeland and generations of Royces from the peaceful countryside of Staffordshire.

Our conversation is so lively, I lose track of time. I finish my wine and am getting ready to thank them for a wonderful dinner when servers bring in a tray of desserts and an urn of coffee. I would be expected to make a choice from Frozen Toffee Latte Fudge Cake, Blueberry Crumble Pie, Pistachio Biscotti or Chocolate dipped Strawberries.

Romulus suggests we enjoy our dessert in the billiard room. The room is furnished with game tables of every kind. Like the other rooms at Royce Estate, this room towers to the heavens. From the lofty heights high above, hang long, colorful pennants.

"Let's play quoits! I am the champion of the family," Sapphire says.

"What kind of game is quoits?" I ask.

"It's similar to horseshoes," Romulus says.

Sapphire's skill is evident with her first turn.

My first time to toss the rings is met with laughter from Sapphire and some encouragement and coaching from Romulus.

Romulus sips his coffee while standing in front of the target to get a better view of my execution. He exhibits enthusiasm in all Sapphire does. He comes to my side, corrects my grip a bit and twists my body so the right shoulder is in line with the target.

I keep my eyes steady on the goal, and toss. The ring lands close, my best one yet. But, instead of an encouraging thumbs up from Romulus, I see nothing but his back as he leaves the billiard room.

"Father, where are you going? Is everything ok?" Sapphire asks.

Romulus does not turn around.

"Is everything alright? Did I do something wrong?" I ask.

"Oh no, not at all. Father is always busy… sometimes is called away urgently."

"Oh," I say, still holding the rings. "I hope I didn't offend him in any way."

Sapphire says, "No way, we are having a great time. We've grown used to his quick exits, nothing to do with you," she says assuring me.

"Thank you for a memorable, fun time Sapphire."

She surprises me with a hug. "I had fun too!" Sapphire says

"Text me and we can do it again," I tell her.

I drive back to White Oak without the usual distractions of my phone, or the radio. I am still thinking about Romulus Royce, strong yet humble, distinguished and revered. I sense a familiarity in his presence, from my dream perhaps. He reminds me of the man on the other side of the frozen pond, especially the energy from his touch.

My thoughts turn to Calista Twinning, the victim of the accident. Logically this former tutor can't be deceased, because she stood in front of me, she was real. There is no wrapping my mind around the outlandish notion of the other explanation. Keefe occupies the remainder of my thoughts.

The next morning is spent attending Sunday services with Tera, Chamous and Pony. Trinity Church is lively and filled with music, although the attendance is dismal. Chamous delivers a good message. It is evident Tera is proud of Chamous. She is happier than ever.

Afterward, I am ready to help Professor Enderlee. He welcomes me with an embrace.

"Quinn, I don't understand your interest in this, you are too busy for this."

"Remember commenting on my home? Let me help make yours the same."

"What shall I do to assist?" he asks.

"When was your refrigerator last stocked?"

"I eat at the shop, so it's been a long time," he says.

"Go on about your business and let me do this for you."

"Ok Quinn, this is…wonderful. I will be in my study, watching the details of the weather moving in."

I pass by the portrait of Rose Enderlee on my way to the kitchen, where a multitude of tasks awaits. I begin by filling the dishwasher and move on to each cupboard. All cupboards are in disarray. I organize his dishes so they are closer to the dishwasher. I find a staggering amount of duplicates and triplicates. I start a box for all of these items. The silverware drawer is now cleaned and reorganized. The cabinets and pantry hold dry goods that have long passed their shelf life. Once I toss those, I am able to organize them. I accumulate a box full of papers and folders. A substantial number of expired medication with Rose's name remained. I examine the bottles for dates and make a mental note.

The refrigerator and freezer are pretty simple, everything out and a wipe down. All appliances, including coffee pot, are in need of a thorough cleaning. I line them up on the counter and spray them down to soak. When the kitchen is organized and cleaned, sanitized and polished from floor to ceiling, I take a short break and make a few phone calls.

After mopping, I remove the simple café curtains and wash them, along with a few rugs, and the room is done. I organize and clean a utility area and breezeway leading to his back door. This task wasn't difficult, as the professor was keeping up with his laundry. Next time I would arrange carpet and drapery cleaning and wash the windows.

The professor was still in his study when I ask where he wants the collected items stored. He decides to have me put them in the yellow room upstairs. I assume the yellow room was Rose's and her space lies undisturbed. A small fireplace sits on the same wall as large windows. A glass, tissues, and pill bottles all rest on a nightstand next to the unmade bed. Her closet is open, exposing her wardrobe. The room is drafty and cold. A desk with papers and folders is next to the window. Her adjoining bathroom is cluttered. I dislike intruding in her private place. I set the box down and leave.

When I come down, I find the professor taking stock of the changes in his grand old home.

"Smells like a spring rain, Quinn."

"I placed the articles from the kitchen in the yellow room."

"Rose's room..."

"I am sorry for your loss, Professor."

"Thank you, Quinn. It's hard for me always having to explain... that is why I refer to her as my assistant," Professor Enderlee tells me.

"I won't disturb the room," I assure him.

"No, I need to do something, two years have passed. She was my light, my joy." He turns away upset.

"Professor Enderlee, let's return the room to the beautiful space Rose enjoyed. Let me help you. I don't have to leave quite yet. Allow me to tidy Rose's room for you?" I ask.

"Quinn, I would like that."

"My pleasure."

The room is much cooler than the rest of the house and I check the windows are secure before I change the sheets and cover the bed with the beautiful duvet and lacy pillows. Next to the bedside a single dry rose in a bud vase I leave untouched. A small gift basket also sits on the table with homemade treats, jam, crackers and a jar of loose tea. The gift tag reads:

"The historian records, but the novelist creates. - E. M. Forster Get better soon, your friends from Literary Club!"

I collect a few glasses, a used teacup and spoon. I wash everything down, dust, vacuum and repeat the process in the bathroom. The fireplace doors rattle from a downdraft in the chimney. The flue's been left open, explaining the chill. On my knees looking up I discover the source of the obstruction. I reach up, and with a firm tug, pull at something which falls to the floor. It's an envelope inside a plastic pouch, with a handwritten note that says:

"To whom it may concern:

If you are reading this, chances are I'm dead. This information cost one man his life, and may cost me mine. This is the information I received from Dow's attorney two years after his death. Only Rand Jolliet knows of its existence. My father must never be a part of any of this! I must protect him from them, please help. Rose Enderlee.

Rose had been in danger and she knew it. Was she murdered? Did the information inside the package cost her life? Does it contain answers, answers to the questions that are on the lips of everyone in White Oak? I need to get this to Rand Jolliet. I put the envelope in my bag and say my goodbyes to Professor Enderlee.

I call Rand when I get into the car. His home is on an acreage on the outskirts of town. As I drive up his long driveway, I am tempted to peek at the envelope's contents, but do not.

Rand answers the door and brings me inside where Cindy Arness is seated at a table with piles of papers. A pencil is tucked behind Cindy's ear and her reading glasses sit low on her nose. Rand's face shows no traces of his bee attack.

"Cindy and I are working on the future campaign. Quinn, would you like something to drink?" Rand offers.

"No thank you, Rand," I say with a quick smile.

"What brings you over, Quinn?"

"I have something belonging to you."

He reads the note from Rose Enderlee, and drops himself into one of the dining room chairs. Cindy and I sit down too.

"My Lord, four years I have searched for this evidence... ever since Chief Dow died," Rand says. He then jumps up from the chair.

"Neither one of you can have anything to do with this. I believe knowing what is inside this envelope is dangerous. Please, leave now." His panicked expression alarms me, and I stand.

"I am not leaving!" Cindy says as she rises. "I care about you, and I am willing to risk danger to help you to get to the bottom of this. I already know more than I should. Quinn needs to go and never speak of this envelope, but I am staying," Cindy declares as she sits back down.

Rand shoves campaign yard signs into my arms and escorts me to the door.

"Here, take these, let them be the reason you came," Rand says.

"You're being watched?"

"I don't know, probably not," Rand says. "Goodbye, Quinn."

He hustles me out the front door. I put the signs into the trunk and make my way back down the long driveway towards home. I won't say anything to anyone.

Chapter Twenty

When I get home, I shower and within forty minutes I am putting the rosemary herb bread in the oven for a quick warm up. I prepare some olive ricotta spread to serve, and chill the chardonnay.

Keefe arrives on time and brings a bottle of Merlot. My phone keeps signaling me to recharge its battery. I run upstairs to connect it to the charger.

Sitting down on the sofa with Keefe feels good after a long day.

"Fill me in on your last couple of days," Keefe says.

"Yesterday, the Royce Estate proved interesting. I asked Sapphire about Calista Twinning, and along with her description of a wonderful teacher and mentor, she also told me Petulah and Twinning were not too fond of each other. Sapphire told me of Twinning's health challenges and the fact she became blind. Days before her trip back to England she fell down a staircase and never regained consciousness!"

Before he can take a sip, his glass stops in mid-air.

"Dead, what? Impossible! That can't be accurate. She fits the description given by Mrs. Murphy as the woman who frequented the library from Royce Estate. Mrs. Murphy didn't mention her eyesight or an accident," Keefe says.

"If Miss Twinning's next of kin were the only ones notified and a funeral service were held in England, and she was without citizenship here, would those in White Oak even be aware?" I ask.

"The attending doctor would declare death, and hospital records are filed. I've yet to find anything with her name, driver's license, address, no evidence she existed in this country."

"Miss Twinning may have not been hospitalized, since the Royces have a residing physician on the estate...no record would exist."

"Quinn, you are creating a good case for an impossible theory," he says nonchalantly.

"Yeah, true. I am piecing together something, but for now I have too many holes."

"Are your duties at the station more investigative, or more

administrative/chief work?" I ask.

"Investigation in our little riverside village takes most of my time."

"Cindy Arness mentioned questions surrounding Chief Dow's death."

"Dow died of heart failure, found near the river after he'd been dead for a few days." Keefe tells me.

"Was he hunting, or . . ."

"His truck was about three hundred yards from his body, the motor was running until the fuel tank went dry, door wide open."

"Foul play suspected?" I inquire.

"Apparently he was spotted driving in White Oak after midnight. He drove to the pier and stopped for some reason, his dog ran off and he left the engine idling and chased his dog. Had a heart attack...case closed," Keefe says.

"When did you come to White Oak?" I ask him.

"A month later. The death was unusual, but suspicions were raised by Rose Enderlee. Her research for a historical book brought her to my office one day, asking how far back the station kept records. With Chief Dow's deep roots in the area, he became a helpful source to her current project. At the time, Chief Dow warned her about exposing the past. His strange comment stuck with her. She questioned why the Chief would be out in the middle of the night, why his dog was never found. The circumstances are odd, but the autopsy listed cause of death as acute myocardial infarction or heart attack, and Chief Dow had preexisting medical records consistent with this."

Keefe snacks on more bread.

I understand the connection between Chief Dow and Rose Enderlee. I am hoping to learn more from Rand. I change the subject to the Royces.

"I met the head of the estate, Mr. Romulus Royce."

"As strange at Petulah Royce?" he asks.

"Not at all," I reply. "He is charming and devoted to Sapphire. He invited me to stay for dinner. I enjoyed the time so much, even learned a bit about quoits," I say with a chuckle.

"What's quoits?" Keefe asks.

"An English game similar to horseshoes, but not as easy as it looks. Sapphire is much like her father. And she, Romulus and Jexis all admitted Petulah is intense, and things are easier when she is away from the estate."

"Did you meet Jexis?"

"Yes, she is the opposite of Sapphire--a non-conformist, independent, but less serious. The symphony benefit this spring is her project, her responsibility. She does a lot of socializing, which is different from her younger sister."

I pour more wine for myself, and offer more to Keefe and he accepts as he puts his feet up on the corner of the coffee table.

He stares at the flames, his thoughts no doubt circulating solutions to the myriad of problems weighing on him.

Without thinking I move the blonde hair skimming his brow. His eyes meet mine, and for a moment I was hoping Keefe would kiss me, but he forfeits the chance.

"What about the younger Royce male? He's the oldest of the siblings," Keefe says.

Our moment for intimacy has passed.

"Yes, Cashton. I met him briefly for the first time at the estate, nice man." I don't tell Keefe I spent a few hours with Cashton, horticulturist, healer and mesmerizingly good looking, reducing me to helpless damsel in a flash.

Keefe's eyelids are closed and his breathing becomes heavy.

I slide the stemmed glass out of his hand. Perhaps the spontaneous kiss at Mocha Joe's didn't mean romance. It was brief, no lingering or words exchanged. What Keefe wants is a friend. It hasn't been long since I lost Alec, and I may not be reading the cues realistically. Perhaps I am only seeing what I want to see. I need friends; I think I can be content as friends.

Plans for dinner were never discussed and now I am hungry. A quick glance at the freezer gives me a few options and I settle on heating some wild mushroom soup. I will offer Keefe some when he wakes up. Before I can get out to the living room, Keefe is answering his ringing phone.

He rises and puts his coat on. When he finishes his conversation

I ask him if he would like something to eat.

"Oh, no thanks, Quinn. I need to get going, make a few calls. I apologize for falling asleep," he says.

"That's quite alright. I take no offense," I say, following him as he opens the door. The bitter cold wind will make this goodbye brief.

"Thank you Quinn, good night," he says with a pleasant smile on his way out.

I am chilled by the night air, and I am disappointed by the cool end to the evening. I lock up and enjoy my hot soup in a cozy chair by the window. My mind is busy going over the weekend activities, and all I want to do is escape. The wind grows stronger. A long, low thunder rumbles. Mother Nature can't decide if she'll deliver rain or snow. While enjoying the rest of my wine, I begin the second chapter of a book. The rumbling and the flurries continue, and lightning flashes in the distance. The oversized chair and cotton throw wrap me in security and warmth. Relaxation leads to sleep, occasionally interrupted by the storm.

I'm not sure how long I am asleep when a jolt of lightning and booming thunder rattle the windows and wake me. Startled, I sit upright. The view outside the window becomes illuminated by the electrical flash. Each episode of lightening reveals dancing, swirling snow. The next boom cracks, shaking the house and shutting the power down. A quick glance out the window confirms the streetlights are doused too. I light a candle when I find the flashlight is without batteries and return to my chair. The fireplace is only embers now. Perhaps the outage won't be long. I wrap up in the throw and set the candle down. Once more another lightening flash lights up the scene outside, I let out a gasp. A hooded figure stands motionless outside the window. Another blast of illumination confirms it. A figure stands statuesque, his cloak whipped by ravaging winds.

I spring out of my chair to back away. I stumble over the end table and lamp, sending both crashing down. Something has sliced my leg, my ankle is twisted. I want only to get away but the injury is excruciating. The next flash of lightening reveals nothing, the figure is gone. In complete darkness, I lay my head on the floor, writhing in pain. I smell smoke! My head is not moving, but my eyes scan in horror as the toppled candle smolders into flames and shoots up the draperies. I use my arms to pull myself towards the kitchen. I must get out now. The fire is spreading, creating an inferno. The smoke grows so thick I'm confused about the direction I'm moving. Each effort sends searing pain throughout my body. Something obstructs my escape, and I use every ounce of energy to shove it to the side. The heat is overwhelming and smoke chokes my labored breath. I raise my head again to pull my body away and my head bumps on something overhead. My hands frantically feel until I discover I'm under the dining room table. I am suffocating. My eyes are stinging, watering and burning. My air is gone. I want to live, but my body can't save me. I lay my head down on my outstretched arm. The fire cracks and whistles as it consumes all in its path.

Unexpectedly, my wrist is grasped with gentle strength. I'm being pulled across the floor, through the thick smoke. Flames shoot up all around me as this savior picks me up and carries me in his arms. Within seconds the clear night air fills my lungs as Cashton rushes me to safety. Pain and shock take their toll, and my head falls against his chest.

Chapter Twenty-One

My eyes open to the concerned expression of my best friend Tera. She squeezes my hand.

"Chamous, she is awake! Quinn, sweetheart I am here, you are going to be ok. You are at the hospital, it's after midnight," Tera says, her sweet and compassionate voice always there for me.

Chamous comes to her side. Keefe rushes into the room.

"Quinn, are you alright?" Keefe asks. He takes a place next to the bed, along with Tera and Chamous.

Chamous explains what is known about the accident to Keefe, "Lightening caused a fire, we think. Someone pulled her out, but the Good Samaritan left the scene. She suffered no serious injuries. I can't say the same for her house."

"The storm was severe, power outages all over town," Keefe says. He takes my hand. "Quinn, thank goodness someone saw the fire. Who helped you?"

"I don't remember," I say. My throat is scratchy, my thoughts confused.

"I'm sorry I left so early." He moves closer to my face. "Are you sure lightening caused the fire and not your cooking?" His handsome smile and lighthearted comment raise my spirit some.

The doctor comes in and announces he will be keeping me overnight for observation, but I will most likely be able to leave in the morning. The news brings smiles to everyone's faces except mine.

"Great, I will be back up here in the morning to pick you up girl!" Tera says.

"I am so glad you are ok," Keefe adds.

I manage a polite smile as Keefe leaves the room and starts visiting with Tera and Chamous in the corridor. What is going on? The fire had nothing to do with the storm. Someone in the window, watching me! The candle toppled, I fell, twisted my ankle, and cut my leg. Cashton saved my life. He pulled me out of the burning house.

From the hallway, Pony waits on the three adult's conversations to end. He holds my gaze, and heads into the room. Pony is upset.

"Quinn, are you alright?" he asks.

"Yes, I am going to be ok Pony, what's wrong?"

"I'm scared, Quinn."

"Why?" I ask in a hoarse voice.

"We lost electricity during our monthly lock-in event at The Barn. Sitting in the dark was boring, some guys fell asleep, and some were rowdy. After the power returned, I went to find a snack in the pantry of a storage room. I hadn't been in the room before, but it had plenty of good snacks and a small refrigerator. In this storage room was another door leading outside. I was startled by a knock on a back door of the little room." Pony pauses and the rhythm of speech slows.

"As soon as I opened the door, a man… put something in my hand and said, "Quinn's house is on fire! She is in trouble, call 911, hurry!" I took out my cell phone and called 911 to report the emergency. I ran back to find Tera in the dark and it was chaos... guys running around with flashlights, laughing."

I'm dumbfounded by his words.

Pony says, "The next thing I remember is being woke up by voices instructing everyone to head to the main church building that was unaffected by the outage. I spotted Tera inside the doors, and told her about you. She lost her cool and began yelling for Chamous. When we got to your house the fire was being put out, and you'd been taken to the hospital.

We made sure you were ok, and Tera asked me how...how I knew about the fire. I went through it… twice, she had lots of questions. Tera saw me sleeping when they checked everyone's whereabouts with the flashlights. She also told me The Barn doesn't have a storage room. The power never came back on, is still out right now. I couldn't believe she was telling me I had imagined my actions! Tera said the experience was some kind of dream. Maybe I sensed you were in danger… or something. How did I know, Quinn? What is happening?" Pony's confusion and fear hit close to home for me, and his emotion is heart-wrenching to witness.

I, too, am in shock by what he is saying. How is this possible?

"I don't know," I answer.

Pony reaches into his jeans pocket.

"This is what the stranger put in my hand," he says, and opens his palm.

My hands fly to my throat to feel for my medal. It's not there. I look straight into his eyes.

"Pony, meet me tomorrow at Fireside Books and keep these details to yourself."

He puts the Saint Benedict amulet in my hands and leaves.

Chapter Twenty-Two

Morning comes without warning. A nurse bustles around before the sun even rises. She removes the IV, and prepares me to leave. She gives me two sacks; one contains the very smoky clothing, and the other my cell phone and my book still marked at chapter two. My phone was not even downstairs with me during the time of the fire, and the book I was reading . . . how or why was this in the bag? I discover only a few bruises and scratches, but my ankle is fine, no pain from a twist or a sprain. My leg is free of cuts or burns. How is this possible?

Tera arrives moments later and we drive to my home, or what is left of it. After talking with the fire department, we are allowed through the tape. My car escaped damage, but when we open the door from the garage leading into the kitchen, we both gasp. The whole living room and dining room are destroyed. Everything is smoke damaged.

"I'm starting over... again," I say tearfully.

Tera puts her arm around me.

"Quinn it's only things; the important thing is you are ok. We can get past this."

"I'm not sure of my next step," I say with sadness.

"Is there any doubt? We shall be roomies again!" she says, winking and squeezing my shoulder. "I assume you will be joining me in the city for a while. You love my loft and the view of downtown and the river."

We head back to the car.

A couple of neighbors come out to greet me. They kindly offer their help.

"Who helped you Quinn?" asks my neighbor to the west.

"I wish I knew," I lied, "a good Samaritan."

We stop at Mocha Joe's to get a morning brew and a muffin before talking through my next step. Professor Enderlee's eyes light up.

"Quinn, thank goodness you are alright! Pony filled me in on what occurred this morning before he went over to the campus. Of course, you'll be staying with me," he says, as his eyes twinkle with sincerity.

"Professor, how kind of you to offer your home, but it would be an imposition," I reply.

"Fiddlesticks, you are like a daughter to me, and my home would give you flexible access to your little project," he says, pointing at me.

"I'm going to enjoy this coffee and consider my options. Tera would like for me to stay with her. Either way, your generosity means so much. Thank you again."

Tera and I take our breakfast over to Fireside Books.

I run through the opening routine, and Tera chooses a few seasoned logs that crackle and burst into flames swiftly.

Carolynn Langford enters, looking stylish and sophisticated as usual.

"Good morning Quinn and Tera," she says, nodding to both of us. "Your house fire is the talk of the town! We are all relieved you're ok, You may not be aware of the small inn near the vineyards. Renovation is close to completion, booking will begin in April, but for now, it's available. Two of the four rooms are done, and day is over at five for the construction crew working on the other two, I don't think they would bother you much. Adam will be at the Inn this afternoon, so stop by and see the accommodations. We would be happy to help out."

"Carolynn, your offer is kind, we will do that."

"Ok, excellent. I also would like to offer seats at our table for the symphony benefit coming up at Royce Estate. You too, Tera, if you plan on attending," she says with a smile.

"Yes, I will take one, Tera are you wanting to attend?" I ask.

"Yes, are you kidding? Seeing the Royce Estate, I wouldn't miss it! Count me in," she says with enthusiasm.

"Wonderful," Carolynn says and leaves the bookstore.

Tera says, "Nice options. What are your thoughts?"

I sip my coffee and struggle for clarity.

"I like the idea of being right here in town. I wouldn't be eating my time up on the road," I say.

"I am in White Oak more than I am in KC," she reminds me. "What about Professor E's offer?"

"Sweet offer…but the inn would be more private. I suppose it will be house hunting next."

"I can help with that," Tera says as she stands up and stretches. "I'm worn out today, and I'll bet you are exhausted."

"Yes, I am. Pony should be arriving soon."

"Pony told me a most fantastic story last night."

"What do you mean?" I say, doing my best to show the proper amount of surprise.

"Quinn, Pony called 911 after having a dream instructing him to do so!"

"What?" I ask, trying to show confusion.

"Like I said, it is a fantastic tale. I don't understand how he knew to make that call," she remarks.

"Some people are very intuitive. I am just glad someone called!"

Tera's phone rings and I am relieved, hoping we could drop the subject for now. When Tera finishes her conversation she's off to run errands.

"I'll be back in an hour and we can check out the inn."

I will get my time to talk to Pony alone, a perfect opportunity. I approach the front window of Fireside Books and view my world through different eyes. I recognize the familiar storefronts of this quaint main street, the town square with leafless trees, and empty benches. But is there more than meets the eye? I am allowing myself to accept more exists, and my fear is replaced with questions. Cashton and the Royce family are somehow part of it all, and so am I. The hooded figure, the fire, the rescue . . . all revolve around me, but why?

Since Tera left, the weather turns foul. The wind blows, sending leaves swirling across the town square. It is the end of March, and spring seems nowhere in sight. Dark, angry clouds move in, threatening to take over White Oak. The few souls outside eye the brewing storm that billows and churns and quicken their steps. Wind blows the rain into vertical sheets, dousing everything. The street gutters fill and swiftly flow. Pony emerges from Chamous's car, and leaps over the mini stream in the gutter and enters Fireside Books.

"Hey Quinn, are you alright? It's a mess out there, and the temperature seems to be dropping," Pony says as he removes his drenched jacket and hangs it on the coat rack.

"Yes, I'm fine, Pony. I am anxious to talk," I say.

The air grows damp and cold, and I am pleased Pony feeds the fire.

We both sit quietly watching the hungry flames devour and increase.

Finally I break the silence.

"After hearing about your experience, I feel encouraged about my own…sanity. And although that makes me feel better, it creates as many questions as it does answers. I am not ready to talk to anyone about this except you."

This conversation could be upsetting to Pony, and change both of our lives. I have to ignore the balance of logic and simply spill it out. I take a deep breath and begin.

"I was not going to survive the fire if a hand had not reached out and pulled me through the smoke and flames to safety. The cut on my leg, minor burns and my twisted ankle vanished before paramedics arrived. I escaped from the house with the clothes on my back and nothing else, yet this morning I was given a bag containing not only the clothing, but my phone and a book I had been reading. I didn't come out holding a book, and my phone wasn't even on the lower level of the house when the fire began. My neighbors claim when they rushed over they found me a safe distance away, alone and unconscious."

"A passerby maybe?" Pony asks.

"No, help did not come from anyone who is… like us. Help came from a different…realm," I say with shaky confidence.

Pony has a somber expression.

"I don't need convincing of a realm … having your St. Benedict amulet in my hand was convincing enough!"

"The man who saved me was Cashton Royce."

Pony is puzzled by my comment.

"So you know him?" he asks.

"Yes, I met him the first time at the Royce Estate."

I could see Pony sorting things in his mind.

"What makes you think you were helped by a different realm?"

I stand and move closer to the fire. Rain becomes sleet, as it coats the windows. The wind howls. I say, "May I describe the stranger who warned you? Black leather jacket, dark hair, olive skin, green eyes?"

"Yes, Quinn, that describes him to a tee. How is that possible?"

I mirror his seriousness when I reply, "That is Cashton Royce. In our world there is no being in two places at once. Cashton saved me in time. From the time the candle toppled until the flames shot up the draperies was only a matter of minutes. He retrieves my phone and book. He heals my afflictions. I am unharmed."

I put a cardigan on to chase the chills and continue. "At the same time he is saving my life, he visits you." There, I said it, crazy as it sounds.

"Cashton is part of the mortal world, Quinn, not a spirit or a ghost," Pony points out.

I pull the sweater tighter around myself and sit down on the fireplace hearth. I swallow hard before continuing.

"I am talking about…Guardians."

Pony is lost in thought, but whatever is on his mind, he does not tell me. He stands abruptly.

"Quinn, you are not getting your money's worth out of me, what would you have me do today?"

I am sure he is either not willing to entertain the ramifications of this theory, or he thinks I am a raving lunatic. I want to tread lightly, because I don't want to scare Pony.

"Pony, I am not unstable, I am fearful to talk to anyone else about this. Please tell me what you know, if anything. I don't think we can carry on with business as usual."

"I know," he says, "I know." He walks over to his bag and removes several books and folders of papers.

"A few years ago, Carmen and I were heading home from St. Louis. Our car slid off an ice covered road, hit a pole and landed in a ditch. Carmen's head hit the side window hard and she was knocked out. Alone and scared, I didn't know what to do. The car plowed into a deep snow bank, doors wouldn't budge. There was no cell service. I thought Carmen was going to die. Hours passed before a young man appeared through the frozen window. He spoke loud enough for me to hear, 'Don't worry! Everything will be alright, I will get help.'"

"Help arrived not long after. I was grateful Carmen was going to be alright, but I was still scared and lonely. The young man who helped us stopped in to see me. He made my night. He sat with me for a few hours, I think. He liked cars and told me all about his restored Chevy pickup truck. His enthusiastic conversation made the time fly. He asked me about school, and my family. I never forgot his kindness or his unusual name, Rocket."

I'm wondering how this story will relate.

Pony continues, "I told Carmen all about Rocket, and how he helped me through that night. She wanted to find this young man to thank him. The nurses were confused when she asked them about Rocket's hospital visit, explaining to Carmen no visitors would be allowed anywhere in the hospital the hours we were admitted. She contacted the state patrol telling them all about the kind young man who helped us that frozen winter night. Carmen was told about a young car enthusiast named Rocket who perished in an accident on that same road years before. Carmen understood, she never made a big deal out of it. She believed Rocket was a Guardian sent to help us. Rocket came to me...twice. The experience was so real. I couldn't accept her explanation. I'll never forget her response--'I don't care if you believe me or not. Faith is always a choice.' I didn't have another explanation. I found out more about Rocket, a young man of 18, who lost control of his truck. A man at the state patrol office told me our experience wasn't the first time Rocket acted as a Good Samaritan. I never talked more about Rocket, but my belief in the existence of Guardians began there."

Pony's story is riveting.

"That is not all, Quinn. When Jessie was leading me to the River People, I felt a pull on my arm, and a whisper telling me to run away. I read all I could about Guardians. My research has given me more than I would ever need to substantiate what Carmen believes. I opened my mind to the possibilities and I believe that is why Cashton came to me."

My thoughts whirl like the wind outside, and I sit speechless.

Pony adds a log to the fire and then asks me to tell him more of my discoveries.

"One of Sapphire's paintings is identical to the cliff where my accident occurred. The clouds, sky, sun, rock, all the same. The scene's vantage point is from the bottom looking up to the cliff's edge.

Sapphire was not at the scene, but the painting looks like she was...she told me she paints from her mind's eye."

Pony says, "Guardians exist? Cashton and Sapphire are... both Guardians?"

"I don't know," I tell him.

"Rocket's spirit helped us, but Cashton and Sapphire are not... spirits; they are part of this world," Pony says.

"What else have you discovered Pony?" I am convinced his knowledge and my witnessing could produce a new reality for us both, change our lives even.

Pony says, "The celestial world is structured by a government, a hierarchy of Guardians. Seven archangels or chief angels sit in protection of mankind. At the foot of each of their thrones is a Fidesorb... seven archangels and seven Fidesorbs. Fides is the Latin word for faith and orb describes its shape. A Fidesorb radiates the brilliant light of faith in our world. Lucifer, at one time, was a high and exalted angel, next in honor to God's own son, Jesus Christ. Next to himself, God recognizes his son as supreme eminence over the entire hierarchy of celestial beings. The angels bow to Jesus. God seated Jesus in the throne alongside his own, as his equal. Lucifer grew envious of Jesus, and considered himself the rightful ruler next to God. Lucifer rebelled and a mighty battle ensued. Lucifer and his followers were cast down from heaven. In their fall from grace they stole four of the seven Fidesorbs. These fallen angels walk among mortals, gaining strength as they spread their darkness to all. The seven archangels continue to wage their battle against darkness and recover the missing orbs of light and return them to their heavenly place."

"Pony would you get me a glass of water?"

"Sure, Quinn," Pony says.

If I choose to deny the existence of Guardians, the world I know will remain the same, but I will be ignoring the plight of those who fight for the goodness of the human spirit. If I choose to believe Guardians exist, my entire foundation of reality shifts. Will I become a warrior of light too? No.... I want the life I led before the mystery woman showed up at Fireside Books. I want to enjoy my bookshop, my home, network in my new town, have a glass of wine with Tera and have our conversation revolve around her social life, and normal, tangible topics. But since my accident I have come to expect something will call me to service…a purpose. And I am fearful as well. I cannot share this with Tera or anyone else because I am not ready to. Before I can go further with my thoughts Tera arrives, just as Pony hands me a glass of water.

"Is everything ok here?" Tera asks, her intuition showing.

I stand and reply, "Yup, we are all good here. Pony a few book orders are left to fill, and the list of tasks is on the counter. If I am not back at closing, you know what to do. Let's go Tera."

Keefe wants us to stop at the station first. He leads us into his office and closes the door.

"We are on our way to check out the Winery Inn," Tera says.

"Being in town will be easier for you, Quinn," Keefe says. "I have some… upsetting news. Cindy Arness was taken by ambulance to the hospital. She has a stab wound, pretty bad shape."

"What happened?" I ask, shocked to hear this development.

"Some kind of... altercation between Cindy and Rand, out front of the attorney's office, witnessed by two others. Rand fled the scene, haven't found him yet."

"Cindy and Rand care about each other. He is not a violent man. This is crazy, everything is crazy! What is happening in this town?" I sit down hard in a chair, a wash of defeat floods over me. When I think of Rand and Cindy I can't fathom what has transpired leading to violence between the two of them. I'm not sure I can take much more today.

Keefe looks at me and says to Tera, "Get her out of here."

Tera takes my arm and we head to the Winery Inn.

Chapter Twenty-Three

The ride to Langford Winery is dangerous as ice forms. Tera is a confident driver, but I am a wreck. I need to sleep, I need to think. I need to be alone. Where will I be putting my head tonight? My life is in chaos. My thoughts are foggy like the night air surrounding the car. Emotions overwhelm me and my eyes begin to fill with tears. As soon as I start wiping them, Tera pulls the car off into a parking lot.

She puts the car in park and turns to me. The car is warm now, only the sound of the rhythmic wiper blades.

"Are you holding together, Quinn?" my good friend asks.

I take a deep breath and sigh. "I am overwhelmed, and I'm tired," I manage to say. Tera is moved by my emotion. Her compassion is sincere.

"Quinn, you don't need to find all the answers today."

Tera only knows a small portion of my concerns.

"Chin up friend. Everything will be wonderful, I promise. Here is a bag of essentials I packed, so no matter where you stay you'll be ready."

I wipe my tears and force a smile.

Tera calls Adam and he is waiting near Bordeaux's for us to arrive. He motions for us to follow him. The air is heavy with thick fog. We are grateful for red tail lights to guide us as we travel down turns and twists. Tera checks the mileage and estimates four miles from the winery.

We finally come to the end of the road and a faint outline of the inn emerges. Damp, cold wind goes right through me. Adam greets us with a kind smile; he seems of pleasant disposition today. We follow him up a stone walkway.

The limestone inn is nestled within the rock bluff. We wait under a large stoop while Adam unlocks the door.

"Adam, I am grateful for Carolynn's suggestion about the inn. I hate to disrupt any renovation that is still ongoing, and I don't want to be in the way," I say.

"Carolynn doesn't realize the project is done, finished last Friday. Sorry about your house fire, Quinn. We are waiting on materials to put some finishing touches in the final two suites, but we are ready to start booking anytime. Let me show you around."

We follow Adam as he takes us through the tiled foyer. An antique mirror with a crack near the bottom is the only feature, along with a brass umbrella holder. The main level is where the old hotel counter sits. Three windows with bar shutters stand open, only showing more fog. The staircase creaks as soon as Adam steps on it. At the top of the landing are four doors.

"I want to show you this one," Adam says, as he unlocks the door to the west. "This is the best one in my opinion. No view from the middle two. They face the bluff. The east one is not as large and is without a fireplace."

The suite's living area hosts a small hearth and mantle with shelves of books on either side. Adam shows us a galley kitchen with enough space at the end for a window and quaint table with two chairs. Another double door off the sitting room leads to an ample bedroom complete with four poster walnut bed dressed in beige brocade. The two windows on each side are covered with old fashioned pull shades and sheer drapery panels. A comfortable looking chair and ottoman stand in the far corner with a reading lamp. The claw foot tub and pedestal sink make up the small bathroom.

Adam explains they will not be booking guests until next month at the earliest. They are happy to host a visitor to test out their project. The inn is rustic, but close to town and available and I am TIRED! I nod my approval and Tera agrees.

Adam and I discuss renting week by week. He gives me two keys, one for the lower level entrance and one for my room. He also offers me his card, and asks me to call if I need anything at all. I thank him more than once.

Tera runs out to the car to get the bag she prepared for me. The thermostat reads only sixty two degrees, and I am freezing. I build a fire with wood already stocked and soon it is crackling and heating as well.

Tera comes up the creaking staircase. She emerges with a medium sized suitcase and a couple of bags.

"Adam assured me you would be safe here. Their break in at Bordeaux's was just kids and they are not pressing charges."

"Great, did he say why?" I ask.

"The two who accused Pony can't be located, so their credibility is on shaky ground. I guess this is good news for Pony! Oh, and you can order meals from Bordeaux's, and someone would run it down to you. He also mentioned to lock the front door at all times," she says.

Tera takes the two bags into the kitchen. Her thoughtfulness touches me. The bags contain a rotisserie chicken, some gourmet cheeses and crackers, a round pumpernickel loaf, a few pieces of fruit, small container of milk, some soup and coffee.

"You are a lifesaver," I tell her. In the second bag she takes out two bottles of wine.

"Man does not live by bread alone," she teases.

We put the items away, and find bottled water in the tiny refrigerator. The drawers are stocked with silverware and filters for the coffee pot.

"Kitchen is all ready to go, follow me," Tera says.

She had assembled a couple of outfits, some sweats, pajamas, socks and toiletries and simple cosmetics. Tera even remembers an extra phone charger and cash. The fire department found my purse, and Tera brought that too.

"It's been so cold, so I packed a sweater, and thought some pain killer might be needed. Do you want me to stay tonight?"

"No friend, go home! These supplies are essential, you thought of everything. I thank you. I am exhausted."

"Ok." She reminds me to text her before I turn in for the night, and I assure her I will.

I follow her down to the front door, and after a hug she makes me promise I will call her for anything at all. Once I lock both the downstairs and upstairs doors, I lean against the locked door and sigh. The only thing on my mind is a bath and some rest. I fill the claw foot tub with hot water and go back to the kitchen to pour myself a glass of chardonnay. The bathroom is steamy and warm from the running bathwater. I sink into the seductive waters and let the warmth envelop me.

I am concerned about my friends Rand and Cindy. I am anxious to visit with Pony and finish our conversation. Tomorrow can only be brighter, I tell myself. The bathwater is soothing to both the body and the mind. The tranquility makes me ready for a night of slumber.

After bathing, I turn off lights, close up the fireplace and crawl into bed. The inn creaks--so many different sounds in this grand old place. Sleep comes and if I dream at all, I have no recollection of it.

The hope of sunshine is dashed when I wake up to more gloomy weather. A text from Tera tells me Pony will open the bookstore for me, meaning I can take my time getting to Fireside Books. I make coffee and hold a hot mug as I stare from the kitchen window. An uneasiness surfaces, knowing I can't see anything in the gloomy mist but I can easily be seen from this well lit room. I turn the light off and lean against the window frame, sipping my coffee.

My eye catches movement in the distance, about 50 yards from the inn, in the trees. Dark figures stand shoulder to shoulder. Is my vision playing tricks on me? Are the moving shapes only shadows cast from wind-blown branches? My nose is on the glass as I watch and wait.

THUD! Something crashes into the window, cracking the pane in front of my face. I'm so startled I shriek and jump back, as a bird falls to its death. Regaining my composure, I look out to the forest, but see nothing. What I need is some fresh air.

The landscaping is not complete, and the grounds around are in disarray. This is an old property. Bushes and trees are overgrown with weeds and tendrils of vines. My steps swish through dead leaves from a season long gone. I step over the raven lying still on the ground. My eyes travel to the deep forest and settle on the place of the shadowy movements. Despite the howling wind I want to get just a little deeper into the forest. My footsteps cannot be heard; the ground is soft and wet. I approach the tree line; obstacles only become visible at arm's-length. Vines travel up the trunks of massive trees. Some of them are wrapped. After walking a distance, I come to a clearing. My shoe bumps something solid and I must go around. After a few more clumsy steps, my foot hits another obstruction. This time I realize the obstacles are grave markers. I am in a cemetery. Enough fresh air for me!

The sound of twigs breaking and water splashing grab my focus. I move forward, going around many grave markers. On the side of a lake a fawn is trapped in the vines at the edge of the water. It fights to live, and then it rests from the struggle. As soon as I get close the effort to free itself starts again. The animal is terrified and I kneel down beside the yearling, trying to soothe her. I touch its soft face and say, "You are into a bit of a mess here, little one." My words seem to calm her. "Let's see what we can do."

I begin to inspect the source of the tangle and free one leg but other vines hold the little fawn down. Its face slips under the water and I submerge my arm into the cold lake water to hook her neck to save her.

The fawn is so frightened now she begins to struggle against my efforts. She is a strong animal, but I am able to pull her to safety. She gets her tiny legs onto the shore and bolts off, unscathed by the experience. I am freezing and wet. I turn to hustle back to the inn, as fast as the fog will allow.

Wings flutter close to me. When I look up, a blackness swoops at me and screeches. With my arms overhead for protection, a bird pecks at my wrists and hands. My heart pounds as I reach the safety of the inn and inspect my injuries. I am ok, only some small surface scratches. I am cold and muddy. I turn on the water so the tub can fill, and I peel off my wet clothes. The water is hot, but I still shiver as I wrap my arms around my chilled body. I clean up and get out. The air is much colder than the bath water. I wrap myself in the robe Tera packed. Along with one of the outfits is her beautiful Italian blue silk scarf. She knows how much I love the accessory; packing it was thoughtful.

After preparing for the day, I loop the lovely scarf around my neck and apply lipstick. I am refreshed, energy renewed. I receive a call from Keefe.

"Quinn, I am out front of the inn to give you a lift to town."

"But I thought Tera would bring my car."

"Quinn, we've had some trouble… with your car."

"Oh, ok, I will be right down." I put the Chardonnay in the

refrigerator to chill, and lock the doors and get into the car with Keefe.

"Quinn, Tera's been in an accident. Fishermen saw a car going into the river. Tera somehow ended up in the water by Grayson's landing," Keefe says in a serious tone with a concerned face.

"What on earth are you talking about? Is she alright?" I plead, panicked.

"The car is retrieved from the river, the seatbelt still buckled but no Tera. Quinn, it's not a good sign."

I say nothing the rest of the ride to the station, and sit trancelike. Suddenly an odd thing happens. A sense of calm melts over my entire being. Without a doubt, Tera is ok. It is a knowing beyond faith. I have never been so sure of anything in my life. When we arrive, Chamous's face tells the story of complete devastation.

He tries to tell me what he thinks happened. His story is broken and confusing.

I take his hand and lead him to the chairs in the corridor. I am calm. I take Chamous's hand and gaze into his eyes and say calmly, "Tera is ok. This is not a prediction. I am telling you I know she is. Please allow your faith to rule your heart, not your fear."

Keefe takes a phone call and the whole station is chaotic with phones being answered and officers talking. Keefe is standing in the middle of it all. "She's been found. She is alive. She is ok!"

Cheers and clapping erupt.

"Where is she Keefe?" Chamous inquires, with Pony at his side.

"She is downstream a ways from Grayson's landing. Come on, I will take you over."

We all get into Keefe's squad car and hurry down to Grayson's landing. We drive down a riverside gravel road and come across emergency vehicles. We park and run over to the side of the river.

Tera is sitting up. She is wrapped in a blanket and they are moving her to a stretcher.

Chamous reaches her side and takes her hand.

"Are you ok, baby?" he asks.

I race to the other side and take her other hand.

"Where did you go, Quinn?" she asks.

"What do you mean? I've been waiting for you at the inn." I tell her.

Again, Chamous repeats, "Are you ok?"

Tera says weakly, "A busy morning." We all laugh at her humor. I am not sure I have ever been so glad to see anyone in my life.

"Tera what happened?" I ask.

"You don't know?" she asks me before she leaves with Chamous in the ambulance. Why would I know about her accident?

Keefe takes Pony and me to the hospital. While in the waiting room Pony is on his phone, and Chamous is pacing.

Keefe says, "Quinn, your car will need to be checked out," suggesting my car was tampered with, I assume.

The doctor comes down the hall, a pleasant smile on his face.

"Tera is fine! She has no injuries, she is feisty and is ready for her friends," he says as he leads us to her.

Tera's hair is tangled but there is color in her cheeks and a big smile as we enter.

Chamous rushes to her side.

"Get over here Quinn and Pony," Tera says in a loud voice.

"What happened?" Pony asks. Everyone is eager for her explanation.

"I took one of Pony's friends home near Grayson landing. After I dropped him off, I came down the steep incline, no brakes at all! As I picked up speed, I realized I wouldn't make the curve back to the main highway. I kept going, and the front of the car plowed into the river. I didn't panic; I lowered the window and then unbuckled my seatbelt and floated myself closer and closer to the shore. It was damn cold! Before long the emergency vehicles arrived and here I am. I drew a bit of a crowd; so embarrassing."

"Quinn, if you don't mind, can I stay with you tonight?"

"Sure, would love the company," I say. "Just one problem, we will need a ride, my car is damp!"

Chapter Twenty-Four

Keefe offers to drive us to the inn, and Chamous brings Tera's car and catches a ride back with Keefe.

Tera wears Chamous's big parka and once inside, she heads to the bathtub. She sheds his coat, revealing slacks and a very soiled and water stained blouse. She turns to ask me about a robe and that's when I see the Italian blue silk scarf around her neck. The sight of the scarf stops everything, I reach up to my throat already knowing the scarf would not be there.

"Quinn, are you alright?" she asks me.

"The scarf . . ."

"You better pour yourself a drink my friend, and be ready to listen when I finish with my bath," Tera says.

I am speechless and stand in the same spot, even after Tera closes the door of the bathroom. I light the fireplace and take my friend's advice and open a bottle of cabernet. Tera does not take long to join me in front of the fire. She accepts the wine and takes a healthy drink.

"Quinn, did you go anywhere this morning?" she asks me, in a soft voice.

"I slept pretty late, walked the property some." She fiddles with the rim of her glass. "The accident didn't quite happen the way I explained this morning," she says and takes another sip of her wine. "My feet are freezing."

"I'll get you a pair of socks."

Tera puts them on and curls her feet back under her.

Then she continues, "I did become submerged in the water and unable to release the seat belt. I started to panic when a hand grasped mine and pulled me right out of the car. I floated along looking everywhere for my helping hand, but found no one. When I reached the riverbank, I couldn't get out of the water. The harder I tried the more tangled in vines and weeds I became. The current held me down and I slipped deeper into the water. Quinn, you stood right there on the shoreline!" she said, with tears in her eyes. "You knelt by the water's edge, your hair falling to one side as you gently untangled me and drew me out of the water. You soothed my exposure with a simple touch. You stroked my cheek and my body stopped the violent shaking. You talked to me, and told me everything is going to be ok. Sirens signaled help approaching when you took the blue scarf off your neck and looped around my throat and you were gone. What happened Quinn?"

"I swear Tera, I did not leave here," I say, confused.

"How do you explain the scarf? I wasn't wearing it, I packed it for you."

Tera deserved any explanation I could muster.

"Dear friend, from what I can comprehend...a Guardian came to your rescue. The Guardian who helped you... loves you very much, but I didn't leave the inn. Tera you must understand, I believe you. I too experienced something unusual this morning, while walking around the inn. I was drawn further into the forest by shadows and sounds. I came across a tiny fawn stuck on the side of a shoreline and tangled in vines. I helped the tiny deer out of the lake."

"This is like Pony's dream, why he made the 911 call. I do not doubt his explanation at all....now."

"Hard to comprehend, I know."

"Yes...no memory of being with me?" she asks again.

"Tera, I don't understand how I helped you with no recollection. I am anxious to talk to Pony about this."

"Why Pony?"

"Pony is researching Guardians and the ....angelic realm. With the experience the other night; he is helping me to put the pieces together. How about we order some dinner from Bordeaux's and I will catch you up to speed?" I suggest.

"Good idea," she says.

We order one of our favorites and the meals are delivered within forty-five minutes.

"I think I was pushed off the cliff, saved in the same way you were...Guardian protection. The mystery woman who warned me was deceased long before the day she came into the shop." This statement stops Tera's fork in mid-air.

"What? Come on, Quinn!"

"That's not all... I met Cashton Royce, and he magically healed a wound I sustained while at the estate, and he is mesmerizing. He's the one who rescued me from the fire, and who came to Pony with my amulet and warning to call 911. The connection I feel with the Royce family grows stronger by the day."

Tera listens intently and eats her meal. She knows everything now. We are silent for a few moments.

"Is that it?" she asks in typical Tera style.

After a short pause, we laugh. It feels good to laugh.

"What do we do next?" Tera asks.

I rub my eyes and stare into the fire thinking deeply about her question.

"I'm not sure, but our lives will never be the same."

My last statement gives us volumes to think about while watching the flames burn down to embers. We both fall asleep.

The next few days are quiet compared to the last week. Tera lets me use her car, while Chamous helps her out with transportation into the city and home. Pony spends his afternoons sharing information with me about Guardians.

Pony and I study the hierarchy of the angelic realm. The tricky part is accepting a new reality.

Business at Fireside Books is slower than usual. The silence and stillness in White Oak is uncharacteristic, and I worry if we are in the eye of the storm.

Tera and I plan to order dinner from Bordeaux's again. I keep her informed on all Pony and I are learning.

"Tera, the fire was not started by lightning. Someone was outside of my window, I knocked a candle over when I stumbled. Someone was in my house the few days before too, and laid out those silk pajamas."

"Damn, Quinn, that's frightening," she says.

"I know, but I won't be intimidated."

Tera is quiet for a moment.

"What happened on the day you found the nightclothes?"

"That was the day we took the bread over to Professor Enderlee. We went to the station and then Tripp Atchison confessed to the hit and run accident. Keefe came over for wine."

"What about the day of the fire?" she asks.

"Hmm...Keefe came over that evening, during the-"

"Stop!"

"What?" I ask.

"Each time after seeing Keefe...?"

"Yes, I guess so."

"Quinn, it's about Keefe! Someone is jealous--an old boyfriend maybe?"

"I was dating before I met Alec, but that was almost two years ago. Seems unlikely."

Tera says, "What about Keefe... jealous former girlfriends, or someone from work? The militant policewoman Bishop from work? She has plenty of attitude. Remember her chiding about Keefe?"

"Yes, I do. She came unannounced into Keefe's office twice when I've been with him. He shunned her explanation and kind of scolded her, but romantically interested in Keefe seems a stretch. Keefe believes she wants a recommendation, so she can advance in her career."

"Baloney," says Tera. "She wants him, and you are in the way. Easy way to find out."

"What are you thinking, Tera?"

"Next time the two of you are together, I will follow her. Keefe will take care of it and the problem will be gone," she announces nonchalantly.

I pour us both another glass of wine and mention Keefe's cold shoulder treatment the last time we were alone.

"What do you mean? Don't tell me you sent Detective Dreamy packing? What happened?" she asks.

"Keefe is looking for...friendship, his actions reflect it."

"No way, Quinn!"

"Tera, I would know if he is interested by now. Besides, this is a complicated time to be in a relationship."

"Just don't close the door on this one forever. We can still figure out if Dawn Bishop is a creepy stalker."

"Sure."

Our wine is gone, and the flames now embers. I try to send Tera to bed, but she's just warming up.

"Are you kidding Quinn, it's only eight o'clock! We will make some coffee if necessary! Let's try to figure out what is happening in our little town, and if the Royces are connected."

We are up late into the night, drinking coffee to stay sharp, and discussing the strange occurrences in town and in our own lives.

I'm not ready to wake up, when a text arrives at seven a.m. from Sapphire.

"I know you are a Guardian. Please meet me."

Her comment jolts me awake.

I text back, **"Where?"**

"At the N.W. corner of estate- old Sawmill....Medicine Bowl Road is the back way... see u in an hour."

Chapter Twenty-Five

I assume an alternate route will take me to the estate without going through the gate. Is Sapphire keeping her mother appeased by suggesting a back way? Medicine Bowl Road is further south of the main highway.

Tera sleeps while I dress. I leave her a note and borrow her car.

Sapphire is aware of the existence of Guardians, but how is she connecting it to me? I travel under a darkened morning sky while relentless gusts whip leafless trees, showing no mercy. Like the sound of popping corn, heavy raindrops hit the windshield drowning out my vision of a patrolman in the road. He waves traffic to stop, his rain slicker flapping in stinging March winds. Many cars are stopped on the bend going to the bluff. My phone rings and it's Keefe.

"Cindy Arness is improving. She is not out of the woods yet, but she is headed in the right direction. The search is still on for Rand. I wanted you to know the latest."

"Keefe, its good news, thanks for calling me. I will call you back; traffic problems up ahead," I say as I hang up. Several emergency vehicles sit with the long stream of motorists. An officer walks along the cars, speaking to each driver. I lower my window enough to hear his message. The rain comes in forceful sheets.

"Obstruction in the road, Miss. We are diverting traffic. Please be patient. We will try to get you moving as quickly as possible."

Drops soak my shoulder by the time I raise the window again. Not wanting to be delayed, I make an impulsive decision to turn around. Now I am heading east. I would need a different way to reach the Royce Estate. I check the radio for weather updates and possible news of what the obstruction might be. The frequencies all crackle with confusing sound bites and high pitched whistling noises. I can't even find an audible station.

I travel two miles and take a southbound turn on a gravel road. I plan to bypass the blocked portion before getting back onto the main highway. I wait for the first opportunity west, and turn. Inside the car a vibration, a buzzing grows louder. I lower the radio forgetting it's not even on. Glancing everywhere I search for the source of the noise. BEES! A nest of bees swarms on the passenger floor mat. My panic escalates and so does the volume of their sound. Any quick action could cause them to attack. Getting out of the car in the driving rain did not seem plausible. I pull off the road, and shut off the motor and sit still. The crawling insects travel into a vent on the console. I move my hand in a deliberate slow motion, reaching to turn the heater off. The bees swarm around the opening. Within a few minutes, they all follow into the vent. With my heart racing I snap the vent closed and all the others. Will it contain them, until I can get out of the car? With the source of heat off, the temperature in the car drops swiftly. With the vents closed, I put the unit on high, hoping for some heat, and maybe to kill the bees.

When I am about five miles west I turn back to the main highway. No traffic. Lightning flashes across the morning sky and more rain pours out of the heavens. Once I crest a hill and begin the descent, I veer the car slightly to avoid running over a dead bird. I squint for better visibility. The highway looks chopped, as the fog conceals low lying portions. A forceful thud hits the roof of the car and robs me of any remaining composure. I shriek and jerk in reaction. A black raven lies motionless on the hood. The pavement is covered with fallen birds. Is this the type of obstruction stopping traffic five miles back?

An ominous blanket of doom covers my spirit, my hope. Instincts tell me I will find answers with Sapphire. I can't avoid running over birds. My tires must be crimson from the blood of these ravens.

My car reaches Medicine Bowl Road and I travel west again. I pray the car is the safest place to be in an electrical storm. I grip the steering wheel with fear, as thunder shakes the ground and lightning crashes all around me. No dead birds on this stretch. I speed up, but the gravel pulls my tires, slowing me down. Low-lying areas become treacherous as formed tributaries of rushing water bully their way across the road. The road comes to an end with only a north turn option. I follow through thick forests as the road narrows, my destination close. Branches and leaves swipe the vehicle as I pass. The forest is drab and misty; gloom slithers around trunks of massive oak trees. The rain is only a sprinkle now, providing better visibility. My left finger begins to throb. There is no bee, but I feel the sting of one and the redness and swelling too. My body heat rises so drastically, I use my injured left hand to lower the window. Cold air floods over me, but does nothing to slow my racing heart. What is happening to me? I loosen the scarf around my neck and keep driving.

A clearing reveals the faint outline of buildings. This is the northwest corner of Royce Estate. I am glad to leave the car to open a small gate. A woman runs from the direction of the main house while I approach the old stone sawmill. My knock on the door is unanswered for a minute, before Sapphire opens the door wide.

"Quinn!" she says breathlessly as she steps forward and surprises me with an embrace. She hustles me inside and closes the door behind us. "I am so glad you are here. Follow me to the North Lodge."

Sapphire takes me out a different doorway, and I hold her hand as we run along the outside wall surrounding the garden. When we reach the back of a building we enter a dimly lit room.

"What is it, Sapphire?" I ask her.

"Quinn, everything is wrong. When Mother returned from England, Father came in the dining room and asked me to give them some privacy. He grabbed her arm and set her down in a chair. He was furious and I heard arguing, but I don't know what the issue was. Afterward, she left and I can't find my father to talk to him. My family is falling apart before my eyes. Something serious has happened between my parents. And . . . I know about Guardians," she says, her green eyes filled with sincerity. Her breathing becomes more relaxed and steady.

"Sapphire, what is this place?" I ask.

"Our lodge for visitors . . . where I'm conducting my investigation."

"Investigation?"

"Quinn, Cashton saved you from the fire. My dreams, my visions have revealed much to me. I know he is a Guardian. He helps people. I saw the trespasser outside your window, the candle, the fire. I saw you safe in the hospital. I also saw a vision of Cashton bending over you as you lay upon the rock floor. He is connected to you, Quinn."

Although she speaks with clarity, her confused expression

remains.

"You rescued your friend, saved her life. You are like Cashton. I've felt different, all my life. Things are becoming clear. Quinn, I need your help with Father."

"What do you mean?" I ask.

She pauses before continuing.

"I asked him a few weeks ago, and he told me as soon as I turn 18 he will share many things with me. My intuition is telling me something is wrong. My family is in danger and I have to help them now, not after I turn eighteen. I don't want to be so dramatic, but a darkness threatens us all! In the tower room, where Cashton spends time, are genealogy charts and pictures of our ancestors. The room is always locked, cloaked in secrecy, but I found a way into the room."

Sapphire takes a deep breath, and when she exhales she is trembling

I ask her if I could make her some tea, and Sapphire is grateful for my suggestion. She has a chance to compose herself and a steaming cup of tea may calm her. I appreciate the hot beverage too, my trip to the estate having been nothing short of harrowing.

"A battle now exists on earth, dark angels spread false prophecies. They destroy lives with deceit, doubt, pain and turmoil. They want entire societies for their dark world. But there is hope, angelic beings exist. The prince of seraphim, Archangel Michael, a patron and protector since the time of the apostles, formed a legion of promoters of the light. Their image is no different than ours. You may see them and not even realize they are Guardians. I don't understand it all. I know my father is connected to the celestial world."

"What do you mean, Sapphire?"

"Hard to explain, let me show you," she says, offering her hand to lead me. I take her hand and she leads me along the walled garden. She takes me to the Dutch barn. This red brick structure with five tall bays is supported by slim piers with gothic arches at either end. We walk under the first of the arches. Sapphire approaches the interior corner and places her hands upon the wall slightly above her head, palms flat and fingers outstretched. The stone under her hands begins to glow and melt, like ice beneath a branding iron. She removes her hands and the stone melts away and she steps through the wall into a dark passage. I am astounded and stand in disbelief at the gaping opening. She reaches out again for my hand with compassion and sincerity in her eyes. I grasp her hand and enter the darkness.

Once inside, the stones become solid again, sealing the entrance. With only a touch, a lamp is ignited, illuminating the passage. I stand wide-eyed as subsequent lantern flames ignite all along the wall. We walk deeper into the stone tunnel, my heart beating faster with each twist and bend. Sapphire leads with confidence. The sound of running water lies ahead. A small boat rests upon a narrow stream being fed by water flowing down the tunnel wall.

Sapphire senses my uneasiness. "Quinn, we are nearly there, don't worry."

I manage a half smile as I position myself in the floating vessel. Sapphire skims the surface of the water and our boat begins to move down this stream. This movement creates illumination from under the water as multitudes of small fish glow a brilliant white.

I am overcome with wonder, but do not speak. I stare at the spectacle of glowing fish following us along.

We come to a fork and the boat veers to the left. A faint sound of music grows louder as we journey towards the end of the passageway. Rock walls become transparent.

We step out to the stone floor. Sapphire places her hands on the crystal quartz wall and melts an opening for us that closes as soon as we enter. We are in a spacious cavern, a ceiling of clear quartz allowing a view of the heavens. The most beautiful music fills the sacred place and my spirit with inspiration and hope. Limestone benches and an ornate cross are positioned in front of the cavern, flanked by thick, pillar candles. Engraved in a stone beneath is "Romulus, Orbis of Sol." I recognize those words from my dream on the silver shore and the beautiful woman.

Sapphire sits on a bench and I sit beside her.

She turns her mystic green eyes to me.

"The phrase is Latin for Romulus Circle of Sun, the name of the legion formed by Archangel Michael. I believe my father is the Polaris, a word meaning leader."

I am spellbound by her statement. No longer can I apply logic to the things I am seeing and hearing. A tingling starts in my feet as gentle warmth travels up my legs. The odd phenomenon holds me captive while I experience a complete blanket of glorious energy covering my chest and arms and face. I want to savor the splendor and never leave.

Sapphire says, "My discovery is premature. I believe when I am 18, I will learn from my father all about Guardians and the Circle of Sun. Perhaps I will even act as a Guardian, like Cashton."

"Romulus is the leader of this... Circle of Sun?" I ask her, my words come quiet and slow.

"Yes, I believe he is, whatever that means," she says in hushed tones.

"Who else knows about this place? Who lit the candles?" I ask her.

"The candles and music are perpetual. I love it here because I feel safe and hopeful," she tells me. "But I never stay too long, so we must go."

She rises and I reluctantly join her as she leads me back to the crystal wall, and places her palms upon the shimmering surface, creating a magical opening for us to exit. Once into the boat, she skims the water with her hand and once more we are gliding and I am mesmerized by the glowing fish trail. We now take the right fork for a time, and arrive at an opening concealed behind a waterfall. I follow Sapphire again, and she grasps my hand as we take rock steps leading us out from beneath the waterfall. We've arrived on the grounds of Royce Estate without a drop of water on us.

Chapter Twenty-Six

We run to escape the wind and rain, the storm still churning and spilling angrily onto earth. The air is biting and I grip my coat tighter as we enter the estate on the south side. Once we are in Sapphire's room, she closes the door and turns to me.

"Mother and Jexis left for a few hours on Symphony business. The benefit is only a few days away. I ran out to the mill to meet you right after they left. I want to show you something else." She leads me to the solarium.

I wonder if Cashton is here and a rush of anticipation washes over me.

The storage room contains bags of soil, tools and a sink. Sapphire moves a few boxes on the floor and lifts a rug, revealing a trap door.

"Follow me," she says. We climb down and walk through a basement level.

Sapphire puts her finger to her lips, "Shhhh," she says.

We climb a rickety, winding staircase. She points to a gap between the stairs and a platform.

"Be careful, I will help you. Let me go first," she says in hushed tones.

Sapphire steadies herself and takes a wide step, securing the railing on the other side. I do the same. We enter a small and dark alcove and the walls grow tighter, until we can go no further.

She pushes her body against the wall, forcing an opening into a room. We are now in the tower room where Cashton stopped the bleeding of my finger. The Royce estate is starting to feel like a maze. The windows do little to light the room. Sapphire lights two lanterns.

Sapphire is all business as she takes a few things from a multitude of books and papers and sits down on the small sofa.

"This is a letter to my father from someone in his hometown." Sapphire reads a few lines. "'You are worthy. You possess a servant's heart. Good luck in Nadellawick.' Many notes have the same type of sentiments, but they never use details or particulars," she says.

Sapphire places a glass serpent in my lap. It takes two hands to hold the unusual item. Tiny gemstones cover the entire piece. This odd figurine, with bat-like wings and ruby eyes, is divided into sections. Each section named is divided by various gems. The back of the beast, identified as Hudovistan, is covered in emerald jewels. The chest of the body is amethyst with the title Sigartoff. The belly of the serpent is topaz and bears the title Moriah. One front leg is crystal clear and says Nadellawick. The other leg is lapis and labeled Ranaconda. A back leg is onyx and reads Fezelopia, and the other leg is opal and it says Aderlucia.

"This is stunning but very strange. What are these words?" I ask.

"Both of my parents have used the word Nadellawick when referring to our region. We moved here because of Nadellawick. The serpent is a map."

"The River People used that word, Nadellawick," I say.

Sapphire shows me an old book.

I open the cover and flip through the few pages of children's poems with subjects like sandcastles and ponies.

"Keep looking, the last page has a short poem, and one underlined portion."

I read the verse aloud, "'Dancing in the midnight sun, knowing that our work is done. Serpents, snakes and stains on souls, found within the darkest hole. Trapped forever, darkness gone, but fear the lover's tears at dawn.' What could it mean?" I ask.

"I think something to do with the reason we are not still in England. Something changed, bringing us here, and now things are deteriorating. The underlined phrase is an emphasis."

Sapphire has put some thought into this.

I tell her, "This reminds me of what Pony told me about the River People! He said when he asked Jessie how this new church started, she told him a story similar to this poem. An undeserving man won the heart of some woman. Despite his evil, she loved him… it was the foundation for the River People, according to Jessie."

"How could one like that be loved?" Sapphire asks.

"Maybe that's the point. Who would ever think someone evil could be worthy of love? The poem says the darkness, serpents, snakes and dark souls are trapped, but the tears of a lover could change it."

Thunder rolls, shaking the whole estate. I am starting to think we should not be in here. We should leave.

Sapphire opens an envelope, its content freezes me. I grab the picture of myself from her.

"Why is my picture here?" I ask.

"No idea!" she says.

I study the photo.

"It could be from my time in Saint Louis. The background might be Danforth campus. I visited Washington University. It was a while ago, when I wore my hair longer."

"Everything in this room bears historical significance to our family in England. Have you ever been to England, Quinn?" Sapphire asks.

"No, may I take this photo, Sapphire?"

"I think you should. I have more to show you, but we can't stay any longer today."

I put the picture in the pocket of my coat and we slip back through the bookcase opening. We shuffle through the very small space to the landing with the hazardous gap to the staircase. We take turns to maneuver across it, and make our way down the rickety steps to the solarium. Once through the trap door, we emerge into complete darkness. I am relieved to be out, but when Sapphire reaches to turn on the lights we discover the storms knocked out the power. We stand holding hands with our faces upturned to view the heavens through the glass dome ceiling. The whole solarium is lit up with each furious flash.

I begin to realize this is not the best place to be standing and lead Sapphire out of possible danger. The darkness prevails once again and we must feel our way out. With the next bolt of lightning illuminating the path, we feel someone is there.

"Mother, are you there?" Sapphire calls above the hammering downpour. "Mother?"

Once again we are forced to make our way until a light shines ahead. Beef is lighting lanterns in the hallway, a welcome sight.

"Beef, I'm glad to see you!" says Sapphire. "Is Mother back yet?" she asks.

"I'm right here, darling," comes a voice behind us.

We both turn. Petulah stands in the arched solarium entrance.

"Mother, you startled me… didn't you hear me call?" Sapphire asks.

"No, daughter, I came from the dining room. Lucky for us dinner preparation was complete before the outage. Sapphire didn't mention your visit, Quinn. Beef, set another place at the table," Petulah orders.

"A full house tonight, with our storm refugees!" Beef says.

"Quinn is delighted to join us," Sapphire says, answering for me as she leads me to her suite. "See you in the dining room in ten."

After we are in her room with door shut she offers an explanation.

"Quinn, I am sorry I answered for you. But she will suspect something if you didn't accept the offer and you need to eat."

She was right. I wonder who the other storm refugees are. After looking in the mirror, we are both surprised by our disheveled appearance.

Sapphire lays out a pair of black tailored trousers, a grey cashmere sweater and metallic leather ballerina flats.

"Here, these are your size, I bet," she says.

She changes into knit leggings, a boyfriend cardigan, both black, and boots. She twists her massive hair into a pile of copper spirals, with tendrils falling about on her shoulders. She applies a quick gloss to her lips.

I emerge in her pre-selected outfit.

"Perfect," she says. "Want gloss?"

However, my appearance does not concern me. I am consumed with the day's experiences. I am tired, hungry and I am confused and overwhelmed. Sapphire reads me well and guides me to a seat in front of the mirror. She says nothing as she stands behind me, her hands on my shoulders. Sapphire's touch is compassionate, it renews and calms me. She sings while brushing my hair. The sound of her mellow voice relaxes my spirit. She applies color to my cheeks and lips and I sense she is pleased. I am grateful. The last several minutes our communication required no words. And from her compassion and tender understanding, I feel solace. She senses my concerns and my confusion, and I recognize a kindred spirit. This time gives me a temporary reprieve from the bedlam.

The hallways of Royce Estate glow with incandescent light. More lanterns make the dining room brilliant. On the far wall, a sideboard supports two elaborate candelabras, each hosting several burning pillars. The fireplace provides not only warmth, but radiance. Opulent oil lamps burn upon the mantle. Three candelabras of stupendous size illuminate the table. Crystal stemware and sterling silver shimmer radiance.

Sapphire and I take our seats and I am offered wine, which I accept.

Jexis enters the room next with her phone to her ear. This time she is dressed, and her long hair is down, silky straight and blonde. Her face lights up when she sees me.

"I didn't know you were coming over. Welcome Quinn. I should have known you'd be here just in time to get snowed in again," Jexis says with laughter. "It's nice to see you again."

"Good to see you too, Jexis." I say.

"Nice outfit!" Jexis says to Sapphire, with a tinge of sarcasm.

"Glad you approve, sister."

Beef is feeding the fire and tries directing the serving of dinner without the convenience of electricity.

"Damn phones, when you need them! No signal!" Jexis remarks. She flips some golden silk over her shoulder, and holds up her empty glass.

"Hello?"

One servant rushes to her side and pours wine.

Jexis snatches the bottle out of her hands.

"I'll just keep that here, if you don't mind," Jexis says gently to the server. She bats her lashes and flashes me a radiant smile.

"What brings you up here, Quinn?" she asks, while fiddling with her phone.

"Sapphire and I are catching up."

"Well," she goes on, "I don't mind you wearing my clothes, I like giving my sister a bad time."

"Oh, I didn't realize the clothing was . . ."

"Oh, no problem Quinn, take them home if you like. My closets are full. Where is mother? I am famished." She uncovers the breadbasket and takes a roll, rips a portion off and begins nibbling.

Beef escorts two men into the dining room.

"Unexpected guests join us this evening, Mr. Keefe Remington and Pony Coldstone," Beef announces.

I rush over to them.

"Pony, Keefe what are you doing up here?" I give Pony a hug.

"Tera couldn't reach you on your phone. I told her I would make sure you arrived and let her know," Keefe explains.

"How thoughtful, Keefe," I say.

Keefe puts his arms around me. His embrace is secure and familiar. Before he releases me he whispers in my ear.

"Keeping you safe." Keefe then speaks out loud. "No way back until morning though, trees down covering our only route back. We'll have to wait for first light to remove the trees."

Keefe and Pony take seats across from me.

Sapphire says, "Means you're snowed in again, Quinn."

I am thinking about Keefe's words. Am I in danger? Does he know something? Is he referring to hazardous travel conditions or my presence at the estate? His demeanor reflects his concern.

Keefe doesn't take his eyes off of me. But, I can't trust my instincts where Keefe is concerned.

I savor the wine while asking Pony how he and Keefe ended up together. Pony is distracted by Sapphire.

"Pony," I say a little louder.

"Yes, Quinn?"

I repeat my question.

"I rode along with Keefe as he checked for the extent of the bird kill. Good news… the issue with the winery, it's all behind me," Pony says with a beaming smile. His attention turns back to Sapphire.

"What a pleasure to have dinner guests." Jexis says, as she pours herself another glass of wine. And then she leans closer to me and says her next sentence under her breath, "And they're easy on the eyes too!"

Petulah enters the dining room, stunning as she lingers for a moment.

Keefe stands and Pony follows, I slide my chair out, and once again Sapphire puts her hand on my leg and turns her face to me, rolling her eyes.

Jexis tries to rise, but she is a little clumsy and misses the opportunity.

"I see some formality and respect in this dining room still exist!" Petulah says, while Beef stands ready to seat her. Wine is poured for her.

"I welcome our visitors, and hope you will enjoy a hot meal!" Petulah says, staring at Beef.

His frustration is obvious as he bumps into a server.

Sapphire breaks into laughter, breaking the tension. I can see this as an opportunity for Jexis to have some fun. But she begins a serious toned exchange about the symphony benefit. Her personality is transformed. She is more erect with her shoulders back. Her voice is steady and controlled. She carries the conversation, introducing Keefe and Pony with formality to her mother. She refuses more wine when offered.

Sapphire rolls her eyes. As the dinner is served, Petulah converses with Keefe about the weather, while Pony stares at Sapphire.

Jexis is quiet and refined and picks at her food.

"What brings you to our doorstep Detective Remington? Petulah asks.

She catches Keefe chewing, so he pauses and dabs his lips with his napkin before responding.

"Romulus contacted the department about the stream overrunning its banks on the edge of your estate, and I checked it out for him. With deteriorated roads, he is concerned about the route traffic will take for the benefit. The stream is now a violent river. Downed trees will prevent our return to White Oak."

"You talked with Father?" Sapphire asks.

"Yes, earlier today," Keefe says.

"Sapphire your father was called away early this morning to attend to an urgent matter. He will be back before morning. Your concerns are unwarranted. The misunderstanding between your father and I was resolved, miscommunication about the symphony event, my error. Everything is fine, Sapphire." She sounds sincere and Sapphire breathes a sigh of relief.

Jexis comments, "Many of the contributors expect to see him."

"Yes Jexis, I agree, and they shall. Our meetings were productive today, but the ride home was long. I will be retiring early. The weather should be clearing by morning; however the forecast for the benefit does not look good at this point."

Petulah asks Beef if the north wing is prepared for guests. Beef responds with all the right answers. She excuses herself and leaves the dining room. The entire atmosphere changes. Jexis snaps her finger and wine is filling her glass.

"Who is up for some Quoits?" Jexis asks, as she backs her chair out from the table.

"No power, remember Jexis." Sapphire says.

"Beef can light it up. Who's joining me?" Jexis asks.

Beef says, "I will have some staff members prepare the game area."

All I want to do is go to bed, but I don't want to appear rude. I make the decision to spend only a short time in the billiard room. This room is expansive, providing enough light will be difficult. The fire pit in the center is burning, roaring.

Jexis lights up the bar area when she ignites the oil lamps. She takes on the bartender role, preparing drinks for us. Sapphire shows Pony how to hold and toss the rings, and Keefe is on the sidelines as the uneven number dictates.

Jexis pours Keefe a brandy. The lighting is dim, but it doesn't stop the fun. Jexis is skilled as she scores points with a martini in her left hand. I am her partner, and when I score a point, she rushes me with a high five and her drink sloshes out one side.

Pony and Sapphire are so smitten with each other they don't notice the rest of us are in the room. Their score reflects their lack of interest in the game, and when it's not their turn, they are talking and laughing.

Jexis and I are a good team, but I am tired and make the announcement I will be turning in. I say my goodnights to Sapphire and Pony and I am surprised by a hug from Jexis. She is feeling no pain. I say goodnight to Keefe, and make my way down the lit corridor to the north wing.

Chapter Twenty-Seven

I am familiar with the north wing, since it is where I stayed before. All I want is a bath, and I am hoping for hot water. The room is lit with candles. The fireplace provides some light too. I disrobe as the bath fills. Lightning still splashes periodic flashes through the window. I am grateful for the hot water, and slip down, eyes transfixed on the glow of a single candle at the end of the tub. The flame flickers and quivers, grows taller and shorter, reflecting and glistening over the bubbles surrounding me. A draft snuffs it out, I am in complete darkness. A few moments pass and the candle reignites, the single blaze reaching higher and producing massive amounts of heat. Within the overgrown flame the image of a man's face appears. It fades out and reappears, each time with more clarity. I grip the sides of the claw foot tub and draw my legs in, attempting to put space between me and the illusion. I recognize the face of Romulus. I shake my head to wake myself from this dream. His image speaks and no longer can I escape; I am frozen.

"Quinn, I mean you no harm, this message is important. Please listen to me. The existence of Guardians is no longer a secret to you. My precious Sapphire is troubled and confused. She will be eighteen soon, but our plan can't wait. The darkness is eager to swallow any light that is left. Petulah is against us. Our bond is severed. I am asking for your help, Quinn. It was our hands touching by the pond in your dream. Your heart is pure. A new revelation turns the tide in the battle being fought for everything good and true. I talk to Sapphire at dawn. Would you be at the Madowent for her after our meeting? She will need support and protection. Please take heed of my warning. Petulah is destructive and will try to manipulate this situation, so keep Sapphire away from her until the benefit. You are capable of great things. With faith and gratitude, I bid you goodnight." Romulus is gone, and the fire reduced to a flickering flame once more.

What did he mean when he spoke of my capabilities? The difference between dreams and reality is blurred. Am I in danger?

After putting on the bathrobe, chills won't stop. A carafe holds hot tea, so I sit myself in front of the fire with a cup.

A loud knock jolts my body. I consider not answering. I want time to process the message from Romulus. I want so much to be fearless, but at this moment I am not. Keefe is at my door.

"Quinn, may I come in?"

I grasp the bathrobe to draw it secure, and open the door for him to enter.

"Did you grow tired of Quoits?" I ask.

"I want to make sure you are alright. Pony and Sapphire stopped participating when Cashton arrived. He and Jexis are deep in conversation at the bar. I hope I didn't wake you."

"No, I am trying to get warm after bathing." I open the door wider for him to enter. "I was relieved to hear the end of Pony's problems with the winery," I say.

"They seemed so determined to accuse him. Yes, good news," says Keefe.

"Nothing of real value taken, so Carolynn says. Is that what changed their minds?"

"The two accusers skipped town," Keefe explains.

"So glad for Pony." I say

"This room is freezing!" Keefe says, as he stokes the fire.

I offer him some tea but he declines.

I lift the cup to my lips, my trembling hands revealing my disposition.

"Quinn, you are shaking! What is wrong?" Keefe asks.

"I'm fine, just cold."

"The temperature in the estate keeps dropping since dinner." Keefe adds more wood and disappears into the bedroom. He returns with bedding. "Quinn, you look tired. Lie down out here instead, let's get you warmed up."

I am chilled to the bone.

Keefe puts the pillow under my head and covers me with the ample mossy green quilt, then the fur throw. The fire roars now. He pours himself a glass of wine and sits on the floor near my face.

I am distressed and fatigued. The warmth of flames and the

snugness of the fur around me stop the chills. It feels good to be warm. I drift in and out, Keefe right beside me.

He sits motionless, except for an occasional blink of his eyes.

Tera is right, he is beautiful. Secure with Keefe at my side, I am grateful for his presence tonight. Tossing interrupts my sleep, with images of the dark figure outside of my window and the nightclothes.

I open my eyes and ask, "Keefe, each time you left my home, something happened. Could there be a jealous woman who is... stalking me?"

"Quinn, there is no one in my life," he says, somewhat amused by my theory.

"I disagree. I think Dawn Bishop is an odd duck, and seems to follow you around like a lost puppy."

"Dawn Bishop? Are you kidding! Why she is the most difficult person on the force. Romantic interest? I think she despises me. She is one weird chick," he says, shaking his head.

"She is difficult to understand, but in her mind, she might be hoping her work performance might win your attention or interest," I explain.

"She does fit some of the characteristics, but would she go so far as to come onto your property, into your home?" he asks. "Damn, your theory does make sense. We can discuss it in the morning...sleep, sleep!" Keefe tells me.

I fade in and out of sleep. Once I awake to find him feeding the fire; another time he adjusts my blankets.

"I am still in shock about Rand! It's tragic." I say in a drowsy state.

"Rand was coerced or drugged or something. There is no other explanation," Keefe states.

"Having Dow's evidence about a secret society in White Oak made him a target," I say, before thinking.

"How do you know?" Keefe asks with concern.

"Rand and Cindy are some of the first people I met and they are good people. When I was cleaning Rose Enderlee's room, I found an envelope with specific instructions to deliver to Rand." I say in my defense.

"Quinn, you should sleep, it's not morning yet."

"I can't, Keefe. I am at a threshold, I am seeking the truth," I say quietly. I surrender my confusion and doubt, and speak without fear of consequences.

"Romulus came to me in a vision tonight. Sapphire needs protection. Before this week, I never knew Guardians existed. Mercy delivered through a Guardian is what saved me. I can't help others, if I can't protect myself." I hold my breath in, waiting for Keefe's logic to surface. I've said too much.

"I will go to the Madowent with you at dawn."

Madowent is the word Romulus used in his message.

Keefe doesn't move, he only stares at the flames.

"Keefe what is it?" I ask.

"I was thinking back to how it all began for me. I think the time has come to share it with you. Many years ago in Chicago I arrested a young man named Roan, a career criminal. Addiction destroyed any hope of a future, thrusting him into a dark world of drug abuse. An assault conviction put him in prison. Word then circulated about important work he did helping others while being imprisoned.

After serving his time, he made his home in a rundown, abandoned gas station in his old neighborhood. During the course of a year he connected with some good people and continued rebuilding his life. This is how I met Father Mopsi, a Roman Catholic priest who helped and supported Roan. With Father Mopsi's resources, Roan renovated the old gas station into a safe house. He made some enemies in his quest to clean up the streets in his neighborhood. But he helped more. He called his place the T- Station which stood for Transformation Station. He made a difference. Local media did a story on the T-Station and with donations, he expanded his unique ministry. On the night of the dedication, Father Mopsi and I attended, as well of hundreds of supporters. Later, after the ceremony, Father Mopsi and I treated him to a celebratory meal. I must admit, the change in his life provided inspiration I needed, with so much ugliness and despair in law enforcement."

Keefe continued, "Tragically, Roan was gunned down when we left the restaurant. He lay on the street dying in our arms, yet spoke of gratitude and peace."

"Keefe, I am sorry for your loss of Roan. It is very sad, he overcame so much." I say.

He explains further, "Father Mopsi prayed over him. I used both hands to apply pressure to the chest wound. While we waited for help, Roan took his hands and placed them over my hands. He looked into my eyes and struggled to speak.

"'My heart is cleansed by his great mercy.' His last word was, 'Your eyes are new from the blood of a renewed soul.' He closed his eyes.

Father Mopsi continued praying. "Roan's spirit rises to glory," Father Mopsi said as his eyes followed something rising above the street.

The paramedics and other emergency personnel asked their questions, and Father Mopsi and I went to the precinct to start the slow process of justice."

Keefe looks to me, holding my gaze as he speaks, only allowing his words and the meaning of them to be absorbed slowly as he proceeds, "At the precinct I was drawn to a woman sitting alone, trembling. Then I saw something I will never forget, a vision. Although the woman's lips did not move she pleaded for her life. I searched all around for a source for the words I was hearing, but the message came from within her.

"The vision continued and I saw a man abusing her. His forceful blow sent her to the ground. He put his hands on her throat. He squeezed every ounce of life from her. She fell away and he let her head drop hard to the floor. My mind was objecting but my body couldn't move.

"The horrible scene vanished as fast as it came. The woman remained seated, the precinct still bustled with reality, Father Mopsi still visited with a police officer, nothing changed... except me. This woman was terrified. I moved toward her and our eyes locked. I sat next to her, asked her a few questions. She opened up to me about her abusive husband. After learning her plight, my vision told me all I needed to know about her future. I suggested a shelter, but she objected, telling me he watches her every move, he would never let her out. I warned her she must take action or he most likely would kill her.

"'Officers will escort you to your home and take you to the shelter. Would that make a difference?'" I asked the frightened woman. She said it would so I told her, "Someone will take you right now." She took my hands in hers and she looked at the blood Roan's injury left on them. Tears rolled down her face, she kissed my hand and said, 'New eyes. New eyes!'"

Keefe continued with a sigh, "Roan's gift was profound, giving me a perspective on the human plight through new eyes. I wanted to help her, because I saw her future. My hands atop Roan's heart, his blood on me, unleashed this ability. Father Mopsi now lives and serves the Royce estate, and that is how I came to White Oak. Our society has eroded. We have followed the tentacles of darkness to realize their roots are in this area."

I am flabbergasted by what Keefe is saying to me.

"We?" I ask.

"Circle of Sun, Quinn," Keefe replies.

It is too late to put the pillow over my head, and turn the hands of the clock back. I want to know more about Guardians.

"Orbis of Sol?" I ask.

"Latin for Circle of Sun," he answers.

"I assume Father Mopsi, Cashton, Romulus...and more?"

"Yes, many more. And many are needed. Chief Dow made discoveries about a dark society, and Rose Enderlee discovered too much. Her death was no accident. Rand is a victim too. Circumstances are escalating. Perhaps this is why Romulus changed his mind about Sapphire. She is learning today about herself and about coming of age as a Guardian," Keefe explains. "The evil is closing in, and although she isn't 18, Romulus knows, now is the time."

"Who is Romulus, what is Romulus? Why is Sapphire in danger?"

"Romulus is Polaris to the Circle of Sun, selected by Archangel Michael. He is the leader, the supreme in command. He is the resolute warrior of light. His many years of service are almost complete. Thick roots of evil lie right here in our area. You have seen it with your own eyes, Quinn. Corruption and chaos are rampant. Our water is tainted, churches are closing, birds are falling from the sky. We are experiencing extreme weather and less light." The concern shows on his face.

"But what does this have to do with Romulus's warning about protecting Sapphire from Petulah?"

"Petulah can't be trusted. Evil has infiltrated this home, this family. Having you snowbound and alone with Petulah was dangerous. I believe she is disloyal to our cause. Don't be afraid, Quinn." Keefe's compassion is tender. I am shocked, confused, overwhelmed.

"To be a Guardian is not something of this earthly realm. It is not something we can control or predict. We don't remove obstacles, we fortify those who are in need, so they can help themselves. The hope and light inside of each soul needs fanning to ignite the flames of generosity, compassion, selflessness. That is what we do as Guardians. The brightest souls are too much of a threat to the evil ones. They are… targeted for elimination. These targets must be protected at all cost, since their possible contribution is too valuable."

Keefe pauses and touches my cheek. "This could be you, Quinn. You could be a target." Keefe stares and waits for my response.

This is outlandish. I throw the quilt to the floor and pace the space in front of the fire.

"This is more than most could comprehend in a lifetime. Processing this information is futile!" I say, exasperated.

"Quinn, we can't analyze using the logic of the mortal world."

"This is my only frame of reference, Keefe. How is any of this possible?" I sit down in frustration.

"Your fall from the stone wall, the fire in your home . . ."

"Cashton saved me from the fire," I respond.

"When I read the report of your climbing accident in the paper, I suspected you survived with intervention from a Guardian. You have... mesmerized me, Quinn," Keefe says, while looking into my eyes.

He catches me off guard with that comment. He reads my confusion.

"I am sorry Quinn. Your life is about to change, and it will take focus and faith to embrace all that is ahead. I thought it would be easier to give you space, since I know what it was like for me when I was trying to figure it all out," he says compassionately.

"I didn't think you..." Tears fill my eyes quickly before I can say any more, the depth of my feelings surfacing.

He leans in and kisses me.

"Nothing could be further from the truth," Keefe says as he moves some of my hair away from my eyes. "Your sweet spirit and your beauty have captivated me since we first spent time together. I am speaking straight from my core. I am in love with you, Quinn." His touch is sincere, genuine.

Before I can figure out what to say, the alarm on my phone lets me know it's morning, time to meet Sapphire. We will offer protection together, Keefe and I.

Keefe instructs me to bring my bag. We won't be coming back.

Chapter Twenty-Eight

Keefe takes my hand and we quietly exit one of the outside doors in the north wing. The air is stoic and silent. Our path is only partially visible in the grey dawn. A gloomy veil of heavy moisture creeps its way around the estate grounds, hovering eerily from ankles to chest. The air is so heavy and oppressive it causes me to inhale deeply, only to discover there is no shortage of oxygen after all. Keefe has a gentle but firm grasp on my hand. His hand is large and confident as he leads me along the stone wall. I had wanted more from our relationship at one point, but so much has happened since then. I did resign myself to the idea that Keefe just wanted friendship. And oddly, that felt more comfortable and secure to me.

The wind begins to pick up and a rumbling can be heard in the distance. When we come to the Dutch barn, Keefe goes directly to the corner and places his palms upon the wall, and I am silent, astounded by the power I am witnessing. His touch easily melts away the red brick of the Dutch barn, creating an opening that we enter. Once inside, the opening seals itself again. Keefe's touch illuminates the lantern, along with multitudes of lanterns, which meander down the winding passage. As we come to the stream, we see Sapphire and Pony waiting.

"Father told me to wait for you Quinn. Hello Keefe," Sapphire says. She embraces me. "I am so glad you are here, Quinn. I have so much to tell you, now that I have talked to Father."

Keefe says, "You two can talk later, we need to get away from the estate now. Sapphire, we will be taking you to White Oak with us. We will take Tera's car and leave mine."

Keefe calls Chamous and asks him to meet us at the bridge on Campion Road, near the Little Blue River. He reminds Chamous to bring a chain saw.

This time we will have to double back and exit through the Dutch barn again where Pony waits. When Sapphire places her palms upon the wall the bricks begin to melt. When we emerge from the Dutch barn, the still surroundings that existed just minutes before have transformed into violent winds and sheets of rain. We quickly get into Tera's car and leave the Royce estate. Keefe sits in the front with me at the wheel. Pony and Sapphire are in the back. The ground is quickly saturated from the heavy rainfall the day before. I am immediately stuck in the thick muck. He and Pony have to push us out of the mess.

The car ride is mostly silent. The rain has subsided some but the wind is loud. Keefe turns on the radio to hear local news warnings of flash flooding in the county. With the massive amounts of rainfall, the area is ripe for problems. The forecast includes more threatening weather.

I am concerned about Sapphire, a young woman who has just learned answers to old questions, and I wonder how she is taking it all. I glance back to see the young couple holding hands. With the car devoid of conversation I hear a weak buzzing and a quick view tells me what I need to know. The bees are back and filing out of the vent. Once they reach a certain point they take flight and soon Pony and Sapphire are swatting at them.

"Keep still!" Keefe warns. "Damn!" he says, as he is stung. "Damn things! Ouch!" He is stung again. He tells me to stop the car and quickly he jumps out of the car, and many bees escape. Everyone jumps out of the car and opens doors, making sure there are no remaining bees.

"Shut the vents, Quinn. And keep them shut for now," Keefe instructs me. He examines himself and finds several raised red sting wounds.

We come to the rain-swollen Little Blue River. A tree has fallen, blocking passage over it. Keefe parks close to the bank, upstream from where the tree has fallen. Chamous is already working with the chainsaw. Tera stands on the other side of the bridge by Chamous's truck, waving as we come to a stop.

Keefe and Pony immediately begin dragging chunks of the tree off the road. I am glad to see Tera, even if it's across the river. The wind whips her hair as she clutches the collar of her coat, drawing it in. The tiny stream has flooded out of its banks and the surging water swells into an angry river.

The vibration in my pocket is my friend calling me. We have to almost shout to be heard over the rushing water.

"Are you ok?" she yells into the phone, as she looks across the river at us.

With raised voice I shout back into my phone, "Yes, I think so. There is so much that has happened, so much to tell you."

She nods from across the river, and blows me a kiss.

The rushing water has almost reached the road of the bridge. A swell pushes some water over the top of the bridge. We don't have much time. Upstream I see movement, people standing in the tree line about a hundred yards upstream. I hold my hair back from whipping my face and obstructing my view. I see two figures standing motionless, their dark robes thrashing and flapping in the wind. Before I can tell Keefe what I have seen, Chamous yells out.

"Come on, the road is clear. Let's get out of here!"

No sooner do the words leave his lips than an immense surge of brown water, filled with debris churning and circulating, runs over the bank and heads for our parked car. The torrent of raging water crashes into it, the powerful force budging the car into movement. With the wall of water and the car heading straight towards us, we all begin running for the pickup on the other side of the bridge. Tera jumps behind the wheel of Chamous's truck and barrels in reverse over the perilous bridge as we all run to it. Rushing water floods over my shoes as I run. Chamous hurls himself into the back of the truck and holds his hands out as Sapphire and I get boosted by Pony and Keefe into the truck bed just as the water catches up. The rear of the vehicle begins to slide under the merciless pressure of the unrelenting force. Keefe and Pony simultaneously heave themselves into the sliding truck bed as Tera floors the gas pedal, causing us to hang on for our lives. We clear the bridge as it is ripped like wet cardboard and swept downstream, along with Tera's car that bobs like a miniature toy.

We speed off against the fierce wind through the wooded forest.

Sapphire clutches Pony with her head down as Tera stops the truck when we are a few miles from danger. Keefe instructs Sapphire and I to get into the cab with Tera. I feel uneasy as I scan the forest while we move from the back of the truck to the cab.

We arrive in White Oak tired and cold but alive. Many of the streets are flooded and I am anxious to reach Fireside Books to check things out. Keefe drops us all off at the bookstore while he heads over to the station. I am surprised to see that Fireside Books is open. We go in through the front door and are greeted by music and a roaring fire.

Professor Enderlee emerges from the back room when the bells on the door signal our arrival.

"Quinn, Pony! I have been worried about you! Are you ok?" he asks with gentle concern and a quick embrace.

"We are now. Professor, I am so glad to see you. What are you doing in the bookstore?"

"Pony gave me his key, and I have been holding the fort down for you, dear," the professor explains with a big smile. "And who do we have here?" he asks, referring to Sapphire. I introduce them and Professor Enderlee extends his hand, which she accepts, while the professor says, "I am honored to make your acquaintance."

This is home to me and it feels good to be here. Tera and I remove our shoes and socks and place them on the hearth to dry and Sapphire follows suit. As we sit down to warm ourselves, Tomesena jumps into my lap and purrs with satisfaction.

Professor Enderlee brings sandwiches and hot coffee.

"You don't have to serve us, Professor!" I say.

"Nonsense Quinn, I am happy to help. Very little business since this horrible bird kill and severe weather. I am considering locking my door for a few days. The whole town is affected by the adverse occurrences here in White Oak. Safety of the drinking water forced the closing of the schools yesterday. Thousands of bottles of water arrived, so school is in session today. I am looking for things to get back to normal soon enough."

"What is normal?" asks Tera.

We enjoy the sustenance while the fire warms us. The day is starting to look up. A few more days till the symphony benefit and we will be traveling up to the Royce Estate again. The others go to Mocha Joe's for refills, leaving Sapphire and I alone as the rain pounds upon White Oak.

"Quinn, my Father is an important man, the Polaris to the Circle of Sun," begins Sapphire. "He is the chosen one to lead a battle going on all around us. His influence and his responsibility are far-reaching. I do not know how this war is waged, but he did explain to me the consequences of defeat, and defeat is not an option. Father has served for many years, but the last three years have been difficult. For the first time he questions the direction of the plan, how he hated repeating it. He explained the importance and emphasis placed upon an orb of light called Fidesorb. One sits at the feet of each of the seven archangels. Four of the seven Fidesorbs are missing. One of those orbs is believed hidden here in Nadellawick. The darkness we see around us is winning the battle right now," Sapphire explains.

"What do you mean, winning?"

"Father explained to me that as more of our society loses hope, our world becomes darker and darker. Each bit of darkness added makes it much easier for the malignancy to prevail. Power and influence, greed and selfishness are elements leading to self-destruction. The tools used to snare weary souls are discouragement, shame, doubt and deceit. We are either on the side of light, or on the side of dark. And those who do not choose are in the middle and that is where the battle rages. The evil ones stand ready to snatch the fickle undecided--those who become attracted to the glamour of the easy fix, the shortcut, the glory. I am sorry Quinn, but you heard a bit of the explanation given to me by my father."

"How is this battle waged? How do we fight?" I ask.

"A certain purity in our spirit grants consideration for Guardianship. Our soul, the essence of our being, will embrace the plight of another or ignore it. Our thoughts, our intentions, our actions are examined throughout our life experiences. We reveal our worthiness through this process. In the eighteenth year, you may be elevated to Guardianship," Sapphire explains. "I don't understand everything either. But Father told me one's awareness increases with experience. As a novice, you do not choose how or when or who will receive your guidance. My father told me when the time comes, when I am faced with a situation, I will be prepared."

Sapphire's confidence has increased since her talk with her father. All the pieces fit now, and she is radiant as she claims her destiny. But although she finds answers, I have none. How am I connected to this angelic realm?

"Sapphire, I need to talk to your father. I want to know what my role is in this battle."

"Quinn, my father talked about you and how I am to trust you. We are to protect one another. He would not reveal what role you play in all of this but said you and I would both learn the answers. He seemed troubled about you; I can't imagine why. But, he is a man of his word, and soon the mystery will be over."

And as she said this she embraced me. Her peace and maturity are far beyond a young woman not even eighteen yet. I am comforted by her embrace and encouraged by words Romulus spoke. I wonder when I will see him again. I am filled with questions.

"Sapphire, you met Pony last night."

"I KNOW! He is brilliant and sensitive, and…handsome!" Now she sounds like the teen I am used to. "We talked almost all night long," she says, biting her lip, her eyes smiling.

The door signals a customer and soon Elliott Kenadie enters.

"Hello Mr. Kenadie," I say as I feed the fire.

Sapphire excuses herself to join Pony.

"What brings you to Fireside Books? You are much too busy for reading."

"You are right, Ms. Clarke. I dropped in to talk with you about the Atchisons. May I have a few minutes of your time?" he asks.

His trench coat is not only damp, but soiled along the bottom edge. His hair is wet and his demeanor quite serious. His eyes are bloodshot. His takes his notebook out of his pocket. There is dirt under his nails.

"Ms. Clarke, when did you last see the Atchisons?"

"Why do you ask, Mr. Kenadie?"

He seems a little annoyed at my question, and pauses before responding.

"They are the front page news, Ms. Clarke. I am a reporter and I'm doing my job."

"The accident must have devastated them both. It might be kind to leave them at peace for a bit."

"Mr. and Mrs. Atchison are missing!" Elliott Kenadie walks to the window and glances out like he is looking for any sign of them. "Last seen two days ago, doing their grocery shopping. The neighbors saw them come home, but they missed a scheduled appointment. Their observant neighbor knocked on their door in the morning to check on them and they were gone."

"They do get around, perhaps went out of town."

"I don't think you are hearing me Miss Clarke. They are missing, I say. The car is still in the garage! The table is set. The television is on, but no sign of the Atchisons. Vanished!" he says, with drama in his voice.

"This is disturbing news. How can I help you?"

"My story will be running tomorrow, and I know the last unfortunate experience with the Atchisons involved you, Ms. Clarke. I am aware they visited Fireside Books and anything about them would make good additions to a human interest piece about them," Kenadie says.

"They seemed nice enough, happy to be retired. They liked to read and are interested in all kinds of topics."

"Ms. Clarke, what kind of periodicals did they purchase? And what subjects did they feature?" he inquires.

"Mr. Kenadie, I don't disclose my customer's preferences. Is there something else I can help you with?"

"Ms. Clarke, I am painting a picture, two of White Oak's good citizens. My story about them may spread awareness," he remarks.

"Perhaps your article will, Mr. Kenadie, but I have nothing to add."

"I am curious about the identity of the young woman with you a moment ago. She slipped out before I could ask her," he says, fishing for information. He peers at me through his spectacles sitting low on his nose.

"I will introduce you next time you are both in the same room." I show him the way to the door. He takes the hint and leaves. His presence is aggravating, and I feel it every time I am around the man. I am shocked by the news of the Atchisons and hope Keefe can fill me in. I slip next door to find a party going on.

Chapter Twenty-Nine

Laughter comes from the group at Mocha Joe's. Chamous, Pony and Sapphire are having coffee with Professor Enderlee and Keefe has just arrived.

"What's going on here, a party without me?" I ask.

"Chamous was telling us a funny story about Pony," Sapphire says laughing. "If I want to know more about him, Chamous is the one I'll ask."

Pony laughs too.

Chamous says, "Now if I want to keep my friendship with Pony I will keep my stories to myself."

"Good idea," Pony says, giving Chamous a friendly slug on the shoulder.

"I served a new recipe I've been working on: Chocolate Filled Croissants. Everyone likes them," the professor says with pride.

"Oh, my goodness Quinn, you have to try one, delicious!" Sapphire says.

Keefe adds, "Chamous is without a car, and Pony and Sapphire want to go to The Barn with him. I am going to give them a ride, and Chamous can bring Sapphire back over to the inn later today. The northern side of town is flooding. We issued a boil order. I suggest sticking to bottled water." Keefe's light hair and coat are saturated.

I still am moved by the compassion he showed me last evening. He loves me, or was it a dream?

"Quinn?" Keefe says.

"Oh, yes, sorry, I am distracted. Yes, good."

"Ok, let's get you three to The Barn," Keefe announces.

Sapphire holds Pony's hand.

Sapphire says, "Don't worry, Quinn, I am in good hands. Be back soon. I can't use my cell phone anymore, Keefe gave me another. I put your number in and will call you so you'll have mine," she says with a smile.

"Oh, ok." I am glad Sapphire is with us.

Professor Enderlee closes up shop for the evening.

So many thoughts run through my mind. I need more answers. I need to retain my focus, keep a schedule of some sort. I need some reality.

"Professor, may I come over for a few hours in the morning to work on my project?" I ask with a smile.

"Quinn, I think you need to table your project for the time being. Your home is lost, and our town is becoming a disaster zone. Perhaps in the summer you can pick it up again," he suggests.

"Nonsense, I will be over first thing in the morning. Keefe can give me a ride. I'll spend a few hours there before coming over to the bookstore."

"Well, ok. I will bring muffins home with me tonight and brew up your favorite joe." He seems happy about this news.

After closing up shop, Keefe comes back to pick me up, and we drive out to the Langford Inn. Some intersections are flooded, some properties look like ponds. Barricades stand on some streets. I receive a text from Sapphire. As soon as the number is saved I asked Keefe about the phone.

"You gave Sapphire a phone?"

"Yes, Romulus is distancing her from Royce Estate for now," he says.

"I want to ask you some questions about yesterday," I mention.

"Quinn, I will be spending the night on your sofa at the inn, so you can ask away," he replies.

"I assume you are my protector again tonight?"

"Yes."

A break in the clouds reveals the moon, and it casts a glow in the valley where the inn is situated. Trees still bare from winter's grasp reach their dark arms skyward. For a moment, all is still. Distant thunder signals more rain is on the way. The inn is drafty, so I put on a sweater while waiting for Keefe's fire to warm us. I open the bottle of wine Tera brought.

"Elliott Kenadie came into Fireside Books poking around for information on the Atchisons. I told him nothing," I explain.

"I keep wondering if their disappearance is connected to the accident on Main Street. My instinct tells me they may know more about Calista Twinning," Keefe says as his phone rings. The conversation sounds like flooding updates.

"Do you think the Atchisons are in danger?" I ask.

"Yes, I do. They are somehow involved with the River People. And we both realize what can happen after learning Jessie's fate. Their safety is a concern, mainly because of a disturbing ritual," Keefe explains.

"Not at liberty to speak about?"

"Heavens no, this bit of information will be in tomorrow's news. Tripp Atchison's notes about the ritual were found inside a book returned to the library. The librarian called the newspaper, not the police! The notations referred to magical methods to conceal oneself. A host must be chosen, a human or an animal with an open wound of some kind. By transforming into a snake or worm, protection or concealment is provided through entering the actual wound! It paints a disturbing picture."

"What in the world? The Atchisons collected information from books on all kinds of religions, but that is bizarre."

"Quinn, we found black robes in their home, the kind of hooded robe Pony described. As I told you before, this is not something new in White Oak. We get calls every few nights about groups of people gathered near the river in dark robes, never in the same place twice. We are getting closer to the figurehead," he reveals.

"I suppose you can't discuss it with me?" I ask with a knowing glance.

"I will very soon," he replies. "We had trouble at the school district office today. The computers locked up, shutting down the whole system. No way to communicate between staff, bus drivers, parents or the public. Bottled water was needed again. What a mess! We went to the office to help straighten things out." He scratches his head and continues, "Significant problems with the city's systems today, too. Staying connected is critical for employees, departments and citizens, with the public safety concerns lately."

"Rand was so passionate about a comprehensive communication system at the chamber meeting. He warned them a system is paramount in a major catastrophe," I tell Keefe.

"We are suffering the consequences of not being connected right now." Keefe stokes the fire and continues telling me about developments. "Madge Botherme came to the station with an impeachment petition for Mayor Welch. She also wants me dismissed as chief/investigator," Keefe says, laughing.

"You find it funny?"

"Believe me, I would like nothing better than to wash my hands of this position!" Keefe claims. He sits on the hearth of the fireplace, stretches his legs out, crossing them at the ankles. He takes a deep breath.

"I bared my soul to you last night Quinn, but I don't know how you feel about me."

He has no problem communicating this issue. I am more reserved with letting him know my feelings.

"Very little time has passed since I lost Alec, and more time can only help heal those wounds. I thought you didn't like me at all, and now you are professing you are in love with me. You don't even know me," I tell him.

"I love you. I usually avoid romantic relationships. I am guarded about who I spend time with. Your spirit is full of light, and you are beautiful, Quinn." He gives me a reassuring, captivating smile. His presence is alluring. But something holds me back. The magnitude of the pressing issues tells me to proceed with caution.

"I like you very much Keefe, but I barely know you. I need more time," I say as I take a sip of my wine.

"Seems fair," he says.

The sound of the rain on the roof is rhythmic and soothing.

"Are River People lurking everywhere? Some robed figures stood upstream watching as the downed tree was being cut…terrifying, but the thought occurred to me, I am with you and you are Guardian…why would I be afraid?"

"We are not invincible, Quinn. There is a plan, a grand scheme. We are not the orchestrators, we are servants. Some Guardians possess certain qualities which are utilized in different ways," he replies.

"Oh," I say. I think about this for a moment, and Cashton comes to mind, and of course, Sapphire, with her visions. "Do you have… qualities besides how you helped the lady in the police station, Keefe?"

"Just the ability to make women fall in love with me!" he teases. "You will learn soon enough, Quinn."

"I have no special gifts that will help me to serve as a Guardian," I announce.

"They will develop and intensify as part of the plan."

"I had a dream, a vision...something when I fell. I've never told anyone else. I came to a woman as I walked along a beach; she was... familiar somehow. She delivered a mysterious message... 'Sun will cease, we can't prepare...hearts are draining…sun, tender grass pushing through bitter soil, follow the way and be quenched.' Her words made no sense at all, like dreams are sometimes. But the woman's face, her kindness, her purity, it was profound." I tell Keefe.

"She could have saved your life," Keefe suggests.

I receive a text from Sapphire and Keefe leaves to pick her up.

"Be back in ten minutes," he says, moving hair from the side of my face and kissing my cheek.

"Please be careful in this weather," I tell him as he is leaving.

Loud cracks of lightning and thunder shake the whole inn. I start bath water and take the wine glasses into the kitchen and rinse them. Through the window I see the small creek that feeds into the lake is over its banks. It rushes, its width multiplied. Keefe needs to be alerted. I place the call, gather my robe and go into the bathroom and shut off the water. The connection does not go through, so I hit retry. I activate the speaker and set the phone down and prepare to bathe. The steam coats the mirror as I stand before it, pinning up my hair.

A man stands behind me!

Without thought, my scream rips through the air as he grabs both of my hands and binds them behind my back with something. I continue to scream for Keefe. He is hurting me. He pushes me to the ground and covers my mouth with tape. I thrash and kick but I am no match for him. Is Keefe hearing this? My screams are only muffled sounds through the tape. The wooden chair from the corner is yanked before me. He thrusts my bound hands over the chair back and forces me to kneel. He puts my bound hands on the seat of the chair as it faces him. He stands in front of me.

Again I am screaming, screaming, but nothing but muffled sounds result. He takes a long serrated knife and begins to saw back and forth on my finger! There is blood and I turn away, trying to knock the chair over, anything I can do. The pain is excruciating, searing through my whole body. He is taking a finger. I cannot watch, I feel lightheaded, everything is fuzzy. He moves away, drops something in the water. Instead of passing out from pain, I do the exact opposite, I become angry. I grasp the chair back and hurl it towards my attacker and while he struggles to avoid falling into the tub. I run out of the bathroom and down the stairs. He's not far behind. I bolt out into the violent wind and rain, and head to the forest. I hear sirens approaching. Gunshots narrowly missing, he's aiming to kill!

"Quinn, get down and stay down," Keefe yells out.

I drop to the ground.

Keefe shouts, "Stop or I'll shoot! Stop or I'll shoot!"

Gunshots echo, the discharge sends shock and terror through my body. The ground is wet and cold and for a moment I wonder if I am hit.

Keefe rushes to my side, "Quinn! Quinn, are you ok?" He looks at the blood and I see fear in his eyes.

"He cut off my finger!" I cry out and jerk away from Keefe. "He's coming."

Keefe grabs my arms forcefully, stopping my movement.

"Quinn, he's been shot, he can't come after you anymore. Calm down, your finger is bleeding, but has not been cut off." He wraps his large hand around my small hand and lifts me from the ground.

My attacker is surrounded by two officers. "Sir, he's trying to talk," one of the officers says.

Keefe says, "Remove the mask."

Dawn Bishop's face is unmasked. Her gun lies a few yards from her fallen body. A weak but defiant Bishop speaks.

"Keefe, I know you love me. Why are you letting her get in the way?" Dawn Bishop coughs and with her last breath she says, "She told me to do it! She is the one who knows! Quinn is in our way."

Those are the final words Dawn Bishop speaks. Her head falls limp and the officer uses his hands to close her eyes.

Tera was right. She wanted Keefe for herself. Another senseless death in White Oak.

Chapter Thirty

Keefe supports me as we walk through the relentless weather. After only a few steps he scoops me into his arms and carries me up to my room. Keefe makes sure Sapphire is delivered safely to the inn. As soon as she arrives and witnesses the commotion, she embraces me.

I am wet and cold, and Keefe suggests tea. Sapphire makes us some while we wait for paramedics to bandage my finger. I am shaken, and although the tea is soothing, I can't stop shaking.

"Who was Bishop referring to....she told me to do it, Quinn is in our way?" I ask.

Keefe takes a call and shares the news with me.

"Dawn Bishop has the mark. Inside of her bottom lip, the embedded beetle," Keefe says. "Someone so twisted working right under my nose!"

Keefe examines my hand. "It's bloody and sore." I reply.

"Quinn, Dawn Bishop pierced your finger with a long hat pin. She wanted you to think your finger was being cut off. She wanted to torture you, and she wanted you dead," he tells me.

I work up the courage to inspect my injury. An old fashioned hat pin with a black pearl is jammed all the way through the skin above the bone where a ring would rest! The sight makes me queasy. Paramedics take over.

I am given a local anesthetic and, after sterilizing the protruding sharp point, the pin is extracted (fancy word for yanked out.) I am bandaged and given something for pain. I am still shaking, from exposure and from terror. The tea does begin to soothe me and my body begins to calm down.

"Dawn was watching our moves. I think someone was influencing her to go to these extremes," I say.

"Dawn came over from Jefferson City about the same time I came to White Oak. Her behavior seemed to change last year. She wanted advancement and grew impatient, while our working relationship became more strained," Keefe replies.

"In her last words she said we. When we discover who that is, we may learn more about the River People," I say.

Sapphire is sleepy and I encourage her to go to bed. She leaves the room and I fall asleep leaning on Keefe and sleep like a baby.

*   *   *   *   *

The next morning starts early and in a mild state of disruption. Keefe is on the phone monitoring the weather and the flooding. The water is rising so fast on the Missouri and the smaller tributaries, that evacuation of the northern part of White Oak is underway. Power is out on the north side as well. Keefe tells us because White Oak lies among rolling hills and bluffs, flash flood warnings are issued.

I ask Keefe if he would take Sapphire and me to the professor's house. I need normal. My finger is not as sore as I predicted.

Upon our arrival Professor Enderlee throws the door wide open and greets us with his sunny disposition. Keefe is on a tight schedule, but he agrees to give me the time I need. He won't leave me or Sapphire without protection.

I am so pleased the professor kept the finished areas in tip-top shape. The refrigerator is still stocked, which lets me know he is eating well. Sapphire and I get right to work. She schedules the carpet and drapery cleaning to be done next week.

Keefe is swamped with phone calls, and clears out when he sees us coming to the study. Professor Enderlee is busy looking out his front window.

I gather all newspapers and magazines and put them in organized boxes in the basement. Then I file papers as Sapphire vacuums the sofa and chair. The room is soon orderly and beautiful.

"Quinn, come here," the professor says with concern. I join him to peer out the window.

He says, "The black smoke cloud covers the entire east side of White Oak!"

"My goodness, what is it?" I ask.

Keefe announces with urgency, "We have an emergency. Quinn and Sapphire, we need to leave. Professor Enderlee, remain indoors, it's the most secure place to be. This cloud may be toxic, so keep everything sealed up!" He shuffles us out the door to his car.

Looming above us, coming from the east side of White Oak, is a voluminous mass of darkness.

"What is that?" Sapphire asks as she peers out of her window.

We speed down the street to the station. I don't like leaving the professor. I am astonished at the flooding. Several streets are impassable. Citizens of White Oak are standing outside their homes looking up at the massive dark cloud. The smoke is thicker as we pass each street.

Sapphire shrieks, "People on the ground! Oh Lord!"

A man is lying in the grass. Another man is on his knees and coughing. A woman and a man run to his aid. The sounds of emergency vehicles are everywhere; it is complete pandemonium. The station is elevated with an empty lot behind it, but 50 yards away flood waters move like a roaring river. Keefe talks to county law enforcement on the phone. When the car stops he instructs us to cover our faces with our sleeves and run inside.

"Try to hold your breath," Keefe says.

The station is chaotic. The phones are ringing; officers are scurrying in and out.

The county sheriff arrives and Keefe advises him to seek all available resources for assistance. This is terrifying.

After his conversation with the sheriff, Keefe takes Sapphire and me down a corridor to the west end of the station to a board room with a kitchenette.

"The smoke we saw coming from the east side of White Oak is from the burning of the dead birds. There is toxicity from this burn. Citizens are reporting to emergency rooms. Curiosity about the growing black cloud is bringing them outdoors, not where they should be. Some parts of the town are without power, creating a tremendous communication problem. The schools should have been closed today. Please do not leave this room. Water is in the refrigerator. You will both be ok here, until we can find out what the hell is going on now. Chamous, Pony and Tera are on their way over." He gives a nod as his phone begins ringing and off he goes down the hall.

Sapphire and I stand looking at each other. We hear constant footsteps and the sounds of crisis. Phones are ringing, voices yelling commands, sirens sounding. The lights flicker on and off.

Chamous, Pony and Tera arrive to shelter with us. Pony embraces Sapphire.

"The professor shouldn't be alone," I say.

"Let's go get him," Pony suggests.

Chamous puts his hand up. "Hold it! It's not safe right now," he says.

"But Professor Enderlee is alone. He needs his friends," I plead.

"Keefe will be back and he'll be picked up," says Chamous.

"I will try to be patient," I say grudgingly.

Tera is talking on her phone. Pony and Sapphire are deep into a conversation. Chamous is on his laptop, trying to get information. This is my opportunity.

Chapter Thirty-One

I am going to the lady's room," I announce.

Tera gives me a quick wave and nod. I leave the room and shut the door. I must think clearly. I have to get to the professor. I enter a storage room across the hall, and turn on the light. At the end of the room is a garage door opening up to the back of the building. I leave a brick under the door to keep it from locking. I sneak around to the sidewalk out front. Traffic is jammed. Cars are parked slant wise in spots provided, but other cars are stopped right in front of the station. Most are shouting through their windows asking for instructions. I walk to the last parked car, and spot keys. Without hesitating I jump inside, turn the key and speed towards the professor's house. He doesn't answer the locked front door, so I move to the side and enter. My finger is throbbing now, but my determination is fierce.

"Professor, Professor Enderlee, we need to get you out of here, Professor!" I call as I run. A quick search of the first level reveals nothing; same with the top level. I run back outside and find his car in the garage. Muffled voices come from beyond his fence line.

I unlatch the gate, I am almost sucked right through the opening by a force so strong I barely can stay on my feet. The gate crashes shut and I am grabbed by a man in a black robe. I am forced to walk into the woods. Soon we come to a clearing. Professor Enderlee is bound to a tree, surrounded by four black robed figures. A large fire spits and sears flames high in the air. Heads of small animals and bloody fur bits are scattered about. One of the men holds a branding iron.

"What do you want?" I shout. "Let him go."

They laugh at my comment. The figure holding my arm grabs my hair and forces me over to the tree. They bring the branding iron close to the professor's chest.

"Please, leave him alone!"

One man rips the professor's shirt, exposing his chest.

"Brand right over the heart!" another shouts.

"Stop, stop!" I scream.

And then I feel power, a capability I've never known. I feel electrified from the inside out. Everything happens in slow motion. The robed figure dips the branding iron in a pool of blood made from the sacrificed animals and holds it over the fire. My injured finger throbs, and my chest burns under the amulet. The protective amulet, my lifelong object of security, burns fire hot against my skin. I reach my free hand to touch it, when the shiny smooth stone back comes loose and it falls away revealing a hidden backside. A circular sun symbol glows and bursts brilliantly from the amulet. The energy from the piece is so radiant I have to look away. The beam from it reaches to a tree, exploding a branch on contact. The laser touches the ground and cuts through it like butter, sending twigs, grass and dirt flying in all directions. I aim it towards the branches of the tree the professor is tied to. A massive limb falls right onto the group, knocking two of the figures down. My aggressor is thrown 15 feet into the air when the destructive force hits him.

Amazed and stunned, I can't believe what I am seeing. A large clap of thunder and crash of lightening ignite the sky as I point my amulet towards the figure with the branding iron. The scorching beam reaches him and the branding iron is hurled deep into the forest. The last figure darts from behind a tree and knocks me down. He pulls a knife, but I fiercely thrust my foot into his chest sending him off me. I send a cascade of fury from the amulet, hitting him dead center in the chest and sending him crashing into a tree.

I use the knife he dropped to cut the professor loose and support him as we rush to the car. I drive to the station and help the professor down to the garage door in the back. I open the door, and shut it behind me. We enter the board room.

"I am sorry friends, he was in danger. The River People were going to hurt him. He is safe, and I am too," I say. I find a first aid kit, and we make sure the professor is ok.

The stunned professor asks me, "Quinn, how....what?"

I put my finger up to my lips. I am not even sure what happened, but I am unafraid. I am ready.

Keefe arrives back at the station in about thirty minutes. "The smoke from the bird kill is toxic, we can't stay."

He leads us out of the board room. The place is packed with people. Amidst the chaos, a group appears from the front double doors, approaching Keefe with a rhythmic gate. They are dressed in professional attire. Two men wear tailored dark suits. One man wears the robes of priesthood. A woman with them is elegant in a black and white knit suit, her black shiny hair in a French twist.

Sapphire jumps up, "Father!" and rushes to his arms. He embraces her and twirls her around. With Romulus Royce are Cashton Royce and a woman I recognize as Dr. Eudora Brazil. The fourth person is a Roman Catholic priest who shakes hands with Keefe.

Sapphire embraces her brother and Dr. Brazil."Father, what are you doing here?" she asks.

Romulus turns to Keefe and asks if we can talk in his office. "Of course sir, follow me," Keefe says, as he leads us to his office.

As we make our way, Romulus puts his hand upon my shoulder. "How are you, Quinn?" he asks.

"I am fine Mr. Royce, I am fine."

Once we are in the office and the door is shut, Romulus says, "I think we all understand why we are here. We are carrying out an important mission requiring your help. The time is now to restore light to the region of Nadellawick. Time is of the essence. We need reinforcement. We must unite now, so we will gain strength in our numbers. When we are one, the fire is powerful and perpetual. When separated from the rest, we are like a glowing ember fading and dying in isolation. Our commission beckons and your protection is of paramount importance."

No one asks any questions. Every person in our group, Keefe and I, Tera and Chamous, Pony and Sapphire and Professor Enderlee want to follow what we recognize is some kind of nobility and what we all understand as hope.

Romulus offers his arm to Sapphire and continues walking to the back of the room. He stands in front of the group and raises his arm. The back of the room no longer is a floor, ceiling and walls, but a towering mountain top. Romulus escorts Sapphire to the edge. Dark churning skies send gusts that whip their hair and clothing. They step in unity away from the security of the ledge, their bodies transforming into majestic white doves as their walk becomes flight. Soaring through the dark, tumultuous clouds, they are joined in the same way by Cashton, who grasps Tera's hand, Father Mopsi, who takes Pony's hand, and Dr. Brazil who holds Chamous's hand. Keefe takes my hand and Professor Enderlee's hand as he leads us to the peak, and as the wind hits my face I am soaring along with them. Soon we all are experiencing flight, soaring like many of us only dream of. As we force our magnificent wings downward we soar ever higher under the heavens.

Chapter Thirty-Two

We come to rest upon a stone ledge at the threshold of the Madowent, and our bodies become as they were. We gather to the front of the room where Romulus addresses the whole group.

"Welcome, my name is Romulus Royce. I am Polaris to the Circle of Sun, selected to lead the crusade in destroying the darkness in our region called Nadellawick. Without interference, the evil will destroy our society. In every pocket of the world these influences corrupt even the best of men. In villages, towns, cities and states, one can find the erosion of character and the epic loss of hope. These despicable entities masquerade as your neighbors, friends and even family. We call our crusade the Circle of Sun. In the heavenly realm sit the seven archangels, and each protects an orb of light called a Fidesorb. The Fidesorbs represent purity, goodness, hope and peace."

Romulus continues, "After the Great War waged in the heavens, the banished dark angels stole four of the seven orbs. These Fidesorbs, in the hands of the darkness, can mean the end to our world. These fallen angels will forever be the enemy of light. Evil must be destroyed in each of our regions. We are the keepers and protectors of Nadellawick. One of the Fidesorbs is in our midst, and with your help we want to recover it, and destroy the black root spreading itself over all Nadellawick. The evil ones wear the mark in secrecy, as cowards would.

"A threshold separates truth and deceit within each soul. The deep erosion in our society began with the smallest of choices, and compounded over time into a tidal wave of confusion, doubt, fear, suspicion, denial and hate. The human experience is made up of millions of choices, some insignificant, some more critical, but all with the same principle. Our choices over time define who we are. We cannot stagnate in indecision, because this, in itself, becomes a decision. An undecided soul forms delicate cracks, providing discouragement a place to flourish."

Romulus looks over those gathered and he smiles and nods to us all. "Those in this room are called upon to expose and destroy the black root and liberate souls. A gathering of many here at the Royce Estate tomorrow evening gives us the opportunity to finish what was started many years ago, and return hope and peace to people destroyed. You are needed. We cannot make the capable willing; we can only take the willing and make them capable. Just as your soul took flight upon the wings of faith, so too will your heart find the way."

"You will need all of your energy, so I am asking you to rest and refresh yourselves at the Royce Estate until the time for the event. This will be one of my final commissions, as the new Polaris takes the reins of leadership soon. I anticipate celebrating victories from groundwork laid for many years leading up to midnight tomorrow night, and it shall be fitting to finish my service as we herald in a new era of hope for the souls of Nadellawick."

Romulus's address is complete, and he walks through the gathering, grasping hands with some, nodding in appreciation to others. His entire presence shows gratitude, although no words are spoken. When he reaches out his hand to me, he uses both of his to grasp mine. His warmth and generosity show in his kind eyes. He next embraces Sapphire, and when he releases her, she smiles with pride, her eyes wet. He turns and walks out of the Madowent.

We are ushered out of the Madowent back down the stone corridor leading out to the waterfall. My amulet is missing, I make my way back, but it's nowhere to be found. I give up my search, not even knowing when I last felt it around my throat. We emerge upon the estate grounds and are led inside to the north wing. Tera and I are shown to a room to share and Pony, Professor, Keefe and Chamous another. Sapphire goes to her own room.

Tera draws a bath. I knock on the door.

"I am fine Quinn," she says above the running water. "I need some time. Go on and get some sleep, and we will talk in the morning."

"Sure, no problem. Good night," I reply.

She needs some time to process this altered reality. I pour a glass of wine and gaze out the window at the handful of groundskeepers preparing the estate for the Symphony benefit. Night is falling and the horizon is filled with white birds making their way to Royce Estate.

I miss the familiar weight of the amulet and the security it provides. Perhaps I don't need it anymore. I will look back on this day and how the world I once knew is forever changed. These supernatural occurrences, the existence of Guardians, my role in this battle, all are new but strangely familiar. My sense of reality is adjusting to accommodate the magnificent and unbelievable possibilities. I wonder if the others feel the same as I.

I am most concerned with the professor, and send Keefe a text.

His reply text reads, "Professor tells me he is mystified, a bit tired, but hopeful. He is ok. Thinking of you, good night."

My finger throbs and aches. My thoughts turn to White Oak. What will be left of our little town?

The next morning Tera and I have our first talk over coffee, knowing our lives will never be the same.

"I am proud to do this," I say with conviction.

She looks over her cup at me.

"I am looking inside, and taking stock. After last night, I am not sure how we can stop the darkness, or if I am strong enough to," she says with a sigh.

"Tera, Romulus explained we are capable. You won't be able to figure this one out. I am scared too, but I can't doubt, after all I've been shown."

"It is the faith in myself that is lacking. I want to do what I can to help. I want to be a part of it," she says with certainty.

Chamous and Keefe stop over before going with Romulus to double check the new route for guests, since the bridge is out. Keefe comes over to me and takes my hand.

"How are you today?" he asks.

"I am thinking a lot about tonight. I am ready to make a difference, whatever this means," I say with a nervous laugh.

"The town is receiving assistance from the state...water is receding some. White Oak is still in chaos. I will return to the estate later. My Lord, Quinn, your finger needs to be seen by a doctor!"

He is right. The finger is very swollen and red.

With Keefe and Chamous on their way, we join Sapphire in her room. She is with Pony, talking intently.

Tera and I will need formal attire for this evening. The Royces have plenty to choose from. We are fitted for gowns in Sapphire's room. I will wear a vintage sleeveless pearl and rhinestone-studded lace gown of silk chiffon with angel wing shoulder panels. The panels are floor length and create a subtle but sheer off-the-shoulder cape effect. The dress is unique, almost regal. I stand looking at my reflection for several minutes, the experience dreamlike.

Tera chooses a pearlescent pink silk halter dress with matching bolero. The dress is backless with pin tuck detailing on the front above the high waist seam. The gowns are chosen and will be placed in our rooms for dressing later. Jexis is occupied with last minute details, and we do not see her.

Sapphire tells us her mother is not around. Romulus explained to Petulah their marriage has suffered and cannot be repaired. For now, Petulah is out of the country for a few days. Sapphire explains this development takes some of the stress out of the day and evening, especially for Jexis, who is more than relieved.

When Dr. Brazil arrives I explain the new injury to the finger she has treated before. The small entrance and exit wounds do not seem to be what is making the finger worse.

"This finger has been a problem," I say.

"I will check it again tomorrow. If this topical treatment doesn't provide some improvement, I will put you on an antibiotic then," she says comfortingly.

The weather is glorious. I can't remember a day like this for so long. Spring has burst out, weary of waiting, showing tender grasses and tiny budding leaves added to yellow daffodils and tulips in pink and red.

The grounds of the estate are manicured and elegant. This weather fills me with hope, but also with anticipation for what the night holds. I feel a strength previously unknown to me.

Hors d'oeuvres will be served this evening in the rose garden, and Jexis is busy giving instructions as Tera and I arrive to see the makeover to the garden. The roses are not in bloom, but that didn't stop Jexis from having a truckload of white roses delivered to decorate with. Beautiful potted rose bushes line the entire garden wall surrounding the rose garden. The scene is breathtaking. A gentle breeze carries the soft fragrance of roses. Tables covered in white linen, and mother of pearl vases laden with dozens of white roses create an elegant finishing touch. It seems light years away from the darkness and destruction of the last few days.

Chamous and Keefe return from securing the alternate route from White Oak and after a quick visit to the station. Beef suggests we enjoy a late lunch before we begin to prepare for the Symphony benefit. Everyone gathers in the dining room, but I excuse myself. I crave solitude. Keefe follows me into the hall and calls out to me.

"Quinn, wait, are you alright?" he asks.

"Yes, I am not hungry. Go back and get some lunch," I say, encouraging him with a forced smile.

"Quinn, let me come with you and talk through things. I want to be there for you," Keefe says as he kisses my forehead. Please don't shut me out. Quinn, I love you." He grasps both of my hands. His sincerity and honesty are apparent in those beautiful eyes of his. I know he cares for me. I feel the strength in his grasp and the security his love gives me. He leans down and kisses me passionately.

The intensity of these feelings, on top of everything weighing on my heart, is too much. I pull away.

"Keefe, I am sorry, I need a little more time. Please understand. I am relying on my faith to sustain me. There is something about my past and a connection to this family. I am unsettled about this. I will explain all of it to you when tonight is behind us. My questions about the Royce family will all be answered, and my life may change again. I can't fall in love with you right now," I say as I turn and walk away.

Keefe stands alone and calls out to me, "You already are."

Chapter Thirty-Three

My walk takes me to the solarium. I move the boxes and rug, and open the floor hatch to make my way to the tower room. My cell phone lights the way. I twist and turn and wonder if perhaps I am lost, but finally arrive at the rickety staircase. I grasp the railing and pull myself up.

I follow the small tunnel-like corridor as it shrinks in space, until I can go no further. I lean my left shoulder into the wall, swinging a portion open so I can duck and enter the tower room. The room is filled with light, unlike the other times when the skies were gloomy and the room was dim. Today the space is stunning, as the sun beams through the windows, bringing it to life. My interest is in the family photos and papers, but the shelves once heaped full of potential answers to my questions are cleaned out. I open a remaining leather binder, with images of young Cashton, Jexis and Sapphire. I turn the page and every subsequent page is empty. I take the only other book, and it is the same thing. I won't be discovering anything today from this room.

I sit down on the small sofa and sigh. My thoughts turn again to the unknown. How will the evil be exposed? Romulus warned us anyone is suspect. What will happen afterwards? Will the guests at the benefit suspect anything? My eyelids are heavy and sleep takes over.

I am again walking on the shoreline. Unlike before, a large full moon paints a glistening shimmer on the surface of the sea, all the way to forever. The mist makes my skin moist. I am floating along, feet skimming the sand. My painful finger reminds me I cannot stay in this most serene setting. I see her again. It's the woman, her face, her hair and her clothes are drenched, unlike before, but her beauty is no less. She approaches me; I am not afraid. Her eyes stare aimlessly, it seems. Once her eyes meet mine, she comes alive, she beams. The woman lifts her hand from her side to touch my face; water drips from her silvery gown. She says nothing.

"Who are you?" I try to say, but I can make no sounds.

The beautiful lady takes something from her neck and places it around mine. She smiles as she fades backwards until she is only a speck on the horizon.

My finger aches. Two bees are stinging me. I swat them away but they are relentless in their pursuit. I begin to run and soon, swarms of bees attack, covering my entire body. I fall into ocean water, escaping the swarm. My finger burns and blood begins to flow, my hands and arms are saturated in crimson blood.

"Quinn!" Cashton says, and comes to my aid. He cups water to rinse my wound, then covers my hand in his. Radiant and soothing warmth flow through his hands, and the pain goes away. Cashton smiles with confidence and I am absorbed by his charm. He leans in to kiss me and I raise my lips to meet his.

Loud, shrill laughter prevents our touch. Coming across the sea towards us, a figure glides over the silver water. It is Petulah. Her dark robes glow in the moonlight. Two snakes around her waist snap their jaws at one another.

"Quinn and Cashton, this is a seductive setting! You belong as one, and of course you will be," she says.

"Leave, Mother!" Cashton says.

Petulah says, "Do not deny yourselves any longer. Before the sun rises passion will rule the night."

She sinks into the water, the snake uncoils from around her waist and slithers on the water's surface towards us, ugly eyes glaring with hate. The serpent lunges at my face, jaws open wide, and I am startled awake.

My finger is throbbing again, and the beauty and joy of seeing the woman is overshadowed by Petulah and her reptile. The dream is upsetting and I go into the bathroom to splash some water on my face. Around my neck lies my amulet. The beautiful woman from the shoreline placed it there. Who is she? This is real. The amulet feels warm, and I feel refreshed.

I go down the staircase, my thoughts turning to Petulah. Is she part of the black root Romulus refers to? But how is it possible, right in Romulus's home? How will Sapphire and her siblings react to this revelation? Or, perhaps it will be no surprise to them. After placing the rug back over the trap door and arranging the boxes I walk to the north wing and prepare for the evening.

A peaceful calm comes over me, a hopeful disposition. Petulah's attempts to intimidate me only strengthen my conviction of defiance. I reach my room, as stunning Tera is leaving. She encourages me to hurry so we can mingle in the rose garden as the guests arrive.

Four ladies approach my door. "Quinn, we are to attend to you," one says.

"Excuse me, attend?" I reply, confused.

"Yes, Ms. Clarke, the night is special. Let us begin, our time is wasting."

I am escorted to the bathroom and one of the young women tends to my hair, another to my complexion, while another works on my hands.

"I don't wear too much makeup," I mention. They don't even respond. After about 45 minutes they help me into my gown and scurry out.

My reflection causes me pause. I am different and I feel beautiful. I fill my evening bag with the essentials. I include the picture of me from the tower room, taking it everywhere and hoping to ask Romulus about it. I say hello to Beef, who calls orders to servants as I pass him in the corridor.

He stops in his tracks and says, "Ms. Clarke, you are extraordinary! I must say, regal!"

"Thank you for your kind compliment," I say.

Guests drink champagne and mingle. The garden is beautiful at dusk. The sun still offers a sliver of golden light before dipping into tomorrow.

Sapphire is elegant and Pony is dashing in a tuxedo.

"Quinn, my goodness, you are stunning!" Sapphire says.

Pony is motionless with wide eyes, and seems a little taken aback by my appearance. Seeming somewhat unsure of what to do next, he gives me a 'thumbs up' sign, as Sapphire embraces me.

"You both look wonderful," I tell them. They are smiling, but seem stiff. "Are you alright?"

Sapphire glances to Pony and he responds. "We are anxious."

"And nervous," Sapphire adds. "What are we to expect?"

"Faith is our shield now," I say with conviction.

Champagne is offered and I accept, as do Pony and Sapphire. The rose garden is breathtaking, and I excuse myself for a walk, taking in the scent of beauty.

Constance Asher from the chamber in White Oak approaches me.

"Hello Quinn, what a beautiful evening this is. You could pass for a princess tonight."

"Thank you Constance, I can say the same for you. How is Operation Reach Out coming along from the health field perspective?"

"Making progress, if Madge would stop interfering and leave me alone to carry out my objectives." Constance is interrupted by Edith Craven.

"Hello ladies, you are both looking stunning this evening. I'm not finding the special seating for my seniors," she says, while giving hand signals to the group waiting for her word.

"Yes, the tables are all reserved. Did you stop at the registration table?" I ask.

"I missed it, what a ninny! Thank you Quinn." She scurries off to tend to a wandering portion of her group.

Constance and I approach Blanche Treadwater from the chamber who is visiting with Mr. Edison, my landlord.

"Good evening," Constance says to Blanche with a smile.

"Hello Constance and Quinn. I am trying to convince Mr. Edison to donate his space on the other side of the corner bakery to our garden club, but he is being a real stinker!" she says, tipping her head back and letting out a hearty laugh.

"Come on Mr. Edison, let's get you champagne," Constance says, leading him away.

"Goodbye Quinn," he calls.

Blanche floats over to an acquaintance and I am left to view the grounds. How peaceful the night air is. I am tapped on the shoulder and turn to see Carolynn and Adam Langford with champagne in hand.

"Good evening, Quinn," Carolynn says with a smile.

Adam nods, letting Carolynn do the talking.

"You two make a handsome couple," I tell them.

"You are so kind," Carolynn says. "Oh, goodness Quinn, something's on your face. Here let me help you." She rubs a spot a couple of times and she laughs and says, "What have you gotten into?"

"Oh, I didn't realize," I say, taking a mirror out of my evening bag to check myself, but see nothing. I brush both of my shoulders.

Adam says, "Carolynn, it's Leslie, let's say hello. Excuse us Quinn."

I return to the peaceful scene but moving branches in the wind give me pause. Is something out there? I turn to find Keefe waiting.

Chapter Thirty-Four

Keefe is sophisticated and handsome in his tuxedo. His blonde hair moves in the gentle breeze and he runs his fingers through it. He approaches me and touches my cheek with the back of his hand.

"Quinn, you are radiant. You take my breath away." Keefe's comment makes me blush.

"I wonder how I appeared before," I say with a laugh.

"Not at all, Quinn, but something is different about you tonight; a presence and a confidence."

"Well, thank you, you look nice too," I reply.

"How is your finger?" he asks.

"It still is hurting."

He raises my hand to his lips.

I smile at him and he offers his arm in escort to our table. I make a stop in the powder room, and Keefe goes on ahead to find our table. I walk down the corridor where Sapphire and Jexis's suites are located. Jexis's door is open and she is running around panicked.

"I can't find my shoes! Damn, I thought my ensemble would be laid out for tonight," she says.

"Can I help you?" I ask her.

Jexis stops everything for a moment, then puts her hands on my shoulders and leans to my ear.

"The circle is mine to break," she says.

"Excuse me?" Her mysterious words make no sense at all, and she ignores my question.

"Can you help me find my damn sherbet shoes? Oh, here is one." She stoops to pick one of the shoes up near a chair by the fireplace. "I am going to slip on my dress. Please keep looking for the shoe. If I can't find the shoe, the whole outfit will have to go!" Jexis is dramatic.

I hunt under the sofa and under a scattering of magazines on the massive coffee table. I am ready to give up when I see the shoe on her patio.

Without warning a shrill sound cuts through the room. I stash the shoe under my arm, and cover my ears. Jexis waves her arms in an effort to clear the air of her cigarette smoke that has tripped the alarm.

Beef begins calling for her from outside her door. Jexis turns to me and says, "Would you be a love and go answer the stupid door?" She attempts to put her cigarette out in the sink. The smoke is billowing and she continues waving her hands, trying to clear the smoke.

I go to the door.

"Is everything ok?" Beef asks.

"She lost her shoe," I say.

"Yes, a regular Cinderella," Beef replies with slight annoyance. "Would you please give her this wine? I will tend to the alarm."

Jexis pours herself a large glass of white wine and drinks half of it in one gulp. She winks at me as she dabs her mouth with a hand towel.

"I better get going, Keefe is waiting at our table," I tell her, shouting over the alarm.

"Wait, do you know anything about fire alarms?" she asks, straight-faced.

"I'm afraid I don't."

"No bother," Jexis says and she aims the pretty sherbet shoe at the alarm and pelts it through the air, knocking the whole thing down and ending the shrill. She scoops the alarm up and marches to the French doors and tosses it out. She takes a long, big drink of her wine, and lights up another cigarette.

"Quinn, your appearance tonight will steal the show. Smashing dress!"

"Thanks, Jexis." I am assuming Jexis will be late, and when she does arrive I am not sure what shape she will be in.

The ballroom is as grand as the name implies. Round tables are all glowing from the light of opulent candelabras gracing each table. The white linen tablecloths hold place settings of fine china, silver, and crystal stemware. Chamous and Tera are seated, elegant in their formal wear, but there is no sign yet of Carolyn and Adam Langford. Chamous and Tera are at our table, and two empty spots, Rand Jolliet and Cindy Arness. At another round of tables, Professor Enderlee sits with Sapphire and Pony. At the table to our left is Madge Botherme. Elliott Kenadie snaps pictures.

Keefe takes his seat while I stop by the next table to give Professor Enderlee a hug.

"Quinn, my dear, you are always beautiful, but you are radiant this night. What is different?" The professor grasps both of my hands and raises them up, showcasing my presence.

"You are more than kind my friend! Only a lovely gown and some professional image work. I am getting quite a few reactions, so perhaps I need to embrace change," I say, as I smile at this man who is so close to my heart. His spirit is so pure and gentle. He embarrasses me by trying to get a picture with his phone.

Tera hops up and offers to take the photo, so he can join with me. Tera snaps a couple of pictures and we take our seats.

Seated at Elliott Kenadie's table is Madge Botherme, engaged in a lively conversation. In the spirit of community and good manners, I meander over to their table to say a polite hello. Immediately I regret the decision.

Madge stands, her Operation Reach Out frog button displayed on her evening wear, and says, "Ms. Clarke, your new image is a reincarnation!" All eyes at their table are on me.

"Thank you, Madge!" I say with a kind smile.

Tera pokes me.

"I wanted to show you your photo." She leads me to the back of the room. I am puzzled at the secrecy surrounding her request.

She shows me the photograph on her phone. "Professor Enderlee is quite dashing. Send it to me, I will cherish it."

"No Quinn, study the photo," Tera insists.

I gasp. In the background of the photo, next to a massive ice sculpture, is Calista Twinning. Red ruby hair, green eyeglasses, orange bag . . .everything as she appeared at Fireside Books. We scour the crowd for her.

"Where is she?" I ask Tera

"No sign of her!"

"Where is the sculpture?" Tera asks, looking everywhere.

"There are no ice sculptures, she is here! Calista Twinning is seeing this thing through to the end."

In front of the ballroom, the symphony is stage left, a podium stands in the center, and on the right the Symphony board members are seated. Waiters with small linen towels over their arms carry trays of champagne-filled glasses, offering a delicious vintage to patrons of the benefit.

Keefe is attentive as he pulls my chair out.

As the lights are dimmed, Jexis makes her way to the podium and you would never guess twenty minutes ago she was not dressed, chugging white wine and smoking like a chimney. Only poised grandeur remains.

"Ladies and gentlemen, welcome to Royce Estate." Jexis is in control and comes across with sophistication and flare. After a hearty round of applause she continues, "Thank you for attending our annual Black Tie Dinner and Concert event, the major fundraiser benefitting our year-long education programs and providing opportunities for young musicians. To find out more about our extensive projects, please visit our website listed on your program. Without further delay give a warm reception for the Music Director of the Kansas City Symphony, Dane Kerrigan."

"Thank you Ms. Royce. Welcome to our spring concert and benefit. Thank you for your patronage. Allow me to introduce talented artists, soprano Mariah Jones and violinist, Herschel Montgomery. For our first number, please enjoy Mendelssohn's "'Calm Sea and Prosperous Voyage.'"

The crowd gives enthusiastic applause. The lights are dimmed. The music fills the night with splendor.

I sip my champagne and wonder how an evening this beautiful can end. I don't wait long before the calm seas form waves, and when two waiters come to our table. One leans down and whispers in my ear.

"Romulus Royce would like a few words with you." The waiter lifts my arm to escort me. Keefe is concerned. I motion for him to stay put.

"I'll be right back."

Chapter Thirty-Five

I am escorted to the billiard room where Romulus is waiting. The two waiters close the door on their way out, leaving us alone. Romulus sits next to me and begins to explain, his sincere eyes looking into mine.

"This is the first time this event is hosted in our home. In the years past the location was in the city. Tonight is very special. Quinn, I am sorry to take you away from the evening, but this is important," he says. "Although raising money for the Symphony's education programs is valuable in its own right, a far bigger reason exists.

"When the Circle of Sun first began working to win back Nadellawick, we needed a gathering bringing out as many citizens of our region as possible. A mock event would be the only way to gather on a large scale with the general public. We knew Guardians would of course attend, but without knowing who our enemies are, a function would bring out most interested parties. The dark angels would never miss a gathering of this size for fear the undecided souls would join the light."

He continues, "You will discover later, these artists of destruction attempt to put roots in every heart without mercy. Through the years we've utilized this function to make our public pleas. Our first year in Nadellawick, I was named as president and board chair for the Symphony. What it meant to those who have ears, is I was being announced as Polaris of the Circle of Sun. This event is our public platform, to display our unity. Our gathering may not reveal our enemies, but finds our allies. This event has been a critical tool. After many years of painstaking work, the worst offenders of light are being isolated, and many are gathered in the next room."

Romulus rises and moves to a balcony overlooking the estate. He gazes for a few moments over the dark forest. He steps back inside.

"Tonight, with God's grace, we will expose them and in the power of His name, even destroy them. I was to relinquish my role as Polaris as a new successor will be named under the guise of President and Board Chair of the Symphony."

Romulus is conflicted. He lifts his glass and drinks some wine and takes a deep breath.

"Many years ago, I was told my first born daughter Jexis would be my successor." Romulus sits across from me and continues. "She does not possess skills required to lead as Polaris. She is immature and her loyalty is unclear. I love her but in my heart I believe Sapphire is more suited for any role of leadership."

Romulus is transformed by these few statements. The concern and doubt show in his eyes, as well as in the rounding of his shoulders. He moves to the fireplace and puts his foot up on the mantle, leaning on his knee. He stares at me with pain in his eyes.

"I doubt the plan for the first time in my life. For this I am ashamed and do not understand how we can put our future in Jexis's hands. It is absurd, and feels… orchestrated. Tonight I will open the envelope from the senate, and announce she is our new President and Board Chair. The public will applaud. Those who have ears will recognize the new Polaris of the Circle of Sun is being announced. The darkness awaits the announcement to mark the next target of destruction, and to know who the leader of their enemy is. Some will be oblivious to what is taking place. I had hoped this would give the needed public display of power and strength to our cause, and be the catalyst to rid our region of these evils. With the announcement of Jexis as the next Polaris, I am afraid the upper hand will now go to the dark side. This was to be our night, but their position will even be stronger than before. This is why I asked you to talk with me."

Romulus seats himself next to me. He places his hand upon mine, and says, "I must accept a dark enemy infiltrated my family. It's been devastating to find Petulah's betrayal. After I lost my first wife, Petulah brightened my world, and became my wife. I was deceived… believing she loved me. She is the mother of my children, but she is a traitor. She knows everything about the Circle of Sun, about me, and our mission. She has sold out to the dark angels, and damaged our progress and weakened the strength of Nadellawick. I can never forgive her."

I am dumbfounded by this news. The callousness of this treason must be a heavy burden.

Romulus continues, "My doubts about Jexis overwhelm me with

discouragement. I suspect our enemy infiltrated our strongholds, and found a way to manipulate the process in the appointment of the next Polaris. Anything less than a solid leader could mean disaster. I am sure they would love Jexis at the helm. She would be influenced. This is only speculation at this point, but it would make sense out of this confusing selection of Jexis to Polaris. What other explanation is there? I am petitioning to remain Polaris until we can discover where this breach occurred. We will find out who the real successor is. In the meantime, I will be grooming a young Sapphire for this honor. She needs mentorship and support. Jexis cannot do this for her. She requires a role model who is strong and positive. Quinn, would you do this for me? Together perhaps we can prepare her for this important position. With me serving as Polaris a bit longer it may give us the time we need. I am not sure if this is the right thing to do, but it is the only way. By doing this I will be able to preserve Nadellawick," Romulus says. His sincerity and his passion are evident

"Of course I will assist you in any way I can. This must be the connection I feel. I am honored you would ask me," I say.

I finally get answers. I will be part of this important transition. I am a servant to the Polaris.

Romulus continues, "When I open the envelope tonight and see Jexis's name, I will announce my petition to remain at the helm for an interim period of two years. No one in this realm will suspect her name was in the envelope. It is all I can do to save our cause," he says. "I will explain what mentorship means, and we can discuss details, but for now we need to get back to the concert." Romulus offers his arm and escorts me back to my table.

The music is coming to a close; most of the time was spent with Romulus. Before the final number, Jexis comes to the podium with what appears to be an addition to the program.

"Ladies and gentlemen, as we enjoy the last number from the symphony, I would like to present a tribute to my father Romulus, our president and chair of the Symphony for many years. This year he will be stepping down and a new successor will continue this strong tradition. Please draw your attention to the screen as you enjoy our last number. Thank you all and thank you, Romulus Royce."

The music touches the heart. The screen depicts a picture of a young Romulus Royce, his first horse, and school chums. The crowd applauds at the image of him on a horse. As he grows older it shows him with a beautiful young woman.

I recognize her! She is the woman from my dream! She is the woman along the silver shoreline!

"Quinn, that's you!" Keefe remarks.

All Guardians stand and begin to applaud and I am not sure why. Tera and Chamous, Keefe and I do the same.

The next picture in the presentation is the same one I carry in my evening bag. Me upon the screen for the whole audience to see. What is this?

There is a wedding photo and this prompts even more applause as the music elevates in intensity.

I am trying to figure out what is happening. The next photo is a family shot: Romulus, the woman and a baby, and this brings cheers from many in the audience as well.

Romulus stares at the screen, tears on his face, moved with emotion. I search Keefe's face.

"That's you, it's you!" he says.

I am so confused.

The number is over and Romulus takes the podium and thanks Jexis.

Everyone stands in applause and Keefe slips over to the refreshment table to get me a glass of water.

"Thank you beautiful daughter Jexis for the wonderful tribute."

The audience remains standing as Romulus continues, "It is touching to be reminded of the love in the eyes of my first wife, who was swept away by flood waters, along with our precious baby girl, many years ago. I have not spoken about them for too long, but perhaps... Jexis thought it's something we can do now." And he smiles her way.

I am beginning to understand. The woman on the screen in front of the whole ballroom is the same woman from my dream. The beautiful woman walking along the seashore, in my dreams, is my mother. Am I the child they believed drowned? How did I survive? Why do they not know she is my mother? She is my mother! My heart beats and my mind is racing. My amulet is so warm and weighs heavy. I must raise it from my skin. And touching it, I understand. This amulet saved me. My mother put it on me, just like she did in my dream. This is how I survived the flood waters. Before my young mother perished, she took the amulet from her neck and she placed it on me, so I could survive! What this means makes me lightheaded. Can this be possible? The amulet I wear on this night provided protection my whole life. The picture of the woman in my evening bag, who I thought was me, is my MOTHER! Romulus is my father! My Lord, Romulus is my father!

Romulus speaks, "I would like to announce the successor to the board chair and president of the Symphony." He opens the envelope and pulls out the contents. He raises his hand to his mouth as if to conceal his shock and pauses. He looks at Jexis, he searches around the room, until he finds me. He says with conviction, "The next to lead the symphony into the future is my first born daughter... Quinn Clarke!"

And with those words, my knees become weak. I search for Keefe, and from where he stands, he recognizes I'm in trouble. He races to my side and is able to catch me before I fall to the floor.

Chapter Thirty-Six

Everything is fuzzy as I regain my disposition. I am no longer in the ballroom. Keefe and Dr. Brazil are by my side to my left, and to my right is Romulus Royce, my father. His face is filled with love, and his eyes shiny with emotion.

He embraces me, for what seems like a long time. His embrace feels like heaven.

"You look so much like your mother, and when I caught a glimpse of the amulet while playing Quoits, I needed answers. Quinn, my precious daughter, please tell me you are alright," he says, as he glances to Dr. Brazil for reassurance.

"Yes, I think so," I say weakly.

Keefe and my father help me to a sitting position on the sofa. Dr. Brazil offers me some water and asks the men to move aside as she flashes her light into my eyes and does a quick evaluation.

"You are fine Ms. Clarke. Stressful situations, pain and excitement can all cause fainting. Strong emotion, distress or shock, can put physical and mental strain on the body. Our blood pressure can drop, and we faint. Your blood pressure is good now, but you may feel the effects of fainting for a while," she reports.

"Thank you, Dr. Brazil," Keefe says.

I turn my attention to my father.

"Father?" I say, looking into Romulus's gentle eyes.

He puts his arms around me and holds me again. He is a strong man with deep emotion.

"How is this possible?" he exclaims

"Mother is in my dreams, gives me messages... I did not understand, but I am beginning to. Last night in my dream, her clothing and face and hair were dripping wet. She put the amulet around my neck and she left. This is what she did before she perished in the flood. She took the amulet from her neck and placed it around mine. Somehow I survived. I thought my parents were dead. I understand nothing about my past, my only link being the amulet. This must be what Calista Twinning knew; the link to my past. The amulet was with me all this time."

"Quinn, we thought we lost you. The pain of losing you, losing both of you, nearly killed me. I can't believe you are alive. Thank you for sparing my daughter, thank you Lord." Romulus's emotions release tears and joy.

He says, "You, you are my first born child. The plan all makes sense now. My precious daughter, we've been robbed of time. You are blessed to be alive today. Petulah had a hand in the death of my wife, and I thought my daughter's life too. I learned her death was no accident! Your mother was murdered, and the fact you lived explains why the enemy is drawn here. When they found out you survived, you became the target most wanted. They would never want us to find each other," Romulus says, holding me close again. "We will take justice for you both!"

"Father, my sisters my brother," I say through my tears. My emotion overcomes me. "I have a family!"

Sapphire, Cashton and Jexis come to my side.

"I am honored to be your sister," says Jexis, who touches my face.

Sapphire kneels before me. She puts her head on my lap.

I cradle her face in my hands and smile through my tears.

"Sister, I loved you before I even knew," I tell her. Sapphire is crying and cannot talk.

Cashton flashes his dynamic smile. "Quinn, we are victims of Petulah's manipulation. The evil ones would love nothing better than an incestuous relationship to stain our souls and discredit you. An unspeakable thing! What kind of mother can do this to her own child? I am honored you are my sister." He leans over and embraces me.

The mesmerizing hold placed upon us is extinguished. The energy felt during prior episodes when I was around Cashton no longer exists. Petulah is not controlling this.

"Polaris," Cashton nods his head in reverence.

This acknowledgement catapults me back to reality and I lock on to my father's proud gaze with a confounded expression.

Romulus says, "Quinn, this is your destiny! All of the revelations coming at once brought doubt, pain and fear. This is what the dark side wants for us... confusion and uncertainty. They would make sure your rise to leadership would never happen, or if it did, you would be unwilling, or unprepared. You will be none of these things. I promise you." He places both his hands on my shoulders. "Everyone return to your seats. The weather is changing and with the storm alerts the concert will be clearing so we can get our guests home. Please congregate to the Madowent after the conclusion of the benefit as we will be conducting the Ceremony of the Ring in honor of Quinn, Polaris to the Circle of Sun."

His words send shivers up my spine. I don't want to be the first ever Polaris whose knees are knocking for all to hear.

Soon the Madowent is packed with Guardians. The room glows from a multitude of fiery torches perched along each stone wall. The front of the room now holds a large stained glass window I don't recall seeing before. The window is round and illuminated from behind, brilliant blue with a massive white dove in flight in the center. A flute plays, Father Mopsi steps up to the podium and welcomes us.

"Good evening and welcome to this special Ceremony of the Ring. Please let me introduce to you our distinguished Senate. Seated to my left are Dr. Eudora Brazil, Etta Mollender, George Tally, Edward Carver, Mason Kidwell and Tristan Pope. Our Senate is the bedrock of the Circle of Sun. Promotion to this important post is a distinction we are pleased to bestow upon our newest member, Cashton Royce."

The whole room applauds, happy with this appointment. Cashton remains cool as he approaches. They rise to grasp hands. When Cashton moves towards his father, their embrace is met with thundering applause and cheers. Cashton takes his place.

"Romulus, would you please come forward?" Romulus stands near the podium in the center of the front, underneath the brilliant stained glass window, and addresses the group.

"My time of leadership as Polaris has come to an end. My daughter lives! I am overwhelmed and filled with pride. And her appointment will move me to the Senate, a move I am pleased with. In order for us to conquer darkness in Nadellawick we must regain the Fidesorb. We have been blinded and cannot see the fires of their ceremonies. Petulah is responsible, and now she is exposed, our blindness is lifted.

We will see the fire; we will have victory."

Romulus's eyes sweep the room and rest upon me. This scene is surreal. I soon will accept a most important role. I question the qualities I must possess to do the things I fear I must do.

Keefe escorts me to the front of the room. I pray He whom we serve will give me everything I need. Romulus takes my hand, and Keefe returns to the rear of the room.

Father Mopsi stands between Romulus and me. Father Mopsi is a large man, his face gentle and filled with passion. He glances up to the heavens and repeats words I do not understand. All present in the Madowent answer back in unison as Father Mopsi speaks again. Father Mopsi raises Romulus's hand, lifting it up high.

The torches perched along the wall flare upwards. The ceiling disintegrates into the night sky. The wide gaping opening exposes churning and furious clouds. The flares of fire develop into mighty columns of power and break up the clouds with ease. The columns contain pure light beaming all the way to eternity. The atmosphere outside the beams is unchanged, but within the great barriers exist only brilliant white light.

My body basks in the warmth of peace, the security of ultimate power and love beyond all understanding.

Father Mopsi puts his hands together in prayer, fingers pointing upward leading the rest of us to do so.

With eyes upturned we stand in awe as glistening pearls of light fill the black sky outside the pillars. Like snowflakes suspended in time, these pearls of light surround us. They appear as multitudes of stars covering the black. Prayers continue in unison, increasing in volume. The pearls began to swirl and circle the columns, round and round. Like small tributaries flowing into one river, the pearls of light move and melt into one beam of traveling brilliance. One beam circles the columns, cutting through the turbulent skies, and the Madowent becomes silent. The trail of light enters and travels down, down, and stops above me.

I am still as an opulent energy lowers more, coming to rest on my hands as they point in prayer to heaven. The power lingers, its brilliance warms my soul, and I bask in incredible happiness and hope. The light beam rises up and ascends into heaven. In its place resting upon my left finger is the ring of Polaris, the Apalacid. Where the pain lived for so long, a gold ring now rests. The face of the ring is a golden sun, the symbol of our legion.

Father Mopsi begins to pray and I gaze on this symbol of leadership with awe. This is the ring, the Apalacid Romulus wore, and now it is on my finger. The pain is now just a distant memory.

Father Mopsi and every soul present share one united prayer, and its message is one of love and hope. Smoke begins to billow from the torches once more and blankets the entire Madowent above the heads of those gathered.

Within the smoke only I view scenes, age old scenes from the battle fought in the heavens brought us to this day. Those protecting Heaven from Lucifer himself hurl balls of fire from their palms. Some Guardians carry pearl handled swords with shimmering silver blades that strike with celestial force. Others with golden disks, which once hurled, emit sparks of rotating electricity. Lucifer falls and takes the weak with him. I observe Archangel Michael as he formed the Circle of Sun. I am shown the details surrounding the death of my mother, and those responsible. I need the experiences and I must understand what those before me have endured. The magnitude is understood. My heart knows. The smoke dissipates and I see the faces of those witnesses to this ceremony and the hope in their hearts.

Father Mopsi finishes his prayer and all the room is silent as I begin to speak.

"It is all revealed to me, all I need to forge our battle and reclaim Nadellawick. I am a committed servant and an eager warrior. The stage has been set for victory. We must take what is ours, and return the Fidesorb to its rightful place. There is little time. May the glory for our victory be His."

The cheers and shouts from hopeful hearts can be heard all the way to heaven.

Before the Madowent is empty, Pony and Sapphire hurl golden disks, becoming accustomed to strange weapons. Chamous and Keefe wield pearl and silver swords, and Tera hurls balls of fire. No instruction is required, they have been provided with everything they need to be fierce warriors. Romulus was right, when we are called, we will be equipped. The Madowent becomes empty as Romulus embraces me as his daughter and his leader. His goodness and character are transparent and his conviction and passion are now mine.

Romulus says, "Quinn, my child. My heart bled for you, and for your mother. My grief has produced an ocean of tears. Your life was spared, but how you survived and how we have been united, is a miracle. A miracle has occurred in my life."

"And in my life as well, Father. I will only know my mother from my dreams. Her heart is pure and beautiful. I never knew her."

"But, Quinn you will be reunited with her when your journey ends on this earth. We will all embrace again as a family," he replies with faith.

"I look forward to that day, Father."

Chapter Thirty-Seven

A large suite is made ready for me in a room on the main level near Romulus. Keefe, Tera and Chamous, Pony, Sapphire, and Professor Enderlee gather around the massive stone fireplace roaring with warmth and light. Keefe is the first to greet me and does so with an embrace. The others do the same.

I sit on the sofa with Tera and Keefe, and the others stand near the fire.

"Latin, Quinn?" Pony asks.

"What do you mean?" I respond, puzzled.

"After the Apalacid was on your finger, it was all Latin from you," he says, and then looks to Keefe with confusion.

"Yes Quinn, you seemed to understand and speak Latin," he tells me.

"I remember Latin at the beginning when Father Mopsi was praying. I was relieved to hear English after...the ring,"

Keefe touches my arm and replies, "No, Quinn, the dialect remained unchanged, you did the changing."

Tera searches my face. She takes one of the filled wine glasses, bringing her attention back to me. She uses a napkin to dab at her eyes.

Tera says in a soft, shaky voice, "We have all experienced a miracle... I am overwhelmed. How will we be?" She dabs at her eye once more and Chamous puts his arm around her. "I still am adjusting to the magnitude of this."

"Tera, our friendship will never change. We move forward together, all of us," I say as I raise my glass.

Everyone raises their glasses to toast.

Dr. Brazil, Romulus and Cashton enter the room.

Cashton says, "We are to meet on Crusader's Bluff. I will escort Jexis and meet you in the tower."

The time has come. We walk to the tower silently, faith masking our fears.

Shrill screaming from outside shatters the silence. We rush

through the south door to discover the source. Beef does his best to comfort a hysterical servant.

"Cashton, Cashton!" she screams.

"What is it?" I demand.

"They took him, they took him!" she cries.

"What do you mean?" Romulus asks with urgency in his voice.

"Cashton thought the horses were out. I followed him to the door . . . many black snakes under the carriage port! The snakes bound his ankles and crept to his knees...squeezing. One coiled around his neck. Black ghosts came and took him away into the forest. He is gone! He is gone!" she sobs.

"Professor Enderlee, take her back inside. Calm her and stay with them," Romulus commands.

He turns to me with concern as we both lift our arms and take flight, knowing we may be too late. The newest members of the Circle of Sun follow. We soar over the tree tops as the full moon casts our shadow below. Our eyes scan and we change direction a few times, when we spot fire deep in the woods near Marcus Landing. Our blindness to their ceremonial fires is gone. We land and gather under massive oak trees, hundreds of Guardians arriving every few minutes. I give my first order.

"We will not be gathering at Crusaders Bluff as planned. We must save Cashton at Marcus Landing. We will take cover within the trees surrounding the River People. We cannot penetrate their circle of fire. Wait for the signal."

A thick covering of fog creeps up the trunks of towering trees. The oaks are dense and impressive in their size. I choose one suitable and place my hands above me, palms against the tree. An opening in its massive trunk is melted away under my hands, creating an opening for myself and Romulus and a few others. The same thing is done throughout the forest by our comrades. The insides of the trees become hollow, providing fortresses for us, and with the swipe of a hand a transparent window for viewing is created.

Figures stand outside the circle of fire, unable to cross, while others stand within the circle. The flames are crimson. There is no yellow or white in the flames, only red.

Silence blankets the dark robes and the air is stoic and heavy.

One of the three robed figures in front speaks, "Bow down in your insignificance. Our Caesar of darkness is among us."

All robed figures go to their knees. On elevated ground beyond the circle, a figure in robes of red appears from within a smoky veil. His voice booms throughout the forest.

"Welcome to our gathering of the Wyvern. I am your Caesar, LaMont."

His dark subjects return to their feet, shouting their support.

He quiets them with an outstretched arm.

"Our legion grows with more dark souls joining our cause daily. Nadellawick will soon be ours!"

This statement brings even louder reactions from the followers.

"To predict our future, one must understand the past. The coveted Fidesorb is in our possession. Success is at hand. Our region will join others in our eventual rise to ultimate power. Can a pure heart find love in the darkest of hearts? Yes! I was loved from afar by one of purity, of light, her love declared only after my death. She mourned at my tomb. Tears were shed upon the thirsty soil of my grave and nourished the evil seeds to life. And so our story continues!"

All of those gathered once again show their loyalty with their loud cheers and yells. The Caesar stands in judgment as the three black robes once again address the group.

I say to Sapphire, "The verse from the book... something about darkness being trapped...fear the lover's tears at dawn. Pony, remember Jessie told you about the origins of the River People?"

One of the three men speaks, "Our Caesar will decide the fate of the donkeys."

The circle of fire changes color as mystical creatures dance within the flames, raising their hands to the skies, and sweeping low as they frolic in their spectacle of honor to the Caesar. The creatures once again return to flames of crimson before a group of robed figures emerges dragging a man who appears unconscious.

The crowd begins to chant, "Caesar, Caesar, Caesar!"

The man is placed in a heap in front of the red-robed figure.

The Caesar says, "Who snared this... mule?"

The group erupts in laughter at the word mule.

A figure comes before the Caesar. Before speaking, his hood is lowered revealing his identity.

"My name is Harold Crumbly and I bring Cale Misock. I befriended him after witnessing an experience turn him bitter. With encouragement, his bitterness has hardened his heart. I insured darkness hovered over his life, and choked out any spot of hope remaining." Harold Crumbly lowers his head and steps back.

"This is good! Cale, what do you say for yourself?" the Cesar asks, his voice thundering.

Harold takes a handful of Cale's hair and pulls his face up toward the master. The evil one laughs and says, "Put Misock in the hole and soon he will receive his mark, our legion grows by one." These words bring cheers from the dark robes gathered. Cale Misock is picked up and thrown into an opening in the earth.

"A gishmot for Harold Crumbly," the Cesar remarks, "record the deed in the Scroll of Acts." Two robed figures provide payment.

Soon another group emerges from the forest.

"We must stop this heinous ceremony," I say.

Two more victims come before the red-robed lord.

"Two mules for the price of one," the Caesar booms in sick laughter. Show yourself sponsor, by removing your hood."

The hood is ripped back and a woman begins to speak. "My name is Madge Botherme, my Lord. I work tirelessly for . . . ."

"SILENCE!" the Cesar shouts.

"But my Lord, I -" Madge Botherme tries to speak again.

"SILENCE!" the Cesar says again.

"I am sorry Lord," Madge Botherme says lowering her head. "Please show mercy on the one who attempted to take the life of the future Polaris."

The Caesar leans forward as if to listen. "You are the one who pushed her? Come now, we didn't know of your evil deeds, did any of you?" the Caesar asks, putting the question out to the group.

There is nothing but silence.

Madge speaks, "Caesar I did not mean to imply I was at the cliff's edge."

"SILENCE, Botherme. Your deeds are nothing more than mere annoyances to our enemy, brushed away like a flies. Do not claim acts belonging to another. Names of the candidates?" the Caesar asks.

"Their names are Tripp and Hailey Atchison. They grow tired of walking a straight path. They choose us," Madge says as she steps back.

"What say you?" the Caesar asks.

"Our souls are ready for rebirth," Hailey Atchison says. "Our allegiance is to the darkness."

"Lead them to the hole, and prepare them for the mark," the Cesar says.

"Record the deed?' Madge Botherme asks.

The Caesar says, "She, who walks alongside those who are on the path to darkness, should not attempt to call it leading." The Caesar points his finger towards Madge. She is transformed into a large toad.

This brings more laughter from the group. A similar scenario plays out, when the next poor soul stands in front of the Caesar.

"Who presents this mule, remove your hood!" Caesar commands.

Elliott Kenadie says, "I bring you Rand Jolliet, conspirator with the former Chief Dow. He obtained evidence of the Wyvern existence. We got rid of Dow and Rose Enderlee, and he is the last of it, I assure you."

The Caesar shouts, "How LONG MUST WE PAY THE PRICE OF OTHER'S STUPIDITY? You assured me Kenadie that Enderlee's death would put this to rest! Why is this creature brought before me, why did you not end his useless life?"

"Lord, I bring him here to show victory! My leaves of poison rendered him insane for the duration of one day, and during that time he attempted murder!" Kenadie says, beaming with pride.

I remember the gift of tea leaves in Rose's room, a gift basket from the literary club, from Kenadie. Tea leaves of poison took the life of Rose Enderlee, another senseless death. My heart aches for the professor.

"Splendid, wickedly splendid. Your potions may be useful after all, Kenadie."

"Lord, he thwarted our efforts, connecting the disasters in

Nadellawick! He should not be praised!"

"Show yourself!" the Caesar says.

Adam Langford stands and says, "Those who serve you should do so humbly."

"You are right, Adam. Let it be known to all, Adam is the one who stood on the cliff's edge. Adam attempted to end the life of Quinn Clarke, the threat presented by the offspring of Romulus, his act never recognized until now," the Caesar says.

"But I failed, Lord. The amulet's protection saved her."

"Romulus's reign is over. Quinn is Polaris now, and we will be given our chance."

The Caesar speaks to Elliott, "Your decision to create a common thread connecting the downward spiral of Nadellawick lacked wisdom. You have no power to make decisions affecting the sum."

Elliott fidgets and responds, "As long as the questions remain about the birds and fish dying and about the water… I merely gave them seeds of doubt."

"KNOW YOUR PLACE, Kenadie! The only reason you are not a memory is due to the lives you are responsible for ending. Throw your mule into the hole to be marked. A gishmot for Kenadie, and the deed recorded in the scroll," the Caesar instructs.

He turns his interest to the special group seated to his left. The Caesar says, "The protector of the Fidesorb, please show yourself."

"I am here my Lord," a female voice from the seated group says.

"What say you?" the Caesar asks.

The woman says with authority, "Safe and secure, the Fidesorb lies dark as death buried where you once rested."

A booming laughter erupts from the Caesar once more.

He says, "This is why you are winning souls for our cause. Once we discovered Quinn wore the amulet, you orchestrated the plan to bring her to White Oak. Loss of employment, putting the bookstore purchase in her reach, all brilliant. Dawn Bishop was another ingenious distraction, Carolynn. I adored it when Quinn questioned her own sanity…sympathy for your crumbling marriage and your drug problem, reeling them in, beautiful! Please remove your hood, you've earned another stripe."

The woman removed her hood and standing before the Caesar is Carolynn Langford, her smile deceitful and cunning. The dark lord approaches her. She lowers her robes, exposing her back with many stripes or brandings.

The Caesar circles around to her back and put his lips upon her shoulder blade. She winces in pain, but her delight is obvious. She raises the robe back over her new stripe.

Tera speaks from her tree hideout, "Carolynn Langford, I was alone with her!"

"What is gained by making me look bad in the public eye?" I ask.

Romulus explains, "Discrediting you would be a good place to begin," he states. "Remember, the darkness would first want to win the ultimate victory, having the future leader of the Circle of Sun join their ranks. They would destroy you, or recruit you."

This ceremony is almost most than I can bear. I want to retaliate. I am ready.

Once again a robed figure escorts a victim before the Caesar. The wind picks up in intensity.

"It's CASHTON!" Romulus announces. I hear their gasps as I dash out.

Chapter Thirty-Eight

There is no time to waste. With every fear converted to action; and with a cause greater than myself, I attack. I feel undeniable strength and incredible power in each step. I raise my hand to the first enemy I come upon, and he is blown to the ground. I put his dark robes on and conceal my face with the hood. Within minutes I am intermingled with those standing. I make my way to the top of the circle, close to where Cashton is being held.

"Who sponsors this disgusting mortal?" A figure moves before the Caesar. The hood is removed; blonde tresses begin to blow in the wind.

"It is I, Jexis, your most loyal servant, betrayed by my own blood brother. He must be silenced forever!"

"Ah Jexis, my fallen angel. Your service is coveted. I enjoy ripping the heart out of those who call themselves leaders," the Caesar says. "Our trial shall begin. Come forward accuser." With those words a dark robe from the special section stands and walks to Jexis and Cashton. She removes her hood. It's Petulah.

"Speak," the Cesar says.

Petulah says, "My Lord, this man is my own offspring. My efforts are unsuccessful in bringing him to darkness. I admit failure in my commission to soil the house of Royce and extinguish the brightest light. Cashton discovered I am the one responsible for Romulus's first wife's death, and he informed his father. My ability to know all happenings in the home of the Polaris Romulus Circle of Sun is gone. I accuse Cashton, and ask for his blood! I also beg mercy on my failure, Caesar."

"Petulah, you are one of my favorite souls of darkness. Your evil and destruction are a pure delight to me. I enjoyed the demise of inquisitive Miss Twinning, with a little mix up in the pills of the hapless Tripp Atchison. Your mistake was bringing Quinn to Royce Estate where her birthright was discovered. Your curiosity and jealousy are more powerful than the web you wove for her destruction. Your years of loyalty are many. I do not consider your mission a failure, because it's unfinished. You may shed the blood of your own son . . . do you not feel your own seed being destroyed along with him?" the master asks.

"No, Caesar, he is the seed of Romulus, there is no part of me in him! I will happily end his life with the sword," Petulah replies.

This comment promotes more laughter from the Caesar.

"Petulah, death of a son at his mother's hand? The deed's value multiplies."

The flames in the circle grow higher and the chanting crowd becomes louder.

With Cashton's hands secured behind his back, Jexis stands behind him, lacing her arms under his and clasping them around his neck. The sword is presented to Petulah and she grasps it with both hands. She first bows allegiance to the Caesar and turns her attention to Cashton.

"Why did you betray me when you could rule with me?" she asks him.

"Go to hell, Mother," Cashton spouts with contempt.

"I'm already there!" she says, causing Caesar to laugh with sick humor at the human suffering displayed before his eyes.

I understand what is happening. Jexis's mysterious words earlier in the evening, 'The circle is mine to break.' She is going to break the circle.

Petulah lunges forward to impale her only son, but Jexis pulls Cashton's body from the sword's point, and falls backward with Cashton onto the circle of flames! Their bodies hit the ground, the fire dissipates and Cashton rolls out and frees his hands.

Jexis takes Cashton's hand, and he pulls her into an embrace as they both reach into their sleeves and pull out discs of gold and whip them into the enemy.

I rush to them, Romulus follows close behind, and thousands of Guardians charge from their tree shelters to flood the darkness.

Pony and Sapphire notice the hesitation on Tera's face and stop her and Chamous before they leave the shelter and join the clash. Sapphire's heart beats rapidly as sounds of battle fill the air.

Understanding how they are all feeling, she reveals her vision to them.

"My vision of victory is clear, we fling disks of gold and shield ourselves from every charge. We enter the battle untested, but we emerge as warriors, do not fear! You must say the words to receive the commissions to defend and conquer . . . *I accept and will defeat!* Say the words!"

The new Guardians leave the shelter and repeat with brave resolve, "I accept and will defeat, I accept and will defeat!" As they aim their disks each is infused with a sanctified measure of skill and instinct to defend the light and destroy those who stand in their way.

The remaining fire in the center erupts into a fountain of fury, flames rising to the heavens and lighting up the scene like mid-day.

Black robed figures with their identities now exposed show their teeth as their faces become cat-like. Snakes slither around their feet which are grasped then transformed to black blades. They raise their shields to defend from the spinning disks of death.

Pony and Sapphire leap on to a fallen tree and send their golden disks shooting rays of destruction into their enemy. They jump through the air towards an advancing line, drawing swords from their sheaths. Like an apparition flowing through a mortal body, these mystical blades slice the victim through, and leave them defeated on the forest floor. Their disks spin back and they catch them in mid-air before hurling them once more through a mass of black robes.

Tera and Chamous come to the aid of Guardians who are outnumbered. They use their golden disks to thin out the enemy and draw their swords on the remainder surrounding the defenders. Tera slices her weapon through two River People who charge at her before falling.

Chamous swings his sword and three more of those aggressors are eliminated.

Sapphire is knocked to the ground and three dark robes attack. She manages to get back to her feet and run towards the forest, the three after her.

Pony sends his golden disk toward them and cuts them down and several tree branches plunge with them.

Jexis has been hurt, and she falls to one knee after sustaining a serious blow. Another dark robed enemy comes from behind, putting his arm tightly around her throat. She grasps her attackers head, pulling it over her shoulder with one hand. She raises her sword and forces her blade down, relieving his head from his body. She charges the one who put her to her knee and runs her blade directly through the middle of his body.

Cashton and Romulus fight through numbers of dark robes, trying to get to the Caesar and Petulah.

I raise my beam of destruction towards a swarm of dark robes rushing from the dark forest, then join Romulus in turning our attention to Caesar, Petulah and Carolynn. They both stand in front of the Caesar, protecting him, their faces grotesque as they bare teeth no longer white, but stained and ugly.

"Our numbers multiply daily. You've failed Romulus. Those present are but a fraction of our forces. Those who perish are easily replaced. They are pathetic and weak," the Caesar gloats.

"The human spirit is inherently innocent at birth, even yours Caesar. The heart and soul reserve choice. Nothing can ever take it away. This ends here, it ends now!" Romulus declares.

And with those words the clouds began to roll and tumble, the wind is fierce and the elevated place where the red robed one stands begins to sink. The entire section of the earth surrounding him falls away and a crater begins to form. A tempest swirls, escalating in intensity as the crater becomes larger and larger.

Romulus and I, Petulah and Carolynn are thrown unsteady as the ground sinks. We descend to the depths of the earth, while our comrades continue to battle above us. We land upon a stable floor of rock, an underworld of stone mountains and valleys, caves and crevices. Flames of crimson burn, surrounding our landing spot. The smells are foul, fueled by layers of decay, their intense heat radiating.

The scene is devoid of any living plant or natural earthly habitat. On a rock ledge above us the Caesar sits upon a throne of misery. Contorted human bodies cling to each other's ankles, wrists, shoulders and throats. Their compressed bodies make up his throne. They wail and moan in their agony.

The Caesar lowers his hood and reveals the form of an ordinary man. Petulah and Carolynn are now unrecognizable. Although they remain in human form, their snarls reveal black teeth, gaunt faces, and skin barely covering their skulls. Their hands are long with stained, claw-like nails, and their feet grotesque with boils festering and draining.

We begin to circle and move around the mountains of rock surrounding us. Romulus casts his mighty hand, releasing a powerful cascade of light directed at Carolynn and she blocks with a shield of fire reflecting it back. I duck to avoid being hit.

Petulah uses her claws to climb up a jagged ledge, trying to gain advantage for the kill.

Romulus strides head-on to face Carolynn. She holds her flaming shield up once again in anticipation of his attack. Romulus grasps the fiery disk, tossing it aside. He puts only one of his powerful hands upon her throat, and lifts her from the ground. Her body liquefies to molten lava in his grasp, reduced to a putrid puddle.

Petulah leaps down and grasps a snake, wielding it like a whip, cracking it towards me. The reptile snaps its eager jaws inches from my face. Grasping the lower jaw of the snake I snap down hard, creating a whipping motion that lifts Petulah off the ground as she clings to the tail of the reptile. I grasp the snake with both hands, freezing it into a petrified staff.

I spot a magnificent flying jeweled serpent, much like the figurine Sapphire showed me in the tower room. The creature screeches, and soars above us, breathing fire from its mouth, barely missing Romulus. Its multi-jeweled body and bat like wings shimmer in the flames as if they are wet. The creature dives down and Petulah crawls upon its back.

I take aim, raising my hand to cast a death beam, but Romulus blocks my arm at the sight of Petulah transforming into the likeness of Jexis. Romulus is shaken by the sight.

"It is not Jexis!" I yell, releasing the destructive beam, but the serpent dips and dives and once more eludes our attack. I stand unmoved, and put both arms out from my side with palms up and with face turned upward I close my eyes and shout, my voice amplified; and the ground quivers and shakes.

"GREATER IS HE WHO IS IN ME, THAN HE WHO IS IN THE WORLD."

Suddenly the mountains of stone begin to crumble all around us. Petulah and her serpent swoop to the ledge where the Caesar sits upon the tortured souls. He leaps onto the serpent's back as evil releases the grip of the throne and the bodies unravel, causing the throne to collapse.

Caesar and Petulah escape the pit of despair. Both Romulus and I raise our arms and take flight in pursuit of those who aim to destroy the earth. We reach the surface and explode beyond to the skies overhead. Our bodies are unchanged with great wings outstretched.

Cashton joins the battle, forging into the turbulent clouds.

The serpent carrying the wicked ones is no match for us as we gain ground. Cashton sends a mighty shaft of light, wounding the red robed Caesar. Blood gushes out of the open wound.

Petulah takes advantage of her opportunity and transforms into a black snake, crawls up his back and enters into the gaping hole left by Cashton's attack, seeking protection.

The serpent moves faster now and leads our chase to the river. Despite several of our attempts to destroy it, the creature dives straight into the swift moving Missouri. Discovering where the enemy will emerge keeps us all engaged, with weapons ready. Moments later the evil thrusts out of the water through the night sky.

I send a jagged lightning bolt, piercing the Caesar's throat. The serpent begins to descend, and the Caesar takes stock of the devastation on the battlefield. He comes to rest in a cemetery close to Royce Estate.

"I am dying. The Circle of Sun destroyed my legion. What is my fate?" the Caesar says. Thinking he would be destroyed first, Petulah in her snake form emerges from the body of the Caesar and coils to the neck of the serpent.

Cashton uses his sword to slice its neck. The creature fights for breath, raises its head to the heavens and breaths a torch of fire into the night sky. Screeching and writhing in pain, its horned feet begin to melt into the earth. His body, with snake still coiled, lies in a heap. He and the trapped Petulah simmer and smoke and become a green pool of liquid.

The Caesar runs his sword into the ground to mark the spot, and the liquid evil soaks into the soil. Left in its place glowing through the smoke is the Fidesorb!

The Caesar stands next to the orb. His robes are torn and bloody. In protection of the innocent, I deliver the fateful blow to end his reign of Nadellawick. I lift the amulet protecting me since birth and aim a powerful explosion of destruction. We all are witnessing the wrath of the Almighty, his power unmatched by any warrior's weapon this night.

The Caesar falls to the ground instantaneously. He is defeated; he is dead. His reign over Nadellawick is over.

I lower my head in prayer and then put my face up to the heavens.

"It is done, it is done!" The fierce wind becomes a gentle breeze, and as the sun begins to rise in the east, Romulus, Cashton and I approach the crimson robed evil one. Cashton uses his boot to move the hood away from the face, revealing nothing but air.

Cashton says, "You destroyed every living cell, there is nothing left to fear! It is a time of great rejoicing!"

Sounds of victory fill the air as multitudes of Guardians rush to the cemetery where we are.

Keefe shouts, "We need help, Tera's hurt!"

The sight of Chamous carrying a limp Tera sends us all racing to her side. Cashton and I support Tera as Chamous lowers her to the ground. Keefe takes my hand as Cashton kneels down next to her.

"The wound is near her heart!" a distraught Chamous says, with panic in his voice.

Cashton places his hands upon her as Chamous and the rest of us pray. Heat radiates into her body from his hands. The bleeding is stopped and the wound miraculously begins to close. Cashton brings his other hand up and rests it on her forehead. Within minutes, she opens her eyes and gives Chamous a weak smile.

We all breathe a collective sigh of relief.

Sapphire holds Pony's waist as they stand shoulder to shoulder. Their clothes are torn and dirty, their faces soiled, but their eyes bright and hopeful.

Pony speaks, "We were met with thousands of dark robes, and

they kept spilling out from the forest like roaches."

"We are warriors in the Circle of Sun and today we are victorious," I announce.

"We are victorious today," Tera repeats.

Dr. Brazil and Father Mopsi now kneel next to Chamous and Cashton.

Jexis and Romulus look on as Dr. Brazil tends to Tera.

Keefe pulls me away from the group, his strong face smudged with dirt, his hair dancing in the dawn breeze. Taking both of my hands he looks into my eyes.

"Quinn, are you alright? I love you. I am honored to be at your service... and that will be enough," he says.

I move some light hair away from his eyes.

"Keefe, I love you too and I need you," I reveal.

He smiles and puts his lips to mine, his tender kiss exposing our love for all to see.

I walk to a raised area of land where multitudes of Guardians are gathered and speak to all. I put my hand over my amulet, the precious object that brought me to this day.

"Brothers and sisters, this dawn marks a new day in Nadellawick. Light spills into each soul, and peace and hope no longer come tethered by the weight of darkness. However, as long as evil still roams this earth, we must remain vigilant in our protection of Nadellawick. Many things will change in our region because of this victory, and tonight we will celebrate those changes. Stay committed to your faith, and fight the daily battle. We give all glory to Him and return the orb to its rightful place."

Romulus brings the brilliant and luminous Fidesorb to me. I raise the precious orb to the heavens, and it levitates silently up through the morning sky.

We watch as long as we were able to. When the light is absorbed into the new day we look to one another. Pony and Sapphire, with arms intertwined, join Romulus, who walks between Father Mopsi and Dr. Brazil. Jexis and Cashton stand shoulder to shoulder, and Chamous supports Tera. Keefe takes my hand, and all of us together turn to the rising sun, and head to Royce Estate, our home.

Epilogue

The chilling morning air is visible in his breath as he grips the red roses and walks to where the sword pierces the ground. The ground consumed the evil, dark Petulah. He steps upon new grasses carrying the frost of a bitter night. Once on the spot marking her grave, Beef bends down and places flowers to honor the woman no one knew he loved. His falling tear melts the frost. His pilgrimage is brief before he turns and walks away. The first rays of morning sun create tiny prisms in his fallen tears. The thirsty soil drinks, mercifully.

Dancing in the midnight sun,
Knowing that our work is done.
Serpents, snakes and stains on souls
Found within the darkest hole.
Trapped forever, darkness gone,
But… fear the lover's tears at dawn.

The End

Author Kim Luke

Author Kim Luke once had to help a customer at her family Christmas tree farm chop down a fresh tree in a business suit and heels. She was comfortable in that attire, the "uniform" of her marketing profession. She was not as comfortable as a Christmas tree farmer, but she's learned to be supportive in this family endeavor. The tree farm is located in Missouri, the setting for both of Kim's two novels in her Circle of Sun series.

A literature major in college, Luke has always enjoyed a good story and loves using her imagination. Of her many passions, writing has been with her the longest. She finds it pure joy, like eating a delicious piece of cheesecake. The cornerstones in her life are her faith and family.

Kim and husband Bob are blessed with three children, incredible in-laws and three grandchildren. The Lukes live with their two Alaskan Malamute dogs on a beautiful 20 acre farm, where they indulge in a love of books, coffee, wine and positive thinkers.

You can connect with Kim at www.kimlukeauthor.com, on Facebook at Circle of Sun or on Twitter, @kimluke. She is also a Goodreads author.

45096761R00141

Made in the USA
Charleston, SC
12 August 2015